/ LIO Fic

17
MORTON STREET

17 MORTON STREET

by
CATHERINE HILLER

St. Martin's Press
NEW YORK

Design by Judy Dannecker

Library of Congress Cataloging-in-Publication Data

Hiller, Catherine.
    Seventeen Morton Street / Catherine Hiller.
        p.   cm.
    ISBN 0-312-04420-8
    PS3558.I4458S48   1990
    813'.54—dc20   89-77947

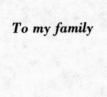

To my family

PROLOGUE: LUCY

TWENTY YEARS AGO AT THE DIN-
ner table, my father told us a story. It took place in Europe,
toward the end of World War II. A woman was imprisoned
and alone. She hadn't seen a face or heard a voice in months:
her food was pushed in through a slot. One night, while lying
on her pallet, she heard a faint tapping. Breathless with hope,
she began counting. She knew no Morse code, but the secret
tapper used the amateur's code: one tap for a, two for b, and
she picked it up fast and tapped back, "Hello."

The tapper was a man. He was also being held in solitary
confinement—but the two prisoners were alone no longer.
Their days were full now. They described themselves, re-
counted their histories. They refined their tapping code to
include footsteps. They tapped and paced in their separate

cells. They told jokes. Soon they began to flirt. He asked what kind of underwear she had on. He told her he loved her. They became engaged. When the war ended, they were freed. They met and got married. As far as anybody knows, they lived happily ever after.

I loved this story. I was eleven years old, and I took it to mean there was hope for me. If there was a war and I was imprisoned, and there was some man also imprisoned, we could tap to each other and fall in love and when he finally saw me, it wouldn't matter what I looked like. I would have a husband and children, just like anybody else.

That first evening with Paul I had eighty blocks in the dark to talk before I turned to face him and tell him good night, but by then his eyes were closed, and mine were too as we embraced.

So much depends on so little! How the millimeters matter in a lip, in an eye! A squirt or two of hormone helps make one fat or thin. A single gene determines if hair will flow or frizz.

As a teenager, I tried to keep a sense of proportion. I was healthy and strong (one gene also decides whether cerebral palsy will strike). I was smart. I had friends. I was loved in my family. I had many reasons to be grateful. Along with bemoaning my appearance, I agonized that I let it obsess me. Such frivolity, I felt, could only be excused by beauty.

I was a homely little girl, I am a homely woman. Plain. On intelligence tests I always scored in the ninety-ninth percentile. At fourteen, in my bed, I would imagine an attractiveness test and torture myself deciding my percentile. Second? Third? As high as tenth?

My sisters, Sara and Perri, of course, made the ninety-ninth. They were girls with flowing blond hair and slender bodies, tender faces. At fifteen, I described myself to a pen pal as a "pudgy girl with brillo hair and a potato face. My eyes are small and brown and shiny." I didn't want him to think he was corresponding with a beauty, nor to clamor for my picture. But he only wrote back once.

Throughout my adolescence, I felt because I wasn't pretty, I wasn't properly female, not a real girl. Whatever I did, wherever I went, I always thought people pitied me—as I'm sure they did, once they'd set eyes on my gorgeous older sisters.

I think my sisters raised me more than my parents did. My father practiced law all day and was tired and remote at night. My mother spent more time on the house than on us. I remember her in the background, waxing the dining room floor or repapering the guest room closet. She also played bridge. My sisters and I were together five or six hours on school days—and longer on weekends. My sisters and I played dolls or jacks or school, hour after hour. Sara soft, Perri sharp, both of them beautiful, beautiful! My sisters and I in town, at the movies, going shopping. When we all went out, people would stare after them.

Given the choice, most young girls would rather be beautiful than brilliant—even the brilliant ones. I wonder if that will ever change. What I know now is that beauty doesn't always matter all that much. I've seen many unattractive women, successful professionals, who are, or seem to be, happy wives and mothers—especially in England, where the plain seem to marry the plums.

My parents did their best with me: my mother said I had an interesting face; my father said I had a wonderful mind. My mother encouraged me to go out for athletics; I was on the Rutland High School tennis team. I remember my special satisfaction when I would beat a pretty girl.

Now I like any close, good-natured match; man or woman my opponent; appearance and age immaterial; winning unimportant. I still play singles when I can. But try playing tennis in winter without a small inheritance!

Of course, I do have an inheritance, the house: Seventeen

Morton Street, where I occupy the top floor. I would never, could never, sell my share in it. Sara has found the perfect way to keep us all together.

I wonder how perfect she's found it this spring.

I haven't been home for over a month now, the longest I've been away since we moved in five years ago. He says the change is good for me, that I am blossoming away from them, but he is always upbeat and enthusiastic. I am often that way these days too.

I have after all been so lucky. Two good men have loved me, and I have loved them.

And I thought I might die without love, unless I charmed a man by rapping on a wall.

PART I

SARA

SARA * · * · · · · · · · · · · · · · · · ·
conceiving Zoe   loving Carlo

1

LATER ON, GORDON WOULD SAY it was all her fault, but as Sara would always point out, she had certainly warned him at the time.

And it wasn't as if they were crazy young lovers. He was forty, she was thirty-six, and they had two sons, Roland, eight, and Rory, four. Married for eleven years, Sara and Gordon had already made love some twelve hundred times, by her later calculation, the night she drew back and said, "Honey, we can't tonight."

Gordon didn't answer. He moved his hand from one of her breasts to the other. He did not like to talk during sex, not even during foreplay. He expected silent acquiescence.

Gordon had come home from work that evening bearing

3

roses and champagne. In the living room, by the loom, he had made a toast: "To Sara, my talented wife."

"And our talented mom," said Roland.

They clinked glasses and Rory spilled some ginger ale on the floor. Sara swallowed some champagne and got a paper towel from the kitchen. As she wiped the floor, she remarked, "Just because I sold a rug this afternoon, I'm no more talented today than I was yesterday."

"Just a bit richer," said Gordon.

"Pin money," she said, "and you know it."

"It all helps," he said.

Sara said, "Dinner's my treat."

"Pay ostentatiously," said Gordon. "Make me feel kept."

"What about us?" asked Roland.

Sara said, "A sitter and chicken pot pie. Ice cream for dessert."

"Yay," said Rory.

"Boo," said Roland.

"I mean, boo," said Rory agreeably. He idolized his older brother.

Gordon said, "Sara, wear the blue blouse. You know."
Sara beamed at him.

"Ma," said Roland, "who's going to baby-sit us?"

"Susan is," said Sara. "And you mean baby-sit *for* us. It isn't a transitive verb."

"It's becoming one," Gordon said. "I hear it used that way a lot."

"Not here you don't," said Sara. "It sounds so ugly."

" 'Baby-sit us,' " Gordon mused. "It does have a smothering feel."

Roland said, "Mom, I need you to sign a permission slip."

"In the morning," she said, going upstairs to get dressed in narrow black pants and the blue silk wraparound blouse—Gordon's favorite because it would loosen to reveal the uppermost swell of her breasts. She opened her jewelery box and

4

took out a slender silver necklace with small blue stones. It had a difficult clasp, and she felt the blood draining from her arms as she tried to join the two ends of her necklace at the back of her neck.

"Let me," said Gordon when he came into the room. Even looking at the fastening, he had some trouble. "There," he said at last.

They left, they ate, they drank, they walked home tipsy through the West Village.

Now, in bed with her husband, she was wearing nothing but the necklace. Neither of them was in any shape to fiddle with the clasp, but she was not so drunk she didn't remember, and tell him—although he later charged that she might have told him *sooner*. Sara said, "Honey, we can't tonight."

Gordon continued stroking her breasts.

Sara whispered, embarrassed in the darkened room, "I ran out of stuff. It wouldn't be safe."

He began caressing her again in a purposeful manner—her announcement neither deterring nor deflecting him. She opened her eyes, flattered and surprised. Now he reached down and opened her legs.

"But, Gordon!"

"I'll be careful. Ohh." And then he was in her. He paused to stroke her hair back from her forehead while he looked into her eyes. She felt she was, at that moment, child and lover, sister and mother. Then he was moving, and she closed her eyes to be with him: his wife. Soon she was sighing and moaning, he knew her so well. Master, she thought, as she shuddered against him.

He left, they both thought, just in time.

But four weeks later Sara took a home test and learned she was pregnant. She came out grinning from the bathroom. She was silly with her sons. She hummed at the loom. She tried to imagine what another boy would be like: maybe a blend of

Roland and Rory—blond and taunting like the one, skinny and shrewd like the other? Or she could have a girl. A girl would be so novel and intimate, so dangerously familiar. . . . Sara thought having a daughter would be the greatest joy and heartbreak of her life. And she would smile some more.

She savored her secret for days, while her embryo doubled and redoubled. After a week, she thought her husband should know. The boys were asleep, and she and Gordon were alone in the bedroom. She was wearing her white lace nightgown, and he was reading a computer magazine.

"Gordon," she said, "I have news."

"Good news or bad?" he asked, not looking up from his pages.

"Good, I think. I hope."

"Well, let's hear it." He put the magazine down. "Sara, what is it?"

Sara said, "I'm pregnant."

"No. No! Are you sure?"

She nodded. "I took a test."

"But I thought that you always . . ."

"Remember the night we celebrated my rug sale?"

"But I was so careful."

"Apparently not."

After a pause, Gordon said, "How could you run out of spermicide? I mean, Sara, there's a drugstore right around the corner."

She said softly, "I don't get it there."

"What?"

"They know me there."

"So . . . ?"

"I don't want the pharmacist thinking about me like that. Thinking I use too much of it. Or too little."

"That's ludicrous."

"I guess you're right." Sara drew a deep breath. "Anyway, looks like we're going to be parents again."

"Oh no we're not. Two kids are plenty."

"Come on, Gordon. You have so much fun with the boys."

"The boys are just fine. I don't need another child. I don't want another child. And I'm not going to *have* another child just because my wife is too ladylike to stock up on diaphragm jelly!"

"Stop shouting," she said.

They stared at each other. Sara saw a tall, craggy man with shaggy eyebrows and intense dark eyes. He had a lot of very straight, flyaway gray-and-black hair. He had smooth tan skin, a hawk nose, and square white teeth. His smile was wonderful, but he wasn't smiling now. He said, softly, menacingly, "No more children."

"Just one more," Sara said.

" 'Just one more,' " he mimicked. "It's not some bonbon we're talking about! With three we'd be outnumbered."

"Outnumbered? What is this—parent versus kid? It's not like that with Roland and Rory. It's not warfare between us and them."

"It's all the obligations," Gordon said. "All the work."

She said, "I'd do all the work." She thought: I do ninety-five percent of it anyway.

He said, "And I'd have all the obligations. The drone. Supporting this circus."

Sara said, "You'd work just as hard without us—and you know it." Gordon had a small software business, developing computer programs for the entertainment industry. He had to work hard to keep up, and he did. Sara said, "Thank God you're successful."

"That doesn't mean you can loll around raising kids all your life."

"It's not exactly lolling," she said with a smile. Sara loved the infant months and early years. Her two sons were aging fast, already well into childhood. Now once again she might have the joy, the *privilege* of living with a baby. Perhaps she would even have a little girl.

"Look at you," he said. "You revel in it."

"Well, what's wrong with that? Just look at the boys!"

"The boys are terrific. Nobody said you weren't a great mother."

"Then we should have another child. Ordinary parents have two, that's their quota, their duty. But great parents . . ."

"Stop being cute," Gordon said. "It doesn't work like that. When are you going to grow up and face the music?"

"The music?"

"The money," said Gordon.

"Oh, that kind of music."

"Maybe even make some contribution."

"But, Gordon, what kind of job could I get?"

He said, "Something in textiles or design? I don't know."

"Well, I don't know either," Sara said, "I don't." Her rugs and hangings earned her two or three thousand a year. She hadn't earned much or fulfilled her promise as an artist, she knew, but if she had three children, *three*, who could call her a failure? Ashamed of the thought, she said, "Gordon? Don't you think another baby would be fun?"

"No," he said. "I don't. We did all that already. The baby food and the stroller and the Pampers in the garbage. And those Wipe 'n Dipe things for their behinds. Sara, think of your *life*. Rory's going to kindergarten in September, nine to three. You'll have some time for yourself . . . time for your rugs . . . or for courses. Time to prepare for a career . . ."

"I don't want more time for myself. I don't want to take courses or prepare for a career. I just want to have this baby. Come on. Don't you want to have a little girl?"

"I would like to have *had* a girl, I guess. But we've had our kids. It's time to move on."

Sara said, "You just lust for that second income you imagine I can bring."

"More cash flow would be nice," he agreed, "but I'm doing

okay. You don't have to work if you don't want to. If you don't mind being the last of the middle-class housewives."

"Not a bit." Sara began to feel hopeful. "You know, I can go look for work when the baby is three. Get executive training or something."

"No baby," Gordon said. "No way." And he left the room, with the computer magazine. Sara heard him running a bath. She got into bed and waited for him to come out so they could continue their conversation, but she soon fell asleep.

In the middle of the night, he began stroking her breasts. Sara, waking slowly, was about to leave for the bathroom when she realized she was pregnant already, she didn't have to take any precautions. It was utter luxury to turn to him then.

The curious thing about their marriage, Sara thought the next morning, was how their shared sexual pleasure affected almost nothing. Or was that commonly the case in long marriages—and if so, why wasn't it commonly known? By day, Gordon, already dressed for work, seemed a different person from the night man who'd groaned in her ear. The morning man said, "So, when are you calling about the abortion?"

"Abortion?" Sara sat up in bed. "Are you crazy? You think I can scrape out our child like brushing my teeth?"

"Millions of women get abortions each year. What's the big deal?"

Sara shook her head. "I just couldn't. You know, I still have Rory's old baby clothes. . . . I always thought maybe . . ."

"No! Get rid of them!" He pushed over a chair. "Call up the Salvation Army!" He strode out of the room. Then he came back to say, "And for God's sake, call Planned Parenthood!"

She pretended not to hear, but that night he asked if she had called. When she said no, he left the house, even though she'd made lasagna for dinner.

She was weaving when he returned. The loom took up a quarter of the living room. She let the shuttle come to a stop. "It won't bother me if you take your meals out," she lied. "Only think up some explanation for your sons. 'Wayor Daddy, wayor Daddy?' " She imitated Rory.

"Tell him Daddy had to get away from Mommy and all her demands."

"I'm not asking for diamonds or pearls."

"I wish you were," Gordon said. "Want a necklace? Afterward?"

"To reward me for killing our baby?"

"How can you mouth this right-wing garbage? You who once marched for abortion?"

"I marched so that mothers could choose. And I've chosen." Only it didn't feel that way—as if, rather, she had been chosen. Chosen to raise a new human being, maybe a girl, chosen to nurse another baby.

"What about *my* choice?" Gordon was asking. "Don't I count?"

Sara looked at him and considered. About the baby in her body, Gordon's feelings really didn't count that much. "I'm sorry," she said. She stood up from her seat at the loom.

He said, "If you have this baby, you'll really be sorry."

Sara said, "If I *don't* have it, we'll *both* be really sorry."

"What is that supposed to mean?"

She was silent. Then she burst out, "Maybe I'll have a miscarriage." She added, bitterly, "You better hope I will."

"Well, I do! After all, it's just a cluster of cells now."

"Why don't you get it over with and punch me in the stomach?" She walked across the room to present her body to him.

He moved back and said, "Please!" Then he said, "I just don't get your great mothering urge. We already *have* children."

"Don't you see? That's just it. I know what it's like to have a baby inside. It's not abstract. And right now it's *not* just a

10

cluster of cells. It's a baby, Gordon, just beginning. And I want it to live."

"One life to live?" Gordon sneered.

"Remember," she said. "You can't force me to get an abortion."

"I'm warning you, Sara."

"What? What's your great threat?"

He grabbed her by the shoulders and shook her.

"He-man!" she jeered.

He flung her down on the couch. Bouncing there triumphantly, Sara taunted, "Next thing I suppose you'll be beating me up."

"You deserve it," he said but left the room.

They scarcely spoke for days. Then Sara came into the study to look for her checkbook and found Gordon sobbing silently over his desk.

"What is it, what?" She was wholly surprised.

"*What?* You think you're the only one who has any feelings? I don't want this child. I don't. I keep telling you. Can't you understand?"

"Shh, Gordon, yes, okay, you don't want the baby." When his shoulders stopped shaking, Sara said, "But why? That's what I don't understand."

"I just don't." He blew his nose. "All the money. All the bother. All the complications."

"Such minor things compared to a life!"

"Maybe minor to you. But it costs a quarter of a million dollars to raise a child to age twenty-one."

"You don't have to pay all at once," she said jokingly. "There's an installment plan." Then she looked at his face. "Honey, don't worry so much." She smoothed his left eyebrow where the hairs were hanging down over his eye.

He pushed her hand away. "You don't get it, do you? I'm already smothered. Trapped. And you want to nail the coffin lid down."

Sara was taken aback. "Do you really feel that way? Honestly?"

He nodded.

The next day, she called Planned Parenthood. Tears ran down her face as she made the appointment.

When Gordon came home, the boys were already in bed, and she told him she'd made the call. "We both have to go there," she said. "For counseling, first."

"Great," he said. "Wonderful. When?"

"Thursday."

"Fine. Don't sound so bleak—we're doing the right thing. A child should be wanted. By mother *and* father."

"I suppose." She was suddenly exhausted. "I'm going to bed now."

"I'll come with you," he offered.

"That's all right, I'm really tired."

"Good night, then," said Gordon. He held her in his arms and kissed her on the mouth. She did not respond.

2

Sara had always pictured herself the mother of girls. The oldest of three sisters, she sentimentalized her childhood and pored over pictures of them all as children. Sweet little Sara. Pretty little Perri. Funny little Lucy. Sara had been good with her sisters and had taken care of them from the start. From the age of nine (Perri was six and Lucy was three), Sara could imagine no future for herself that didn't involve raising children. She ruled out certain professions—medicine, law—because they meant too much time away from the kids she was planning to produce.

She did well in high school and college and art school. But until the age of twenty-five, Sara was waiting to get married and have children. Waiting, she wove. Two of her wall hangings won prizes; one of her rugs still hung in a small museum.

13

But Sara felt her true vocation would be motherhood. She judged the men she dated as future fathers—and she fell in love with Gordon.

Did she really want to marry a man who liked to take afternoon naps? A man who rarely noticed what she was wearing or looked in the mirror himself? A man who read road maps in bed, and put a blue bulb in the refrigerator—to make the food look colder? Love and biology amazed her. By their third date Sara knew (intensely, inexplicably) that she wanted this man to father her children—her *girls*, if she was lucky. In Gordon she saw a man who was overwhelmingly *good*: a virtuous man with good genes, a good heart, and a good sense of humor. He even smelled good. She loved it at night when he finally turned away from her and went to sleep. Then she could throw her arm around his shoulder and burrow against his broad back, face against featureless flesh; it made her feel so settled, so secure. She really did want to stay with Gordon, she always concluded. But the next day she would marvel again at the mate she had chosen, whose outlook and interests differed so greatly from hers.

They got married. The years passed. They had a baby, and another, little boys. And motherhood exceeded even Sara's expectations. It was so good she wanted to do it again. Grow a baby. Feed it. Burp it. Everything.

Yet here she was in the waiting room of an abortion clinic. She and Gordon, waiting for obligatory counseling, sat one seat apart from each other. Sara was filling out the lengthy questionnaire. Gordon was doing some work on his lap computer.

"Look at this," she said to Gordon. She showed him the form and pointed to the waiver that she had to sign, absolving the clinic of any blame should the procedure result in complications or death. "Death," she said aloud.

"It's just an insurance formality," said Gordon. "No one dies of an abortion anymore."

"That's not entirely true, you know."

"Sign the thing, Sara."

She went back to her seat, signed the form, and returned the questionnaire and clipboard to the receptionist. There was only one other couple in the waiting room: Hispanic, twenty years younger than the Lenoxes. Although the clinic was almost empty, Sara and Gordon had to wait forty minutes before an abortion counselor was ready to see them. Since it was the first time they had ever sought counseling, either singly or jointly, Sara found herself looking forward to the process and to Gordon's reactions. She hoped the counselor would be wise and that Gordon would see that they should keep the baby.

At last the receptionist looked up. "Mr. and Mrs. Lenox? Ms. Watkins will see you in Room 303." Sara waited as Gordon folded up his computer.

When they opened the door, Sara saw that their counselor was not the seasoned therapist she'd been hoping for. Ms. Leola Watkins—identified by a nameplate on her desk—was in her early twenties. Perhaps new on the job, she had a list of questions she kept consulting. Sara and Gordon had to answer in turn. Gordon interrupted Sara twice, for which he was gently rebuked. Ms. Watkins seemed much more sympathetic to Gordon's side of the story than to Sara's. When Gordon spoke, Ms. Watkins nodded. Sara thought that maybe this was the wrong place to get counseling: perhaps the counselors always urged pregnant women to abort when the spouses disagreed.

When Gordon finished presenting his case, Ms. Watkins said to Sara, "You've got to be willing to compromise."

"There *is* no compromise," Sara said. "Not about this."

"Ms. Watkins means, overall," Gordon said. "In long-range goals. So, you wanted three children but you'll only get two. That's a compromise."

Ms. Watkins watched approvingly.

Sara said, "I don't want to compromise like that."

Ms. Watkins said, "You have to consider your husband's needs, irregardless."

Sara's eyes met Gordon's and they both looked down, repressing laughter. He was more successful than she.

"What's so funny?" Ms. Watkins asked Sara.

"Well, 'considering his needs,' " Sara improvised. "I mean, it seems I'm *always* doing that! How do you think this baby started? It wasn't *my* idea to make love that night."

"It never is," Gordon muttered.

"That's ridiculous," Sara said. "I never refuse you."

"And never make the first advance."

"How can I?" she protested. "You don't give me a chance."

"We're getting off the subject," Ms. Watkins said.

There was a short silence. Then Sara said, "Let me tell you what I dreamt last night. I dreamt I had this abortion you both want me to have, and they scraped the fetus out of me. Then—right there in front of me—they chopped the fetus very small so they could feed it to the rats. There were all these rats in cages all around. . . ." She couldn't go on.

Gordon passed Sara his handkerchief. He and Ms. Watkins exchanged looks. Ms. Watkins said to Sara, "That's just a dream, you know. You don't really think we—"

"Of course not," Sara sobbed. "But the dream shows how strongly I feel."

Gordon was already standing up. He said to Ms. Watkins, "There's not much point to this counseling."

"You both have to want it. And your wife has to want the abortion."

"I'll never want that," Sara said.

Ms. Watkins said, "Whatever you decide about that, I think that as a couple, you have major life problems to resolve. I recommend that you get further help, irregardless."

Sara honked into the handkerchief and brightened up perceptibly. They left Ms. Watkins's office.

"You're such a language snob," Gordon said when they were alone in the elevator. "Just because she says 'irregardless.' "

"I know. I'm ashamed." She tucked her arm into his as they walked into the lobby. "But thank you for getting me out of there."

"Well, that was a terrible dream."

"It was all so real," Sara said. "The nurses were stuffing these bits of chopped baby into the cages, and all the white rats were showing their teeth." She drew back her lips.

Gordon closed his eyes. "Please."

They walked down Second Avenue. It was a sullen February afternoon.

"So?" Sara said, hoping, knowing.

"So," Gordon said, "Sara wins again."

3

I**T HURT TO STAND, SO SARA SAT** on a stool near the stove and stirred the chicken-lemon sauce. In her ninth month of pregnancy, she was cooking dinner for her sisters and her sons (Gordon was out of town). Sara regretted that she hadn't sent out for some food, but a home-cooked meal was part of the tradition.

Whenever Perri or Lucy came home from a trip, they had their first dinner at Sara's. Tonight Perri was returning from a Europe shoot. Lucy was joining them. Sara knew that in their different ways she and Lucy—captive housewife and plain academic—made an excellent audience for Perri's tales of heat and lust. Professional travel, whether once as a fashion model or now as a documentary filmmaker, was just another chance for Perri's romantic adventures. Sara hoped that in Perri's new, more serious mode, she at least had the sense not to fool around with the crew.

Lucy let herself in with her key and called, "It's me." She came into the kitchen. "Sara," she said in a worried tone, "you look so tired."

"I have every right to look tired," said Sara. She put her hand on her belly and felt a kick. *His* kick, for Sara had a feeling the baby was a boy. "All mothers are tired at this stage."

"You weren't this way with the others."

"I probably was, you just forget. Anyway, I'm older now. Elderly, really, for this."

"An elderly thirty-seven," said Lucy, who was thirty-one.

"You just wait."

"Till I'm pregnant?" Lucy asked rather sharply.

"Why not?" Sara replied.

The doorbell rang. Lucy said, "I'll get it."

Sara heard her sisters murmuring at the doorway. Then Perri burst into the kitchen sporting a short new haircut. She had two shades of color on her lips and three around her eyes.

"Sara, darling, you're so pale!"

"And tired looking," Sara said. "Lucy's been telling me. You, however, look terrific. All made up just for us."

"Not at all," said Perri. "I find it soothing to apply cosmetics. Meditational."

"Ha," said Lucy, who never wore makeup.

"Girls," Sara said sternly, the way she'd stopped their squabbling as children.

Perri said to Sara, "You do look rather big."

"Perri, I'm due in a week. Of course I'm big."

"Let me set the table. Where are the boys?"

"At a friend's down the block. Gordon's in L.A. till tomorrow."

"What if you give birth?"

"I hope I do. Gordon would be *thrilled* if I gave birth without him."

"Come on, now." Lucy patted Sara's shoulder. "That's not true. You said he was great with the others."

Sara suddenly burst into tears.

Lucy led Sara to a couch in the living room. Perri turned off the gas so their dinner wouldn't burn. Sara gasped, "He hates me for having this baby. He hates me!"

"No, no," Lucy murmured. "He'll get over all that."

"I should have had the abortion."

"But you couldn't," Lucy said, stroking Sara's hair.

"I couldn't because of the boys." Sara sobbed. "Because I'd had babies in me before, because I couldn't let them scrape or suck away a life . . ."

"No, no, of course not," said Perri, who had had her first abortion at seventeen and her third the year before. "You're such a great mother, it will work out."

"The housework," Sara said, blowing her nose. "The shopping, the cooking, the cleaning, the laundry."

Perri said, not for the first time, "You could get some help."

"I don't like the idea of a stranger doing my dirty work."

Lucy pointed out, "She wouldn't be a stranger for long."

Perri said, "We both think your drudgery is somewhat self-imposed."

Sara said, "Oh, is that so? You've discussed it? Well, try discussing where I'll get the money. Gordon's not going to pay for anything extra right now. He considers this baby extravagance enough. Besides, he thinks I deserve constant exhaustion—at the *least*—as payment for this baby. He keeps saying, 'They'll outnumber us!' As if family life was a constant battle between parents and kids!"

"More like kid against kid when we were young," Perri said.

Lucy said, "They used to believe three years between kids

was the best possible spacing. Now they've decided it's the worst."

"Why?" Perri asked.

"The older one's at just the wrong stage to accept someone new, so the little kid gets picked on. The little one counters by appeals to the parent—which only makes the older one more jealous. The siblings are likely to fight a lot—at least that's this year's theory."

"We hardly fought at all," Sara said. Perri and Lucy laughed. "You both exaggerate," Sara insisted. She led with her belly to the kitchen. "Perri, how's your film?"

"Terrific. We got just what we needed—and more. An unexpected interview with Barbara Drowell in the British Museum. Haney and Frim in a pub. We almost didn't get that one, because our equipment—"

Roland and Rory burst into the kitchen just as Perri was warming to her subject. "Mom, I'm hungry," Rory said. "When are we going to eat?"

"Hi, Aunt Perri," said Roland. "You're back!"

"Did you get me a present?" Rory asked.

"*Rory*," Sara said.

Perri said, "Yes, I brought you *both* presents. Silly things. For silly boys."

"Hooray!" The boys began jumping around her.

Perri grinned at their greed.

"Appalling materialists," Sara said.

"Aha!" said Roland, pouncing on the shopping bag with the presents. "Where's mine?"

Perri reached in and brought out paper parcels for her nephews. "One for you and one for you."

The boys tore away the paper. "Oh, fresh," Rory said. He put on a plastic headpiece that made him look as if an arrow had penetrated his skull and come out the other side. "What did you get?" he asked Roland.

But Roland had left the kitchen. When he returned, he was

wearing fangs. A bloody wound gaped on his cheek, and a strand of phosphorescent snot hung to his chin. He tugged at Sara's arm. She saw him and screamed.

Roland cried triumphantly, "Busted!"

"I'll bust you," Sara said. "And you, too, Perri! What disgusting presents!"

"Ma, we think they're neat."

"You've probably started my labor."

"Well, you said you were tired of being pregnant," Roland replied.

Sara said, sotto voce, "He doesn't miss a trick."

After dinner, the women went upstairs to see Lucy's new couch, which had taken twenty-two weeks to arrive. Lucy had the fourth floor of the townhouse they shared; Perri, the third; and Sara, because of her family, had the parlor-floor duplex. The basement and the garden were shared space: off the garden was a small room where guests sometimes stayed.

Lucy had the stairs but also the stars and the sun. There were three skylights in her apartment: in the living room, kitchen, and bedroom. Perri had a little terrace near her bedroom. Sara had rococo ceiling moldings. The sisters had bought the small building five years earlier, after the death of their parents in a car crash in Connecticut. Sara had been outraged that the drunken driver of the other car had survived.

At the time, the three sisters lived separately in Manhattan: Sara, Gordon, and Roland in a small apartment in Murray Hill; Perri in a high-rent high-rise on the Upper East Side; Lucy in an airy Columbia University–owned apartment building where she'd been mugged twice. It was Sara's idea to use their parents' estate to buy a place together. She searched for months and finally found Seventeen Morton Street in southwest Greenwich Village, a neighborhood of old trees and old houses. Five minutes from midtown (at least at night by cab), it was an oasis in the city. The buildings were low and tidy and there were flowers in the window boxes. It was not the tourists' Greenwich Village—it was a quiet pocket by the river, an area of bourgeois bohemians, rich gay couples, lucky people on rent control, Puerto Rican supers and their families.

Seventeen Morton Street, Sara felt, had worked out very well. It had kept the three sisters together—independent but close. It had proved a good investment. And it meant that whatever happened, Gordon could never kick her out of the house, not that he would. Still.

"Marvelous couch," Perri said. "Even if you did have to wait all those months." She slipped a hand in her pocket and brought out a joint. "I love to smoke here. It's so cheery. Especially compared to my place."

Perri's apartment, on the floor below, was all mirrors and metal and various shades of gray. It had been done five years earlier, at great expense, by an architectural designer. Sara thought it was about as personal as a corporate lobby.

Lucy said, tactfully, "Your place is dead elegant."

Perri said, "I'm starting to think it's just dead. You've got all this . . . color. Warmth." She gestured around her.

It was true: even at night, the living room glowed. The walls were painted pale peach, and the wide-planked floors were stained the color of honey. There were apricot silk curtains at the window, and the new yellow leather couch faced the marble fireplace. A bonsai tree and a sculpted stone ashtray rested on a low rattan table.

Sara said, "The couch is just great. You do have a gift for decor. My place is twice as big and half as nice."

"Nonsense," Lucy said, "you've got all those great rugs."

"And roomfuls of clutter and mess."

"Well, your family . . ."

Perri dropped a match in the ashtray. Lucy moved the bonsai tree to the bedroom. When she returned to the living room, she held out her hand.

"Thank God you still smoke," Perri said. "Everyone else I know's quit. Here."

"I only smoke with you and with Paul." Lucy inhaled.

"It's funny that Paul should smoke grass," Sara mused. "It doesn't seem to fit."

"Oh, he's a great hedonist, for a fifty-year-old man."

"Fifty, Lucy, really?"

"Next month."

"How long have you been seeing him?" asked Perri.

"Four years."

"Four! I thought more like two."

"I didn't tell anyone at first. Then I got tired of you two thinking I never had a man."

"Heavens, Lucy, why should we think that?"

"For obvious reasons," Lucy said, turning away.

"Not to me," Perri said. "The joint."

Lucy passed it and said, "Do you remember that time Uncle Jack came up from Charleston to spend Christmas with us?"

"Sort of."

"I'll never forget it. I was nine. I came into the living room to find him posing you two by the Christmas tree. You both laughed and his camera went click. Click and click. I sucked a candy cane and waited for him to ask me to join you. Perhaps I moved forward. 'Hey, Lucy,' said Uncle Jack, 'you're blocking the light.' Then he took a whole roll of you two by the window. And one shot of me at the end."

"I don't remember that," Sara said.

"I do," Perri said. "I never liked Uncle Jack. Here."

Lucy extended her fingers for the joint.

Sara said, "Lucy, what long, slender fingers you have. Why don't you wear nail polish and rings?"

"What—*adorn* myself?"

"Things good with Paul?" Perri asked.

"Wonderful. When I see him. He's been in Nantucket for weeks."

24

"Will he ever leave his wife?"

"I doubt it."

Sara said, "You know, you're only thirty-one years old. Maybe you should try to meet someone else."

"I don't want to meet someone else."

"Maybe someone more appropriate," Perri said. "Someone to settle down with."

"Really, Perri. Get serious. Why don't *you* settle down?"

Perri said to Lucy, earnestly, "You mean, we're in the same boat?"

"Hardly," said Lucy.

Sara felt a pang for Lucy. Perri, at thirty-four, was gorgeous, even better looking than Sara. That Perri chose not to marry, but rather to fall for men who would never love her, did not liken her situation to Lucy's.

In fairy tales, the third and youngest daughter is the beauty, but it was quite the opposite with them. From the age of fifteen, either Sara or Perri could enter a store or a classroom and, at will, command attention and desire. Lucy was different. Her eyes were small, her nose was big, her hair was unruly, her body was thick. Lucy was the ugly duckling who would never be a swan. It was only in graduate school, when Lucy began publishing papers, that she was no longer pitied by her peers. Indeed, her success was envied by her male colleagues—especially when she got the Columbia University job. Still, Sara knew that few women would trade places—and faces—with Lucy. So when Perri came out with the "same boat" remark, Sara felt angry on Lucy's behalf. Perri could have a new boyfriend a week. Lucy had had one in her life.

"Don't you mind?" Perri insisted. "That he's married?"

Lucy said, "Not as much as I once did. It's really not so bad. I have a lot of time to work. I have someone to love. And I never have to cook."

"Oh, Lucy, you're so practical! Don't you ever scream and weep and moan?"

"Of course I do, Perri. I just don't pride myself on it."

"What do you pride yourself on?"

"My mind," Lucy said without hesitation. She held the joint out for Perri. "You know, sometimes I can actually feel my brain sorting through information, making connections—it's the biggest thrill of all."

"The biggest?" Perri wet her bottom lip with her tongue and rolled her eyes salaciously.

"Yes, Perri, the biggest. Just because we're sisters doesn't mean I'm as sex-mad as you are."

"No one's as sex-mad as I am," Perri said. "Want to hear what happened in Stockholm?"

"I suppose there's no stopping you," Sara replied.

"Actually, I need Lucy's advice about something else."

"Mine?"

"Well, you wrote that *Times* thing on women and power. You're the authority."

"Perri," Lucy protested, "I'm an authority on developmental psychology. The Op-Ed piece was a one-shot."

"Well, it got you a lot of attention. Now listen. I'm having these problems with Fenley. You remember our deal?"

"You were going to be coproducers, right?"

Perri nodded. "Right. He was the experienced producer, but the Writers Union film was my idea. So I worked for six months without pay and raised most of the budget—and now that the film's being made, it's like I no longer exist. He just goes ahead and does whatever he wants."

Lucy said, "What? Doesn't he even consult you?"

"Never. And he hates when I ask what's going on. 'Stay merry, Perri,' he says, like this rhyme is some kind of hilarious joke. 'I've made films for twenty-three years. Just leave it to me.' But that wasn't our arrangement! We were going to make the film together. And this was going to be my film school, so I could learn about producing films. But I'm learning very little except Fenley's dirty jokes—all of them awful."

26

Lucy said, "If *you* think they're bad, they must really be terrible."

Perri threw a cushion at Lucy. "Come on, Lucy," she said. "Help me. What do I do? Do I pout? Do I punch? Do I weep? Do I flirt?"

Sara and Lucy exchanged a look. Feminism hadn't much affected Perri.

"There are other options," Lucy remarked.

Going downstairs to her own apartment, Sara felt pain with every step—a dull ache high in her legs. Regrettably, however, she could detect no intimations of labor. She was certainly tired of being pregnant. This time around, it hadn't been fun. She was older now and Gordon was angrier. She hadn't dared complain of the various discomforts of pregnancy lest he jeer and gloat. She would never get into this fix again. Six weeks earlier she had signed the consent forms. They had to be signed in advance, to make sure you didn't tie your tubes in a passing pique, impetuously.

Sara finished cleaning the kitchen, and put Roland and Rory to bed. Then she took a long, hot shower. Very hot water sometimes induced labor. She shaved her legs so they would be smooth for the medical staff. She put on a thin cotton nightgown and got into bed.

It was 11:01. Orgasm, too, had been known to bring on labor. Gordon hadn't approached her in months, but Sara had recently made a shocking discovery: when she touched herself it was blissful as never before and as never with anyone. Perhaps the baby rested on some inner pleasure zone. Perhaps the guilt she felt (unnatural mother and mother-to-be!) heightened the excitement. Sara soon was gasping at the grand finale. She lay on the bed, shuddering and wondering: What does the baby feel now? It was 11:04.

4

SARA WENT INTO LABOR SUNDAY morning, so Gordon didn't have to miss any work.

They left for the hospital at nine. On the way to the taxi, Gordon bought the Sunday paper. "Oh, good," he said in the cab as he thumbed through the paper, section by section. " 'Personal Finance.' " He opened the supplement and turned to an article headlined, "The Real Costs of Having a Child." He held it out to her and said, "Look at this."

Sara was timing her contractions. "Every five minutes," she said.

Gordon skimmed through the first couple of paragraphs. "This guy says you have to consider not just how much the child costs, but how much your money would earn if it were otherwise invested. The real cost of having a child is over half a million bucks!"

"Gordon," Sara said, "I really don't feel very good."

"You're not supposed to," he said. "You're in labor. Remember?"

The pain passed. "Remember with Roland?" she said.

"Roland took forever! I'm hoping today to be home for the game."

"You're really a beast," Sara said, but Gordon was too busy reading the article to respond. Sara remembered being in labor with Roland, how calm she had been after the pains had begun. She had finished writing a letter to Lucy, who was then at Stanford. She had tidied up the apartment, and even sorted some dry laundry. When Gordon came home at seven, the pains were coming every ten minutes, but she was serene. "Your hospital bag," said Gordon. "Are you packed?" Sara had been packed for weeks, and she answered, "It's by the door." Outside, they walked up their street to Lexington Avenue to get a cab. Gordon dashed out to the middle of the avenue, and Sara, suddenly in pain again, leaned against an abandoned corner building. There were no cabs in sight, but a car, coming up the street, slowed down to stop beside Sara. A man rolled down his window and said, "Hi, there. Want to party?" Gordon came back for her then, and Sara stepped into the taxi Gordon had hailed. He put his arm around Sara and said, "Darling, how're you doing?" She giggled and replied, "Some man just tried to pick me up."

That had been nine years ago, and she had been too young and smug to fear childbirth. But in the final hour with Roland, she had forgotten about her Lamaze. She'd grabbed Gordon and begged, "Get me that doctor with the needle." But no doctor came and she found herself wrestling with two nurses. "They just want to put your hospital gown back on," Gordon explained. "Tell them to fuck off," Sara said. "It's my pain and I have to be naked!"

The last part with Rory had been equally intense: waves of cramping pain, and then the pushing out, the hugeness, the baby.

Now, as the taxi stopped for a light, Gordon said, "I hope I can sneak out for some breakfast."

"Don't count on it," Sara said. "It's coming fast. Oh. *Oh*." The taxi lurched around a corner.

"Come on, you're an old hand at this," Gordon said. She closed her eyes and was silent until they reached the hospital.

"Girl or boy?" asked the taxi driver.

"We don't know yet," Gordon said. "But we'll keep it, whatever her sex."

"Very funny," said Sara.

Because of Sara's intuition that the baby was a boy, she had chosen not to learn the baby's gender, although she'd had amniocentesis. She didn't want people to feel sorry for her during pregnancy. She also hoped Gordon would be consoled by the hope of a daughter. But in all of Sara's dreams the baby was a boy—a sweet, warm infant who looked like a blend of Roland and Rory. Another male. What a mistake, people would say. She broke up her marriage to have a third boy.

In the labor room, Gordon read the sports section and half of the magazine section while Sara's cervix dilated from five centimeters to nine. Twice, when asked, he held a wet wash-cloth to her face. Now and then he said, "Wow" at the strength of her contractions as displayed on the monitor screen. It was just like Gordon, Sara thought, to appreciate the new tech-nology of birth while all but ignoring his laboring wife. Would he ever relent? "Sara wins again," he had said those months before. Some victory.

Then a pain wave crashed so hard inside her it smashed all thought away.

When he next examined Sara, Dr. Silver was surprised to

find Gordon still reading the paper. "She's ready," he said. "Hurry up." He thrust a green scrub suit at Gordon. "Change in the bathroom."

The nurses shifted Sara onto a movable bed. "I gotta push," she muttered.

"No, wait till the delivery room."

"I can't wait," she moaned and it was upon her, she was pushing from the top of her head through her chest, through her gut, pushing and moaning.

They were running with her down the hall and to the delivery room. They shifted her onto another bed and put her feet in stirrups. A nurse curled Sara's hands around grippers to help her bear down. There was a moment of respite. She opened her eyes. Dr. Silver was saying, "I'm making one small incision."

Sara felt no pain, only a warm spurting.

Then she had to push again, and everyone around her bed cheered her on. She was the center, the heroine, the star. All the faces were smiling, nodding, waiting, the people were saying, "That's it, keep it up, very good, harder." And Gordon's face was nearest. "Almost there," he said. "Doing fine."

Sara shrieked jubilantly, "This is it!" And then she was yowling, straining, turning inside out, it felt, to let the head pass through.

Dr. Silver pulled the baby out. Sara felt all slack and rubbery, like a collapsed balloon. Dr. Silver exclaimed, "Oh!" (an Oscar presenter pleased that a favorite has won). He said, "It's a girl."

The baby began mewing, weakly, dryly. "Are you sure?" asked Sara, stunned. "A girl?"

"Oh, yes," said Dr. Silver. "You'll see for yourself in a moment. I'm cutting the cord now."

"You see," Sara said to Gordon. "We got our girl. Now aren't you happy?"

"She's blond or bald or both," he said.

"A fine little baby," said Dr. Silver. "Take a look." He held the baby up, and Sara stretched out her arms.

"I have to hold her," she said, and the naked baby was placed on Sara's breast. "My girlie," she said, weeping. "My tiny girlie."

Dr. Silver took the baby back. "Mommy gets you later." He gave the baby to a nurse. "We still have some more work here," he said to Sara.

"Get something to eat," Sara told Gordon. "I'm okay for the rest of this."

When Gordon returned, eating half an egg sandwich, Dr. Silver was washing his hands, and the clean and tightly swaddled baby was in Sara's arms. "Take a few minutes," said Dr. Silver. "I'm going to get the anesthesiologist."

"Can't I wait a little longer?" Sara asked.

"It's easier not to," Dr. Silver said. "See you soon."

Easier for whom? Sara thought. Then she and Gordon were alone.

He asked, "Are you sure you want to do this?"

"Certainly," Sara said. "I just wish it wasn't now."

"Because, I could do it instead."

"It's okay," she said. "This was our deal. I'd have the baby. And I'd have the operation."

"I'm not sure it's right."

"You've got to be kidding," Sara said. "After all our fights about having a third child—you can't want a *fourth*—can you?"

He shook his head.

"Well, then?"

He said, "It's irrevocable."

"So? We've had more than our quota. I can't imagine wanting still more." Now I've had my *girl*, she thought. She said to Gordon, "You amaze me."

A nurse came and took the baby from Sara.

"You look like you should rest," Gordon said. "Not go under the knife."

The anesthesiologist came into the room and said, "I'm Dr. Weinreich."

"You can still change your mind," Gordon told Sara.

Sara stared at Gordon, baffled. Then she turned to the young doctor. "I'm Sara Lenox."

Gordon said, insistently, "I don't feel right about all this." He came to the bed and took her hand.

Sara suddenly understood. "You have some premonition, and you're scared about this operation."

Gordon nodded.

"It's a simple procedure," said the anesthesiologist. "I do ten of these a week. Take a moment, if you want." He left the room and went down the hall.

Sara said to Gordon, "Don't be silly. Premonitions usually mean *nothing*. The whole time I was pregnant, I was sure the baby was another boy. She was always a boy in my dreams."

"Really? You never said anything."

"I knew you'd be disappointed."

Gordon tightened his grip on her hand and said, "Still, sometimes these flashes come true."

He meant, something could go wrong today. Sara knew what she had to do. She said, "Listen, if anything goes wrong, just remember—it's my choice, and I want to do this."

"Are you absolutely sure?"

"I sure don't want to go through hell again with you." They were chopping up her fetus to feed it to the rats.

"I'm sorry," he said. "I guess I've been hard on you."

She nodded.

He said, "I can't help myself sometimes."

"I know. But you have to try."

He was silent. Then he said, "No matter what, I love you."

He was gripping her fingers so tightly they hurt, but she

didn't mind. She swallowed the tears in her throat. She began stroking the back of his hand with her thumb.

Dr. Silver walked into the room. "Are you ready now, Sara?"

She nodded.

Just before they wheeled her away to be sterilized, Sara said, "Don't worry, Gordon. You'll see. Everything will be fine."

5

Sara awoke in the recovery room to see Gordon reading the "Arts and Leisure" section by the window. "Gordon," she said, but it came out "Hrgha." She tried again. "Gordon."

He came to her side. "Sara?"

"You see."

"See what?"

"I'm okay. It worked out. We're over it all." She drew his hand to her face and held it there. In fact, she felt awful.

Dr. Silver walked into the room. "So, how's it going? How do you feel?"

Sara tried to smile. "Not terrific," she said. "How many stitches did it take?"

"Not that many," he said—evasively, she thought.

Dr. Silver said, "You're going to feel tender inside for a while, maybe a week or two. And of course, you'll have gas, some abdominal pain. I'm putting you on a liquid diet till Tuesday."

"You never told me about any of this."

"Tubal ligation's an operation—a surgical procedure. It's a trauma to the body—on top of the trauma of birth."

"You're telling me. I feel like I've been beaten inside."

"In another hour, when the anasthesia wears off, you can have some Demerol."

"I feel like I've been cheated."

Dr. Silver took off his glasses and put them in his pocket. He said, "How have you been cheated?"

Sara said, "The other times after giving birth, I was *happy*. Now I just feel battered. And I can't even feed my baby till tomorrow."

"By tomorrow, you'll be ready for her. It was a routine operation. Perfectly straightforward. Like your delivery. You'll be fine. Tell her that, Mr. Lenox."

"You'll be fine," Gordon said.

But Sara turned to the wall to hide her wet eyes.

"The baby's perfect," said Dr. Silver impatiently. "You have nothing to cry about."

She heard him say to Gordon, "It will pass. She'll be all right in twenty-four hours." He left the room.

Gordon pulled a chair up to her bedside and sat down. He said, "Sara, listen. You're just having some chemical reaction. You'll be better tomorrow."

"Promise?"

Gordon nodded.

Sara said, "Tell me about the rabbits, George." She wondered why the only line she remembered from *Of Mice and Men* referred to an unfulfilled dream.

Gordon said, "All right, just a minute." He thought for a

short while. Then he took her hand. "Okay. Next summer, I'll take a two-month vacation and we'll rent a house at the beach. Roland and Rory will swim and fish and play ball. I'll play golf and grill fish. And you and the baby will sit on the beach under the red and yellow umbrella. You'll be watching the waves. . . ."

Her eyes were closed. "That's very nice." Soon she drifted into sleep.

For two days, Sara slept a lot. The abdominal pain ebbed and flowed according to the pills she was allowed, but the weariness was constant. Feeding the baby was all she had energy for—and looking at her, gazing at her face.

When Gordon came to visit Tuesday afternoon, the baby was in the room with Sara. The infant lay, neatly bundled, on her back, in a small bed with transparent plastic sides.

Sara said, "Go have a look at her."

Gordon walked around Sara's bed to get to the isolette. He looked down at his daughter.

Sara said, "Don't you see it?"

He remained silent.

"It's more apparent every day. She looks just like you!" Sara said.

"She looks like every newborn baby. Like a mouse, or a plucked chicken." Then Gordon's voice became almost affectionate. "Goo goo. Hello. Her eyes are open."

"Look at her eyebrows and mouth," Sara said. "Yours!"

"If you say so." He put his hand close to the baby's face and moved his fingers back and forth. "So it's Zoe," he said. "You're sure?"

"We've had Zoe in mind three times now," Sara said. "Of course I'm sure."

"She's following my fingers," Gordon said. "What about Laura?"

"Zoe," Sara said.

37

"All right, all right." He left the baby's side and returned to the chair near Sara's bed. "I heard about something today," Gordon said. "How would you like an au pair?"

"Your mother's coming to stay again," Sara said. "You know that."

"I mean afterward. In October. Someone to live in."

Sara stared at him in great surprise. "You mean just to make things easier for me?"

"Well, don't you complain about how much you have to do? About the laundry and the dishes? About needing time at the loom?"

"Go on," Sara said.

"Don has this Italian friend in Florence," Gordon began. (Gordon's company had developed several computer programs for Don.) "The friend has this kid, Carla, who's a graduate student at NYU. She has no place to live, maybe we could work something out in exchange for some help, let her live downstairs, in the garden room. . . ."

"But that's supposed to be shared space."

"Ask your sisters," Gordon said. "I bet they won't mind."

"What if we don't like her?"

"Then we won't hire her. You can interview her."

"Okay." She lay back against the pillows.

Gordon said, "It makes a lot of sense to have an au pair live downstairs. We don't lose our privacy—she's not really living with us—but she's there when you want her."

Sara said, "She can teach the kids Italian."

Perri came into the room, dressed all in blue. She wore a big shirt and slim pants and a belt with a large silver buckle. She rushed to Sara's side and embraced her hard. Sara thought she heard a gulp in Perri's throat.

"Perri! What is it? Not Roland? . . . *Rory*?"

"It's Lucy. Something horrible happened. Paul died in her bed this afternoon."

"Oh, *God*." Sara sat up. "How terrible!"

Perri nodded.

"What happened?" Gordon asked.

"I'm not sure. They made love, they fell asleep—and when Lucy woke up, he was dead in her arms."

"Then what?"

Perri said, "Then she called me, and I went up and we made things look respectable."

Sara said, "You touched him?"

"I had to. It was no big deal. Then we called the police and they took him away. She went with him to the hospital."

"Poor Lucy," Sara said.

Perri nodded. "Let me see the baby," she said solemnly. She strode over to the isolette, peered in, and gave an involuntary smile. "Gordon, she looks just like you."

Sara said, "You see?"

Gordon shrugged. "Maybe." He and Perri had never got along: he thought she was zany and self-centered, a poor influence on Sara. She thought he was dull and dreary, a clod.

Perri was still staring at the baby. She said, "Can I hold her?"

Gordon said, "You'd better not, you're not even supposed to be here in the room with her."

Perri said to annoy him, "I'll grab her later." She said to Sara, "She's adorable. I'm envious."

"You'd better hurry up and get on with it," Sara said.

"I just keep meeting Mr. Wrong," Perri said, with some satisfaction. They had discussed this often. Perri was very tolerant of her own proclivities.

The baby began a snuffly sort of mew. "Hungry girlie," Gordon said. He turned to Sara. "Mommy? Someone's calling."

"Do you think you could pass her to me?" asked Sara. There was an edge to her voice: you always had to *tell* Gordon this sort of thing, he would never volunteer.

The baby mewed again, and Gordon reached into the isolette. "She's so little, it's hard to get a grip."

"She's not *that* delicate," Sara said. "You're holding her like a poached egg. You've forgotten your technique."

"I didn't think I'd need it again," Gordon muttered, awkwardly placing the baby in Sara's arms.

"Low blow," Perri said.

Gordon said, "What was that?"

"You heard," said Perri.

Gordon turned to his wife. "I'll tell Don you're interested, Sara."

"What?"

"About the au pair." And he left.

Sara closed her eyes and shook her head. She looked lost and forlorn.

Perri said harshly, "*You'll* be okay. It's Lucy we have to worry about."

"You're right."

"Paul was the only man in her life. I mean, *ever*."

"It's not going to be easy for her," Sara said. "You know, I stare at the baby for hours, hoping she'll be pretty. I never did that with the boys."

"We were the lucky ones," Perri said. "It's a wonder Lucy doesn't hate us."

"Apparently, looks matter less as you get older."

"Big deal," said Perri. "Everything matters less as you get older."

The baby began her mew again, more vigorously, and Sara undid the top of her nightgown and brought the baby's moving mouth against her nipple. Sara hurt three ways as her baby sucked. Her nipple was sore, her stomach was burning, and her abdomen was cramping.

Her episiotomy only hurt when she walked, as did the tops of her legs. This Carla might work out very well. Sara thought:

I'll certainly need help this time around, even after Gordon's mother leaves.

"Perri," she said suddenly, "how would you feel about my having an au pair live in the basement?"

"In the room by the garden?"

Sara nodded.

"That's fine with me," Perri said. "If she doesn't mind the damp."

6

T<small>HE AU PAIR CANDIDATE TELE-</small>phoned a week after Sara came home from the hospital.

Sara said, "Hello?"

She heard, "This is Carla. Carla Rinaldi." It was a low, lightly accented, musical voice. "Don told me to call . . ."

"Of course," said Sara. "I'm looking forward to meeting you."

"I could maybe come this afternoon? Is that a good time for you?"

"That's fine. Around two?" Zoe was due to be fed at one and would certainly be finished by two. Sara wasn't especially modest, but she didn't want to conduct a job interview barebreasted.

"Two o'clock is excellent."

42

"What do you study?" Sara asked before saying good-bye.

"Urban forestry," was the reply.

What could that be, Sara wondered—planting trees on terraces? Smokey the Bear rides the subways? There were so many strange subjects these days. She knew someone who had studied media ecology.

Gordon's mother Lydia came into the room, wearing a bibbed apron. "Sara? Lunch is ready."

They ate in the dining room. Lydia took off her apron and gave her daughter-in-law some fresh cream of broccoli soup.

"Wonderful soup," Sara said. "Hint of nutmeg?"

Lydia nodded. "Sara, dear, have you ever hired anyone to help you before?"

"Just baby-sitters. And a wallpaper hanger."

"This is different," Lydia said, patting her mouth with one of the cloth napkins she insisted on using. "You must make it very clear in the interview just what you expect from this girl. You have to spell out every single thing you'd like her to do. If you add chores later on, she'll just feel badly treated and abused. After a while, you can always lessen her duties, but if you try adding to them, you'll have trouble.

"Another thing," Lydia continued. "These au pair girls sometimes need taking care of themselves. Here they are, eighteen and in a new country, with new customs, new freedoms, they get frightened, they need help."

"This is a graduate student. She sounded very self-assured on the phone."

"I hope so," Lydia said.

While nursing Zoe at her left breast, Sara tucked a clipboard under her right one and made a list of the various chores the au pair could do. Carla could help her with shopping and laundry and housework. Depending on her school schedule, she could take Roland and Rory to the park in the afternoon. Perhaps she could iron and mend. Certainly, if she was home in the evening, she could baby-sit. Sara herself would cook and look after Zoe—activities she enjoyed. And she'd have time for the loom.

The bell rang at two o'clock sharp. Sara imagined a black-haired young girl waiting by the curb until the exact time. Lydia was taking her afternoon walk ("After fifty, dear, the secret of beauty is lots of interests, lots of fun, and plenty of activity!"), so Sara answered the door.

It was, she thought, some mistake. A blond young man in a well-cut tweed jacket was standing at her door. "Yes?" she said, puzzled. "Can I help you?"

"But I'm Carlo," he said. "Carlo Rinaldi. Have I not understood? Am I late?"

Sara blushed. "Not at all. Please come in. I was expecting . . . I thought . . . never mind. So!"

"So," said Carlo. They faced each other, smiling.

He was of medium height with olive skin and eyes of pale brown. He was a very handsome boy, she thought—and not really a boy. Surely he was twenty-three. "Please sit down," she said, tugging at her sweater to make it lie smooth. Two weeks after giving birth, she was only about ten pounds above her normal weight. ("A pound in each cheek and two in each buttock and tit" was how Perri described it. "Very flattering!") Sara was suddenly conscious of being an attractive woman talking to an attractive man. "Why don't you tell me about yourself?" she asked, as if they were on a date.

"Well, I am the second son of Luigi and Franca Rinaldi of Florence."

This information, though important to Carlo, didn't mean very much to Sara. She prodded, gently, "Your father is a friend of Don's."

"That's right, from their student days. I grew up in our family's palazzo and went to high school in Florence. Then I got my bachelor's degree from the University of Turin and published one book in Rome. Now I am studying here at your New York University for a graduate degree."

44

"After that you will teach?"

"Maybe not. I hope to get a job in urban planning."

"New York could use some of that."

They smiled at each other. Sara thought they should get down to business. "So, Carlo. You want a job as an au pair."

"It is a way to live for less. I don't want to take any more money from my mother."

"And your father?"

"My parents are divorced," Carlo said. He added vehemently, "I have nothing to do with my father."

"Well, he's friends with Don and Don's friends with us. . . ."

"The connection is enough remote," Carlo said huffily.

"That's true." Sara wondered why she was probing his story so intently. She said more gently, "You know, it's a little unusual for a boy, for a *man*," she hurried on, "to be an au pair. Have you had much experience with children?"

"Well, but certainly! I have cousins, nephews, nieces. I love children. They love me! I can, how do you say, *amuse* to them?"

Sara nodded, smiling. "That's right, amuse."

Carlo continued. "And they amuse to me. Children are much more interesting than adults."

"My feelings entirely!" Sara said, but never before had she admitted as much. "And babies? Do you know how to take care of babies?"

"Not so much," Carlo conceded. "You can teach me, can you not?" He looked into her eyes. His were very bright.

"Yes," said Sara, pulling her eyes away from his at last. "I suppose I can."

"This is a so beautiful house," Carlo said. "Where will I sleep?"

"You would sleep downstairs," Sara said, lightly stressing the conditional. He seemed to think he was hired already.

45

"There's a room off the garden, where my mother-in-law's staying now."

"Can I see it?"

She led him downstairs, past the laundry machines and the ironing board, to the garden room. Sara opened the door, and for a few moments they stood on the threshold, peeping in as if they were children on forbidden territory. The walls were white, the hooked rug (one of Sara's) was forest green, and the windows looked onto the garden. In one corner of the room, there was a small stove and refrigerator. A table doubled as a desk, and a new electric heater had been installed against the damp.

"The couch opens up to a double bed," Sara said.

"I am but a single man," Carlo said.

"Yes, well . . . The bathroom's over there."

Carlo looked in. "Fine. Bellissimo! I shall enjoy to live here. I can, perhaps, go into the garden? Take in the morning coffee there?"

"But of course! I do that myself, when it's warm." She pictured them both at the white wrought-iron table. Gordon almost never went into the garden. "We'd better go upstairs," Sara said, "so I can hear the baby if she cries."

On their way to the interior staircase in the basement, Carlo pointed to a closed door. "What is in there?" he asked.

Sara opened the door and turned on a switch. It was a small wood-paneled room that housed a hexagonally shaped hot tub. She rolled back the cover and a cloud of steam rose into the air. Underwater lights made the green water gleam. "I sometimes have trouble with my back," Sara said. "My husband had this built for my, um, for a birthday."

It had been her thirty-fifth, in fact, the "midpoint" she'd been dreading because, as she'd told Gordon, "Everyone knows that the second half of life isn't as good as the first. Your health declines. Your pleasure ebbs." Gordon's card—which accompanied a dozen hot-tub catalogues—had read,

"To my better half, for *her* better half and greater pleasure, greater health in all the years to come." It was true that Gordon had hoped that the hot tub would lead to hot sex, but it was also true, Sara thought, that it had been a wonderful, extravagant gift. Now, watching the water with Carlo, Sara tried to remember the last time she and Gordon had been in the hot tub together.

Upstairs, Sara asked Carlo, "What's your schedule? When do you have classes?" The telephone rang before he could answer.

"Sara," said Gordon, laughing, "I've just spoken to Don. There's been some misunderstanding about the au pair. It's Carlo, not Carla!"

"I know," Sara said. "He's right here."

"Well, don't be prejudiced against him just because he's a guy."

Sara smiled. "I'm not," she said. "Not at all."

Gordon said, "If women can drive trucks, men can take care of babies. It might even be better for Roland and Rory."

"You don't have to convince me," Sara said. "I agree." It was rare, these days, that they agreed about anything.

"So it's all set?" he asked.

"I think so," she said. "Yes."

There was a key in the door and Lydia walked in.

Gordon said, "I'll be home for dinner around eight."

"See you then," said Sara.

Lydia and Carlo were by the front windows, agreeing that it was a perfect autumn day. Lydia said, "I walked all the way out to the edge of the pier, and the air was like pink champagne."

Sara smiled. "This lady can get drunk on the wind," she told Carlo.

"That is a good thing," said Carlo. "Love for life!"

"Tea anyone?" Lydia asked on her way to the kitchen.

"I have a class," Carlo said regretfully. "I am desolate."

Sara walked him to the door. Carlo said, "Shall I give to you a telephone call? And you can let me know?"

Sara said, "I can let you know now. My mother-in-law leaves next Sunday. You can move in any time after that."

Carlo broke into a big smile. "I am so happy," he said. "I am much looking forward to meeting your boys."

Sara watched him leave. He went bounding down the front steps like a schoolboy himself, his beige hair bobbing.

In the kitchen, Lydia, who was spooning tea leaves into a heated teapot, said, "Is *that* your new au pair?"

"Seems so," said Sara.

"A handsome young man," Lydia observed.

"He says he loves children," Sara said.

Lydia asked, "Did he agree to all this?" She pointed to the clipboard that rested on the counter. On the top sheet was the list of chores Sara had drawn up earlier.

Sara said, "He agreed to do his best," and she went to look out the back window. Outside in the garden, two sparrows were flying near the rosebush. Sara knew her face was red. Somehow, while talking to Carlo, she had forgotten to mention the housework.

7

Sara and Zoe were together in the upstairs bath. The baby hated bathing alone. Five weeks old, she would squawk until she turned almost eggplant in hue when she was lowered into water. But if Sara got into the tub with her and held her close the whole time, Zoe didn't mind the bath at all.

As for Sara, bathing with Zoe was bliss. Another—her last—nestling baby to comfort and nourish. Sara would let Zoe nurse in the bath, even if it was between feeds. Nursing was lovely now, easy, fulfilling. Just by existing, she satisfied this child, this little daughter, just by granting the baby bodily access.

Now Zoe sat back, half-immersed, against Sara's thighs. Her eyes and mouth were wide open; she looked birdlike and alert; she drooled into the water. With water-wrinkled hands, Sara washed the baby's arms, murmuring, "Wash you up, my buttercup," whatever nonsense came into her head.

Roland banged against the bathroom door and bawled, "Mom, Dad's on the phone."

Sara shouted back, "Tell him I'm coming!" She stood up with Zoe. She wrapped the baby in a towel and placed her on the hamper top. Sara formed a sort of baby security fence with her thighs as she put on her terry-cloth robe. Then she lifted Zoe onto her shoulder and stepped into the hallway, leaving wet footprints. As she passed the boys' open doorway, she glanced in. Roland and Carlo were playing chess on the floor while Rory watched. Carlo looked up at her in her robe. Sara hurried on down the hall, conscious of her naked feet leaving footprints.

When she got to the phone, the line was dead, but Gordon called her back two minutes later. "Well, it's happening," said Gordon. "Disaster."

"What's happening?" Sara was terrified. Illness, death, World War III?

Gordon said, "We're being audited."

"Is that all?"

" 'Is that all?' You idiot!"

"Don't call me an idiot!"

"Don't talk like one, then! Do you know what this means? I'll be busy for weeks, we'll owe thousands of dollars, they'll think it was fraud. . . ."

"We'll all go to jail, I suppose," Sara said. "Is there anything else? Or did you just call to *share* this wonderful news?"

"With my wonderful wife. Don't expect me for dinner." Gordon hung up.

Sara slammed the phone down after he did. She stood up, pulling hard on the ends of her robe belt. She put the baby in the crib. Then she went out to the hallway again, looking in at the boys around the chessboard on the floor.

"No, Roland," Carlo said, pronouncing it the French way. "Take back the move. You must ask of yourself why I moved the horse."

Rory said, "Daddy calls it a 'knight.' "

Sara said, "Carlo, would you like to have dinner with us tonight?"

Carlo said, "Oh! But certainly. That is so kind."

"Seven, then," Sara said. "And Roland. Bishop to knight five."

She went down the stairs and into the kitchen. It would be Carlo's first dinner with them, although he'd been their au pair for two weeks. Sara, who was fierce about her privacy, had made it clear to Carlo that normally he would be on his own for meals. At dinner, she wanted the freedoms that only come with family: she wanted to quarrel with Gordon or snap at the kids—unobserved by outsiders, witnesses.

But dinner wasn't only psychodrama and bad manners. Sometimes a question from one of the boys sparked Sara and Gordon, and they would go on defining and debating and discussing the best mode of explanation until the child was sorry he had asked the question in the first place. But information surely was absorbed. Sara had recently read an astonishing study that found that the single most important factor in predicting academic success was whether or not the child lived in a family where they all ate together and spoke at the table each night.

Sara went down to the kitchen to cut vegetables for a stir-fry, a dish she now made guiltily because of the oil. Americans, she knew, ate too much fat. Cooking wasn't as much fun as it had been before she'd learned that so many things were bad for you. She marveled that magazines could go on printing recipes that called for sticks of butter and pints of heavy cream. Surely these recipes should include a warning from the Surgeon General about arteriosclerosis. Sara opened the refrigerator and brought out the vegetables. She sliced small mounds of pepper, onions, broccoli, mushrooms, tofu. Carlo came into the kitchen holding Zoe awkwardly at his shoulder.

"I think this is a hungry girl," he said. The baby was sucking on his neck as if she could create a nipple there by suction only. "Is it time for her feeding?"

"Not really," Sara said. "I thought she would nap. Why don't you try walking back and forth with her for a while. . . ." Sara opened the refrigerator and brought out a bowl of marinated chicken pieces. Garlic and ginger wafted up at her. Zoe began crying.

Carlo walked with the wailing baby to the living room and came back with a small round cushion from the couch. "May I use this?" he asked Sara.

"Sure . . . what for?"

"Well, I thought, you see, for walking . . ." He stuffed the pillow inside his sweater and placed the baby against his artificial breast. He patted Zoe's back. "I've been watching you," he told Sara.

Sara was baffled. Was he mocking her bosom? Admiring it? Or being wholly ingenuous? The idea that you had to have breasts, real or false, to walk back and forth with a baby . . . ! Sara found herself snorting with laughter.

"Am I so funny?" Carlo asked. "I am overcoming my lacks."

"You don't need the cushion. Let me show you." Sara held out her arms for Zoe and demonstrated to Carlo how a baby could be held by a person without breasts. While passing Zoe back to him, Sara's hand happened to touch Carlo's. She felt her face flush. She had to remind herself that she had no interest at all in younger men, not even blond Italian ones.

Sara had never been drawn to younger men. To interest her, a man had to be older and seem wiser than she was. College boys on the street did not stir her fancy. But when, at a party, she saw a full head of silver hair and a certain sorrow in the eye, she had to cross the room and meet the man. Her only flirtation since her marriage had been with an older man. There had been several lunches—nothing more—but what food for the dream machine!

"There," she said to Carlo. "Now try walking her back and forth."

Zoe screamed louder than ever.

"I'll just have to feed her," Sara said.

Carlo said, "Would you like a glass of juice?"

"Why, yes." Sara was grateful that he had asked. A nursing mother had to drink a lot of liquids, and Sara drank enough throughout the day by sipping at a glass of milk or juice while she nursed. When she sat and drank and nursed, she thought: I'm just a liquid-processing machine. It was not a bad thought.

Carlo poured her some apple juice over ice and asked where she would sit.

Sara liked to nurse Zoe in a low armchair in the living room but had never done so with Carlo around. Her breasts were like melons, her nipples like plums. She didn't want to repel or arouse him; she didn't want to feel self-conscious. On the other hand, she planned to nurse Zoe for another six months; she couldn't keep hiding herself in her bedroom because of this handsome male au pair.

"I'll sit in the armchair," Sara said, walking to the living room. Carlo followed her and put the juice on a nearby table. Sara sat down with Zoe and picked up the shawl that lay on the arm of the chair. Although Carlo was walking back to the kitchen to wash the salad, Sara made a sort of tent with her shawl. Inside, she lifted her sweater, unhooked her bra, and applied little mouth to large nipple. Then she draped the shawl around herself and Zoe more comfortably. She knew that some people—Perri, for instance—thought her modesty excessive, but Perri didn't have the plumber in her past.

One afternoon when Sara had been nursing Roland in the Murray Hill apartment, a plumber had come to replace the shower head. Lydia had been visiting for the afternoon; Sara and the baby were on the living room couch. On the way to the bathroom, the plumber caught a glimpse of breast. "My God," Lydia said. "Your plumber looks transfixed."

The next day the man telephoned Sara to see how the shower was working. He said, "I want that shower to be very hot for you, know what I mean? Good and hard against your—"

Sara hung up in a hurry, but he called again the next afternoon. By chance, Gordon was home, so Sara said, calmly, "Perhaps you should speak to my husband about all of this. Gordon?" The man hung up and never called again, but for years she worried that something would go wrong in the bathroom and the landlord would send that plumber to her apartment again.

Of course, she lived in a different place now, but Sara had not forgotten what breasts could do to men. The shawl made nursing more discreet.

Carlo came into the living room as she was burping Zoe mid-feed. "Shall I cut up a cucumber for the salad—Eeee!"

Zoe was spitting up. Curdled milk fell to the floor. Sara said, "Get paper towels."

Carlo returned and began wiping up the mess. Watching him, Sara felt deeply embarrassed. Those globby curds of white were still warm from Zoe's body—and her own. She waited until he left the room before affixing Zoe to her other breast.

That night, because of course Europeans drink wine, Sara brought out a bottle of Chardonnay. She lit a fat sage candle she'd been saving for years. As she poured the boys' milk into a pitcher, she admired her table. She put on lipstick and earrings before calling Carlo and the boys. It seemed only natural to put Carlo in the chair where Gordon usually sat. Rory said, "Mommy, you're wearing perfume." Sara served the rice and heaped the chicken stir-fry over it.

"Such beautiful colors," Carlo said, and gave a small, refined, inquiring sniff at the steam from the food on his plate.

When Rory was served, he began picking out the mushrooms and moving them to the side of his plate. When Roland was served, he picked out the tofu.

"Mmmmm." Carlo closed his eyes. "What do you call this excellent dish?"

"Chicken wok," Roland answered. "Here, Ma." He scraped his tofu from his plate onto hers. "Passthesoysauceplease."

Carlo laughed. "What is your hurry?"

Sara said, "I keep trying to civilize him—without success." She reached for the soy sauce and moved it very slowly toward her son. She said to him, "I keep telling you. The faster you ask, the slower I'll pass." The bottle inched its way over the table.

As soon as it was within reach, Roland grabbed it from her hands. "Hey," she said indignantly. Roland smirked. She shook her head in feigned exasperation. In truth, she liked to let their squabbles end like this, with Roland (or Rory) thinking he had somehow bested her. Children were really so powerless, Sara thought, it was only fair to let them save face in the little encounters. Rory shoved his mushrooms onto her plate.

"When I was a little boy," Carlo said, "if I dropped a spoon or a fork, I had to go eat in the kitchen."

"By yourself?" Rory asked.

"Well, the cook was there and the maids, but it was exile. A disgrace."

"Just for dropping a fork," Roland said, "like this!" He knocked down his fork with his elbow and guffawed at the clatter.

Sara gave him a look and he mumbled, "SorryMa, justkidding."

Carlo said, "My father was very strict, very harsh."

Rory asked, "What's 'harsh'?"

"Hard," Carlo said. "Mean."

Sara said, finishing the wine in her glass, "Like a wind that comes howling in winter."

"Like the sound of a key in a lock," Carlo said as they heard the key turn.

Gordon opened the front door and strode into the dining room to find them laughing by candlelight. The crystal wine glasses gleamed. "What are you celebrating?" he demanded of Sara.

"Nothing—I thought you were coming home late."

"Changed my mind. I hope there's some food left for me."

"Of course there is." In truth, there wasn't much left, so Sara surreptitiously scraped what remained on her plate back into the wok. "Gordon, sit down."

"Where?" Gordon said, looking pointedly at Carlo.

Sara pushed an extra chair to the table and got Gordon a plate and cutlery from the kitchen.

Gordon said, "The food doesn't look hot anymore."

Sara said, "I'll heat it up for you, then. You *said* you were going to be late."

"I was too depressed to stay on. This is just the beginning. They'll investigate everything, personal, corporate, going back ten years. It's a fucking nightmare."

Sara thought it was very bad-mannered to allude to private matters in front of guests—even worse than the casual obscenity, which he knew she loathed. "We're being audited next month," she explained to Carlo.

"Audited?" Carlo asked.

She told him what the word meant, and asked about Italian tax practices, a subject she thought might interest Gordon. Carlo chatted on, but Gordon didn't say a word until he'd eaten his reheated portion of stir-fry (which was partly Sara's and so contained Rory's mushrooms and Roland's tofu).

When Gordon did finally talk, it was only to say, "I should never have listened to that fool of an accountant."

As Gordon began getting up, he leaned forward and banged the top of his head against the stained-glass lamp that was hanging low over the table. "Jesus Christ!" Gordon yelled.

"What an idiot place for a lamp!" He pushed the lamp so it swung back and forth.

"Careful," Sara cried, catching it so it didn't hit the wall. "It's a perfectly good place for the lamp. You're just not used to sitting there."

"Well, whose fault is *that*?" Gordon asked.

"It's all *my* fault," Sara said. "Your every little boo-boo— the audit"— she was about to add Zoe but, instantly editing, just said—"everything."

Gordon glared at her.

Rory said, "May we be excused?" The boys often left the table first.

Carlo said, "And I must go too. I must a book read for class."

Sara said to Carlo, "Of course you may go. I'm sorry about all of this . . ."

"Don't apologize for *me*," Gordon said.

Roland said, "Ma, may we *please* be excused."

"Yes," Sara said, "everyone can leave." She stood up and blew out the candle—harshly. Then she shouted, "Go on. Get out of here. All of you. Now."

8

It was saturday night, and Gordon was in the study, examining his tax records. The audit was eleven days away. "How many times can you chew on those miserable figures?" Sara asked. "Why don't you take a couple of hours off and come to the movies with me."

"Why don't you stop this puerile whining," replied Gordon. "I've got to know where I am. I'm spending two days in Toronto next week and I can't work on the taxes up there. Have you found that receipt envelope yet?"

Sara said, "I would have told you if I had." Certain of Sara's cash purchases at the stationery store or post office could be deducted as expenses; throughout the year, she threw the receipts into an envelope so she could add them up at tax time. They had a record of this total for the year of the audit, but someone had mislaid the receipts. Each thought the other had misplaced them, and Gordon asked her twice a day if she had found "those receipts you lost" yet. She couldn't see why these receipts were so important; the figures added up to $243.17. In that same year, through a series of honest mistakes he kept explaining to her in excruciating detail, Gordon had underreported his income by some $20,000. Given that significant an error, she couldn't see why he raged about the crummy cash receipts.

"I'm going to the Waverly," Sara said. "There's a ten o'clock show."

"You shouldn't go out at all. You should find that envelope you lost."

"Oh, get lost yourself, Mr. Misery. Gloompot."

"What if the baby wakes up? Don't expect me to take care of her!"

"Certainly not—you're only her father! Just let her scream!" Sara got her jacket and left the house, although it was only nine twenty-five.

She bought her movie ticket early, then decided to have coffee somewhere. Next door to the theater, there was a doughnut shop with greasy crullers on display and one of those mass-produced signs proclaiming "The World's Best Coffee." She walked inside; the place was empty except for two tough-looking men who stared at her bosom. She wondered what she was doing in such a seedy place; people came from all over the world to sit in charming Greenwich Village cafés—and here she was all alone in this ugly plastic dump that served food she didn't like. It occurred to her, with relief and surprise, that she could leave, and she turned and went out the door.

She crossed Sixth Avenue and walked one block east. Couples strolled up and down MacDougal Street; it was date night. A boy and girl of eighteen, wearing the same hairstyle and outfit, blew bubble gum as they paraded by. An artist chalked a picture on the sidewalk.

Sara went into the nearest café. Vivaldi played, the lights were soft, and the room was crowded with attractive and animated people. The waitress led her to a table and gave her a menu.

"Just a cappuccino, please," Sara said.

"Whipped cream?"

"No. Well, yes, I'm afraid. Yes."

The waitress smiled and left. Sara looked around. Everyone was talking or listening intently; it all felt very European. She congratulated herself on leaving the doughnut shop and coming to this place, just a minute away. She didn't mind being the only one alone. She thought, I'm so alone anyway. Gordon is gone for me now. She repeated the phrase in her mind, sobered by its feel of truth: Gordon is gone for me now.

The door of the café opened, and a man who looked like Carlo came in with a young woman. Then Sara saw that it *was* Carlo. Oddly embarrassed, she would have turned away, but he saw her first and said, "Hello, Sara." He smiled and came toward her with his date, crowing, "Long time no see."

Sara smiled. He'd uttered the banality proudly, obviously pleased with his mastery of American slang.

"May I?" Carlo asked as he sat down.

"Of course. But I have to leave soon for a movie."

Carlo and his friend sat down. "This is Lorraine," he said. "And this is Sara, my landlady."

Sara said, "You could call me something else."

Carlo said, "My boss?"

"That's even worse!"

"You're the one with all the children," Lorraine said.

"Only three," Sara said, with a certain pride.

"Lorraine is in the urban forestry program with me," Carlo said, "pushing bees."

"Bees?" Sara asked.

"Our helpers, our friends," Lorraine said. "There should be bees in every public park."

"You might say," said Carlo, staving off hilarity, "she has a bee in her bonnet."

Seeing Carlo laugh made Sara laugh too, and Lorraine herself forced a smile. She was surprisingly plain, Sara thought, for a girl friend of Carlo: pale, big-nosed, plump. Yet sometimes very handsome men were not drawn to beauty themselves. Maybe, possessing it, they sought other things. Maybe, too, Lorraine wasn't Carlo's girl friend, just a fellow student.

Sara said, "I'll be late for my show." She stood up.

"*Ciao*," Carlo said.

It seemed to Sara then that he looked very hard at her waist, as if examining her narrow, silver-buckled belt.

When she got home after the movie, Sara heard a curious sound coming from upstairs: a regular creak and a sort of hum. She heard the baby babble and Gordon murmur something. Sara tiptoed upstairs and looked into her bedroom. Gordon was in the rocking chair with Zoe, holding her close. He cooed to the baby, "Now, who's my little squidge?"

Then he saw Sara. He stopped rocking and said, "Here you are. Take the baby. She's been up for an hour. I had to change her. Now I've got to get back to the taxes."

Sara opened her blouse and took Zoe into her arms. She didn't bother with her shawl; Gordon would only look at her body if it were strewn with cash receipts. She thought, Maybe men and women react oppositely to stress, women wanting more sex, as relief, and men wanting none.

When Gordon finally came to bed, Sara reached for him with perfumed arms. He patted her head and shoulders and kissed her on the forehead. "Good night," he said, definitively, and turned away from her. He permitted her to hug him from behind, however, and she pressed her bare breasts against his clothed back, excited by the contrast. Perhaps if she kissed his neck very tenderly, really concentrated, it would get to him. She devoted herself to a tender tendon hollow. She couldn't tell if Gordon was aroused, but *she* certainly was. She touched his cheek. She stroked his head in the exact way she liked her head stroked, but he didn't respond. She sighed and rubbed her cheek against his T-shirted back. She realized he was sleeping. Soon, against all expectations, she fell asleep herself.

Sunday morning, Gordon was in the shower when she awoke, and Sunday night in bed was very like the night before. But early Monday morning, he woke up early and drew her to him, pulling her from a sea of sleep. Her dreams clung to her like seaweed. Gordon was lifting her nightgown, and she was hardly awake, and then he was in her. As usual after a sexual hiatus, it was too short, and now she was fully awake. He offered his usual alternate; she tendered her usual refusal. Knowing he was through cut something off in her, made sex lonely, somehow sad.

Gordon got up and began to pack. At nine, he left for Toronto. Sara went to the dentist at two. For once, there was no wait in his office, and she came home an hour early. She opened the door and found Roland and Rory watching "G.I. Joe." They were so riveted they scarcely noticed her entrance. She went upstairs to look at Zoe, but the baby was gone from her crib. "Carlo," Sara called. "Carlo?"

"He's downstairs!" Rory called up to her. Sara came downstairs again. Living room, dining room, kitchen, where were they?

"No, Mom, *downstairs*." Roland pointed toward the basement.

Sara went down the stairs quickly, past the washing machines, to Carlo's room. She opened the door. Carlo was at the table, bent over his books. Directly over his head, Zoe's portacot was suspended by a rope through its handles to a ceiling hook that usually held a hanging plant. Through the mesh sides of the portacot, Zoe could be seen, on all fours, raising her head. Carlo, unseeing, was rocking her with one hand, taking notes with the other.

"Hello," Sara said.

"Oh!" He jumped up. "You gave me a surprise!"

"Ingenious rigging," Sara remarked.

"So I can rock her and work all at once," he explained.

"Yes, but she's awake and lively now. She doesn't want rocking." Sara lifted Zoe out of the cot. She put her hand down the diaper. It was wet and cold. "When did you last change her?"

Carlo looked at her.

Sara said, "You haven't changed her at all. But I've been gone for three hours. You have to check these things, Carlo, I mean it."

Sara went back upstairs with Zoe. She rested her daughter on the changing table and took off the old diaper. "You didn't want rocking, you wanted to play," she told Zoe. She grew indignant thinking of Carlo mechanically rocking Zoe and letting the boys watch junky TV all afternoon. After all, Sara thought, Carlo was getting a mighty good deal: choice lodging and even some cash in exchange for baby-sitting weekday afternoons and some weekend nights. And he wasn't much help with the housework. Indeed, when Carlo gave the boys a snack, he left the three dirty plates and glasses on the counter or, at best, in the sink.

After dinner, when the boys were in bed, Sara went downstairs and knocked on Carlo's door.

"Please. Come in." He went to close his door behind them, but Sara said, "Leave it open so if Zoe wakes up I can hear."

Carlo had been studying and eating. Books were open on the table. A few oily, cooked lettucelike greens could be seen on the side of his plate: collards, dandelions, what?

Sara said, "I didn't mean to interrupt your dinner."

He pointed to his mostly empty plate. "I am finished. Would you like any coffee?" He was already pouring water and inserting a filter into an electric coffee maker.

Sara said, "Sure. But it's not a social visit." She swallowed. "Carlo, I'm disturbed about this afternoon."

He turned on the coffee machine and said, "Will be ready in two, three minutes. Please. Sit down."

Sara sat down stiffly in the only chair and Carlo sat on the bed. Sara said, "You're here to take care of my children, not to tranquilize them."

"Again?" he asked, puzzled.

Sara said, "You know the boys are not supposed to watch 'G.I. Joe.' And putting the baby's bed up there . . ." She looked up. Now the plant pot was back on its hook.

"I had to study," he said. "I have a big test tomorrow, and I am behind."

"I'm sorry to hear it. But you're neglecting my children. Zoe's got diaper rash now." Carlo looked at her incomprehendingly, so Sara explained. "Pink and sore between her legs because you didn't change her diaper."

He looked chagrined. "I am so sorry. Poor little one. I didn't know! It won't happen again."

"Good."

"Coffee's ready," said Carlo.

She said, "Maybe some other time. I see you're studying."

He got out two cups. "It's okay, I need a study cut."

"What? Oh, study break." She grinned.

The coffee was both thin and strong. Carlo had his black, but Sara, who liked hers light, found that no reasonable amount of milk could make it golden. What milk she'd used had made her coffee sepia, tepid.

Carlo said conversationally, "It's very interesting living here. With your family."

"Interesting? How?"

"The whole thing. Your boys. They're so intelligent. And you and your husband. So intense."

"Intense," mused Sara, somehow flattered.

"Oh, yes. And you and the children, so tender and loving. It makes me think of my family." Carlo fell silent.

Sara found herself saying, rather inanely, "It's natural to feel homesick now and then."

"No," Carlo said. "I mean my family to come. The wife I will have. And the children."

Sara smiled. "Well, Carlo. You're just a kid. You have plenty of time to think about all that."

"How many years do you give me?"

"I don't know. Twenty-two. Twenty-three."

He shook his head.

"What, then?" Sara asked.

"I'm twenty-nine."

"Really!" She stared at him. "Not just a kid," she murmured. Twenty-nine was certainly a man. An erotic pang went through her. Her friend Ruthie was dating a man of twenty-eight, a man not nearly as handsome and gallant as Carlo.

Carlo said, looking into her eyes, "What perfume is that you are wearing?"

Then they both heard Zoe's waking cry. Sara said, "I must go." But she didn't. She stood there in the doorway, looking in at him and at the dinner plate beyond. "Carlo?"

"Yes, Sara?" He moved a step closer.

And she forgot whatever it was she'd been going to say. "What, what, what is that vegetable you were eating? Those leaves?"

"Loosestrife—it grows in vacant lots downtown."

"Really. Is it any good?"

"But of course. Next time I'll cook some for you."

"Yes, that would be nice."

They stared at each other.

Zoe's cries grew more intense. Sara said, "I really have to go."

"*Ciao*, then," he said and squeezed her shoulder.

9

ONLY A SHOULDER, THE LEFT; and through cloth, a white cotton shirt; and but a brief squeeze, surely just a friendly gesture; only natural, as she was leaving the small space they had shared alone, as they were so rarely alone. Only a shoulder, then, just a large, glowing knob sending rays down her arm and body. Just a nothing touch, she reminded herself, not a kiss or caress. But as Sara slowly climbed the stairs, her head felt thick, and she could barely hear Zoe's cries.

The baby had worked herself into a fury and had to be patted and walked before she was calm enough to be changed. Then Sara got into her bed with her daughter. Zoe began sucking and patting Sara's breast, and Sara's left shoulder still glowed. Carlo. Twenty-nine-year-old Carlo. Twenty-nine was almost thirty. Sara smiled. She was no blushing virgin; nor yearning, dissatisfied matron; and she and Gordon had good sex. So why had Carlo's touch so disturbed her? Not disturbed, she thought—*thrilled*. Remembering, she felt it again. Zoe was sucking Sara's breast very deeply and rhythmically now, and Sara was thinking of Carlo, of his olive skin and beige hair and square hands. And a sexual feeling was building and spreading and warming and swelling—

Sara abruptly pulled Zoe off her nipple. The baby opened her round blue eyes in protest. Sara tried to breathe normally. She thought, That was so weird. I came so close. She brought Zoe to her shoulder and patted her. Zoe burped obediently, but Sara did not put her on the second breast right away. She wanted to regain her composure. She walked around the room. She drank some grapefruit juice. Then she let Zoe resume. Sara was fine, now, but she had a *New York Review* at hand, just in case.

Why would it be wrong?

Too bizarre. Incestuous.

Who would know?

I would.

Coward.

Maybe. Enough.

Sara opened the *Review* but she couldn't concentrate. Gordon was in Toronto and Carlo was alone downstairs, just two floors below her. She thought of his eyes. And Sara suddenly remembered the time she saw the fox.

She had been alone in a field in the late afternoon. Gordon was napping in the camper they had borrowed for the weekend. They weren't married yet, and she felt cross that on this weekend in the country, he had chosen sleep over walking with her. At twenty-five, Sara didn't believe that his physical needs could, or should, differ much from hers—except sexually. He was lustier than she was—which neither of them minded.

Sara walked in the sun through the high, buzzing grass. She was thinking that the insects droned *electrically* when she came to the top of a rise and saw, perhaps thirty yards away, the wholly unexpected animal.

Sara had never seen a fox before, not even in a zoo, and she felt a pounding in her ears. The fox wasn't red or orange, as in books, but beige, a sand-colored beige, with white on the throat and nose. It had a driftwood sheen.

The fox didn't see her at first, and then, all at once, it did. For a long, terrifying moment, it looked her in the eye. Then it turned, and she screamed, and it loped away elegantly and was gone.

Or did she scream before it turned? She felt a fool for crying out like that. The look between them had been intimate and deep; her senseless scream, a harsh and stupid cry in the still air.

Sara sat on a rock and looked back toward the far field and the camper—a small blue oblong she could scarcely see. Gordon would be sorry he had napped and missed the fox. But if he had been with her, they would have been noisy, talking and clomping, and she might never have seen the fox at all.

She walked back to the camper, stopping now and then to pick the wild blackberries that grew on thorny bushes in the field. The berries were dark and bursting, blistered, sweet. She ate a few herself, then gathered some for Gordon. She scratched her arm going for an inner cluster and carried them carefully, between loose fingers, back to the campsite.

He was up when she returned, stretching by the camper door. "Close your eyes and open your mouth," Sara said. Gordon closed his eyes and yawned. She put some blackberries on his tongue. He spat and coughed and spat again.

"I hate berries," he said.

"You hate berries?" She was astounded.

"Hate them all," he replied.

"You never told me that. I know you're allergic to

strawberries—but blackberries, raspberries, blueberries?" Sara stared at him.

Gordon said, "I'm not really allergic to strawberries—I just say I am so I won't have to eat them. People always serve them up as some great treat."

"So you make them feel sorry for you!"

"At least they don't point and stare."

"Not to like berries," Sara marveled, "the candies of the field. How can I marry a man who doesn't like berries?"

"Your idea," Gordon said.

" 'Smiling smugly,' " Sara said. "You could have refused."

"More fun to accept. If you're grateful."

She began pummeling him. He held her wrists easily and brought his mouth to her neck. Then he tripped her backward and lowered her onto the ground.

She said, "Wait, the ants, the stones . . ."

"Then get into the camper."

"Must I?" she asked, unbuttoning her shirt as she walked into the camper ahead of him. In truth, this time she was excited herself. Gordon pressed up against her. Later, she thought, she would tell him about the fox, and the long look, and her foolish cry.

Somehow, though, she never did. The moment for telling had passed, and as the hours and days and weeks went by, she came to savor her private fox. It loped through the fields of her mind. It was her first secret from Gordon.

It was not her last. The year after Roland was born, Sara had a few secret lunches with an older man, but in the end, she didn't find him compelling enough to lunch with him in private. And when Rory was two, Sara's first boyfriend, Michael, moved to New York, and Sara welcomed him to the city, over several months, in ways that had to stay secret from Gordon. Then there was the time she'd secretly taken tennis lessons to improve her backhand. She had hoped to stun Gordon with her improvement; instead, he merely said, "You're a little late on your forehand." Sara mostly kept it secret when she went on diets and when she had her period. She could surely be discreet about Carlo. Keep it secret. *It?* What? A surely social squeeze?

She felt a surge remembering. Zoe, asleep, let the nipple slip out of her mouth. Sara placed the sleeping baby in the crib and tiptoed out of the bedroom. She saw herself in the hall mirror and paused. She looked soft and sort of stupid. Happy. Dopey. Ten years younger and twenty years dumber. Sara went down the hall to her bedroom singing "Careless Love" exultantly and out of tune.

_10_

SARA AWOKE THE NEXT MORN-
ing knowing something was different, but it took her some
moments to realize just what. Then she remembered. She
touched her left shoulder lightly, experimentally, as if expecting it to be tender. Then she pulled the down comforter
up around her neck and gave herself over to reverie. It was
only seven-thirty. Gordon was in Toronto and she was alone
in bed; she could lie there for twenty minutes and think about
Carlo without interruption.

There were many avenues down which to promenade. There
was his past: his childhood, his adolescence, his university
years. She didn't know much and had to imagine everything:
his mother's face, the size of his house, the shape of his dining
room table. There was his body: the set of his shoulders, the

curve of his back, again there was much to imagine. There was the curious circumstance of his employment. How was she going to face her au pair and ask him—no, dummy, *tell* him—to do one domestic chore or another when she felt so befluttered, so beflustered, at such a disadvantage in his presence? Sara discovered that the idea of her own helplessness was itself very arousing. Finally, there was the *moment* to imagine: the thrilling *acknowledgment* moment, when neither could deny any longer what was happening. Not a consummation, it entailed one. Sara could imagine acknowledgment between her and Carlo happening in various ways and was dwelling on way number three, which took place in the garden, when there was a knock at her bedroom door.

"Mom? Can I come in?" Rory's voice was surprisingly deep, given his age and seeming fragility. At five, he had what she thought of as a ghetto face: huge eyes, thin cheeks, an olive pallor no matter how long he played in fresh air. Only on the coldest winter days did his cheeks acquire a pinkish tinge. It was a face from a "Feed This Hungry Child" poster when he rolled his big brown eyes at her, which he did too often.

"Come on in," Sara said. Morning cuddles were a family tradition.

Rory got into bed with her and burrowed against her nightgown. She caressed his spear-straight hair and stroked his knobby back under his pajama top. "Mom?" She knew what would follow. "Could you *scratch* my back? I have an itch." He always said that. She moved her nails in circles on his back. Rory closed his eyes contentedly. His eyelashes were thick against his cheeks.

His eyes flew open as Roland entered the bedroom, wrapped in his blanket, which he invariably used as a robe. Roland climbed in on the other side of Sara and lay, loglike, next to her. Sara wasn't sure at what point to phase out cuddles. Ten? Twelve? Fourteen? But that would mean banishing Roland while cuddling Rory and Zoe. How could she exile her first-born, her sturdy, happy son? Maybe he would be the one to keep away, but at nine he showed no signs of embarrassment about morning cuddles. He certainly wanted to be on hand to ensure that Rory didn't get more than his fair share. Sara patted Roland's hair. She understood how hard it sometimes was for him to be the oldest, and she had been glad to see that Carlo was equally affectionate with both her sons—even though, for the moment, Rory was significantly cuter.

Now Roland let her tousle his curly hair. As usual, he began to tell them his dreams. Last night, he'd been flying in the schoolyard up above the other children when he realized he wasn't a bird, he couldn't really fly, and down he fluttered and woke up just before he would have gone *splat*.

"Gross," Rory remarked appreciatively. Rory claimed never to remember any of his dreams.

"But, Mom?" Roland said with wonder. "Before, in the dream, when I was flying? Really doing it? It was great. And so easy! And I bet flying's really like that."

"How do you know what flying feels like to a bird?" Rory asked. "How could anybody ever find out?"

"They can map the cellular structure of a bird's brain," Roland offered.

"That's not the same. That's not being bird."

" 'Being bird.' The guy can't even talk," Roland exulted.

"Can so," Rory said, pinching his older brother's ear. Roland yanked Rory's arm around and back. Rory howled.

Sara said to them, "Out, out." Fighting meant the end of cuddles.

"We're sorry," Roland said.

"Yeah, Mom, we'll stop," Rory said. "Really."

"Well . . ."

"All right, we'll stay," Roland decided. They settled in around her as before. There was a knock on the bedroom door. "Yes?" Sara called, expecting to see Perri or Lucy.

But Carlo appeared, looking down on them in the bed.

Sara sat up hurriedly, drawing the comforter up under her chin. Carlo was wearing a drab plaid shirt and drab green pants and he looked wonderful.

"Sara," he said and he smiled. "I am sorry to intrude like this when you are so comfortable with your sons. But I forgot to say yesterday. There's a reception for the students in my program this afternoon, so I cannot pick up the boys from school."

"I'll get them, then. Take the afternoon off."

"I should have told you sooner."

"That's okay. Say *ciao* to the dean."

They smiled at each other.

Roland looked at the clock and squawked, "Yikes. Eight o'nine. We're gonna be late." He bicycled his legs out of bed and left, trailing his blanket behind him.

At this, Rory too jumped out of bed and left, so there were no children to break the smiling stare Sara and Carlo were locked into; second after expanding second, she was just drinking him in. At last he said, "So. Have a nice day, Sara," then turned and left.

It wasn't quite the acknowledgment moment, but it was certainly a stare. Sara got out of bed slowly, blushing to her navel. Downstairs, she began making breakfast. He could have telephoned, she thought. He could have called but he wanted to see me. He wanted to see me in bed.

"Mommy!" Rory said, laughing.

Roland lunged for the toaster and hit the eject. Out came the pot holders Sara had inserted.

"Jesus," Sara said.

"Talk about absentminded! Wow, Mom," said Roland, delighted. Her sons always enjoyed her mistakes.

She said, "I guess I got mixed up because the pot holders are square, like slices of bread."

"You could have set the house on fire," Roland gloated.

"Would they burn?" Rory asked.

Sara said, "Here's your juice."

Roland said, "Wait till Daddy finds out."

"I'd rather Daddy didn't find out," Sara said without emphasis.

"I won't tell," Rory said.

"Okay," Sara said. Roland said nothing. She said to him, "Your juice."

He swallowed, licked the corners of his lips. Then he smiled and sang out, "Mah-ahm. Mom."

"What is it? What?"

"I hear someone waking up." Roland had the best ears in the family: from the floor below, he could hear Zoe when she first awoke—when she was still cooing and burbling. He knew that Sara liked to get her out of bed before she started crying: she claimed that this way she encouraged her to be cheerful.

Sara ran up to get Zoe. Then the morning got very busy, and until she left for school with the kids, she thought of Carlo only two or three times.

Out in the street, though, everything seemed amazingly relevant to him. There were men to compare him to, and women to imagine by his side. The shops had shirts and jackets he might wear and clothes for her to wear for him. Coming home from the school, she noticed a secondhand copy of *The Italians* on a blanket on the sidewalk. She turned the corner and almost pushed Zoe's stroller into Marian Gold.

"Sara! Hello. Is this baby yours? I didn't even know you were pregnant!"

"It is. I was."

"She's beautiful."

"Little frog," Sara said. "How's yours?" She had forgotten the name of Marian's daughter.

"Karen's really into gymnastics. She goes three times a week. She's good."

"She was always very graceful," Sara said. A silence came between them on the corner. Sara felt embarrassed, almost ashamed. Maybe Marian did, too.

Marian said, "Great to see you."

"We must get together," Sara said. Smiling, they parted. Sara's cheeks felt numb from her grin. Once not so long ago, Sara and Marian had seen each other two or three times a week, at meetings or workshops or demonstrations. They had been antinuclear activists together, organizing, mobilizing, fund-raising. They had put out the newsletter of their organization, Families for a Future. They had run ambitious projects: a citywide peace essay contest, a weekend conference on the chances for a future, a family concert at the Felt Forum. Their logo had made *Time* magazine.

And then, inexplicably, a year after the largest peace demonstration in American history, the antinuclear movement seemed to collapse. Was it because senators and governors now used freeze rhetoric? Was it because the public seemed adequately persuaded—now it was up to the President? Whatever the cause, although the world wasn't a single kiloton closer to safety, Sara, like many, suddenly found that protest was less important, certainly less urgent, than before, and she took a smaller role within her group. No one else took her place. Marian continued working for the group another year, but then she, too, stepped back. Sara hadn't received a mailing from Families for a Future in two years. She and Marian, who had vowed commitment to the cause for the rest of their lives ("for our children, for your children, for their children"), had become antinuclear dropouts. The Soviets and the Americans had just agreed to pull medium-range missiles out of Europe, which Families for a Future had urged long ago, yet Sara and Marian, meeting on the street, spoke only of their children.

After they parted, Sara reproached herself. She really should get active in the movement again. How could she indulge herself in a silly little crush when the world still lay poised on the edge of destruction? What importance was Carlo compared to nuclear annihilation? What importance was anything?

Then she saw a special on Cremeni mushrooms and thought one day she'd make Carlo a mushroom omelette. A construction worker called, "Why're you smiling, gorgeous?" Her smile grew wider. At thirty-seven, which was not far from forty, Sara didn't really mind when men called out flattering things. Sara thought the general level of street tribute had risen, but she didn't know if that was because of feminism or because she flaunted less flesh as a mother of three than as a single woman prowling. When she was twenty, men sometimes said, "You oughta get arrested." She wondered whether Carlo found her unbearably sexy. And then it was reverie all the way home and for much of the morning.

Her days could accommodate dreaminess—the baby was little and the boys were in school. From nine to three, Sara was alone with Zoe. When the baby took a long afternoon nap, Sara wove. And weaving was dreaming time too. On this day during Zoe's nap, Sara began to weave a new hanging that would have, for its center, a fox.

When Gordon came home the next evening, he gave the boys toys from Toronto, windup tanks that climbed upon one another, gears gnashing, lights flashing. He brought Sara a scarf in a tangerine color she never wore.

Rory asked Gordon, "What did you buy for Zoe?"

Gordon said nothing.

Roland said hastily, in defense of his father, "Zoe's too little for presents."

When the boys were in bed, Gordon turned to Sara and said, "I hope you found those tax receipts by now."

Then Sara remembered all that was wrong in her marriage. She said, "Your hopes are dashed."

"Aren't you cute. Well, I'm going to find those fucking receipts since *you* can't be bothered." He went into the study and opened her file cabinet. She ran in after him. Gordon was pawing through the folders.

"Stop that, sewer-mouth," she said. "Those are *my* things."

He continued to thumb through them. "You probably stuck the receipts in the wrong folder."

"Would you leave my papers alone?"

"We have no secrets, do we?" asked Gordon. The drawer was very full, and some crumpled papers fell out. "You really have a lousy system here."

"No one asked you to judge it. No one asked you to scrabble around in there. Leave that stuff alone! Tell me about Toronto. I haven't seen you for days."

"The audit is Friday. You really don't get it, do you?" He was still rummaging through her papers.

And then something terrible happened. In a file labeled "PTA 1986," Gordon found the missing tax receipts.

He said, "Here they are, you asshole."

She shrieked, "I told you never call me that!"

"Then don't act like an *asshole*." His voice dripped contempt.

"How eloquent you are. And how exactly does an 'asshole' act?"

"Shit passes through it. Just like when you tell me you've looked for those receipts and you haven't gotten off your fucking ass." He knew vulgarity enraged her, but he wasn't prepared for what happened next.

"You know what I think of your lousy receipts and your rotten disposition?" She grabbed the folder from him and ran to the open study window.

He ran after her shouting, "You'd better not!"

But in a rage she thrust the folder outside and opened it upside down, so that twenty or thirty cash-register receipts (for such items as stationery supplies, $6.24) fluttered out into the night.

"You fucking bitch!" he yelled.

78

For a moment, she thought he was going to hit her, but then he turned around and raced downstairs. From the study, she saw the garden suddenly light up. Then she saw Gordon darting here and there on the wet plants to pick up the little white paper slips.

Five minutes later, he was at the front door with his overnight bag, which he hadn't unpacked.

Sara asked, "Taking a trip?"

"You bet," he said, opening the door. "I'm out of here."

"Fine. Go. Great reason for ending a marriage."

"I have a couple other things in mind," Gordon said without turning his head.

And that was it. He didn't slam the door, he left it open, the lip of the lock hanging out against the doorframe. Sara, staring until image became symbol, wondered if this open door meant he was coming back. Or did it mean, frankly, he didn't give a damn—let anyone come in?

She closed and locked the door. She climbed the stairs and walked into the baby's room. Zoe was awake on her back, hands near her face. Sara thought, almost idly, It's happened, Gordon's gone. In her crib, Zoe was slowly rotating her fists and staring at them, mesmerized.

_11_

W<small>HEN RORY CAME INTO SARA'S</small>
bed the next morning, he woke her up asking, "Where's
Daddy?"

"He went to work early," she said. The lie came automatically, for Sara tried to shield the boys from worry. As she
scratched Rory's back, she realized she really didn't know if
Gordon was gone forever or just for the night; she might never
have to tell the boys at all that he had left. Separation, she
remembered reading, is harder on children than on their quarreling parents: most kids, given the choice, would rather their
parents stay married—even tempestuously—than break up.
And she and Gordon didn't even quarrel all that much.

Oh, but that _coldness_ of his and his boring and petty
concerns! Just for herself, she was glad he was gone, she was

tired of living with hatred! Fated, she thought grimly. It was bound to happen like this from the moment he'd said, "I'll be careful." Never mind. She had Zoe and the boys. And Carlo. . . ? Sara felt a sudden shame. She knew she was taking Gordon's departure calmly only because of the handsome Italian au pair who was yearning for her—unless she was completely self-deluded. So the morning after her husband's departure and the possible end of a twelve-year marriage, Sara felt mainly relief—and an underwash of guilt.

When she told Perri on the phone that Gordon had left, Perri marveled at Sara's composure. "Of course he's a lout," Perri said. "I've been telling you for years. But I thought the two of you were close. I thought when you were alone you had some compelling rapport. I thought your world would collapse if he ever moved out."

"Apparently not," Sara said.

"I can't believe your nonchalance," said Perri.

Sara said, "Neither can I."

"Unless you're having an affair," Perri said.

"You're such a sex fiend." Then, to her own surprise, Sara laughed. "In fact," she said, "we've never even kissed."

Perri said, "So there *is* someone else . . ."

"You make it sound so trite!"

"I don't mean to," Perri said. "But many highpoints are trite—graduation, getting married, giving birth, one's first affair . . ."

"I told you we're not having one," Sara said heatedly. "And Gordon and I have been having a horrible time this past year. This new person has nothing to do with all that!"

"I have to look at some footage now." Perri giggled. "Fenley's making gestures—some of them obscene."

Carlo brought the boys home from school. Sara was wearing faded jeans and a soft blue sweater the color of her eyes. And, no, she thought, as they said hello, I'm not imagining those looks. But then he turned away and she thought: *Am I?*

Roland said to Carlo, "You gotta see these tanks my father brought us from Toronto."

Rory said, "Bring mine down too."

Roland climbed the stairs two at a time.

Carlo asked Rory, "Was your father away long?"

"Yeah," Rory said. "About a week."

And it was then that Sara knew for sure. For Carlo, involuntarily, looked up at Sara, stricken. His eyes said, unequivocally, *Your husband was away all week and you never even told me!* His face became yellow from shock as he and Sara locked eyes.

She was about to tell him it had only been a couple of days when angry buzzing filled the room. Roland had returned with the tanks, and Carlo sat down on the floor, evincing enormous interest in the toys. Sara watched his stiff back. She wanted to touch him, make him relax. But she also took a certain satisfaction in his shock. He cared for her that much. . . . He had been that sure she cared too. . . . At this last thought, something in her said *Ha!*

"Mommy," Roland said. "I hear her."

Sara ran up the stairs. Zoe was on her back saying, "Mla. Mlaag."

Sara looked down at her. Zoe no longer looked like Gordon: she looked like a dainty duchess. "Madam," Sara said, bowing to her daughter. "May I have the honor of tending your behind?"

Zoe said "Mlaag" again, and Sara brought her to the changing table.

"Milady," Sara said. "How you're filling out!" It was true: the baby had true buttocks now, as opposed to the concave shanks she'd had at birth. Sara felt a surge of pride: every ounce the baby gained came directly from her.

Sara nursed the baby in the rocking chair, and when she

brought her downstairs, Carlo and the boys had already left for the park.

When they came home, Carlo went down to his room and the boys came into the kitchen and saw the box on the counter. "Yay, pizza!" said Rory.

"Where's Daddy?" Roland asked. When Gordon was home for dinner, he insisted that Sara cook a full meal. "It's the least you can do," he would say. The previous week she had challenged him: "What's the *most* I can do?" "You can never do enough," he had said, referring to his letting her keep Zoe.

Now Sara said to the boys, "Daddy had a lot to do at work. Catching up from Toronto."

Roland said, "Ma, I need a watch. I really do." And Sara didn't have to make any more excuses to her children.

But she felt she owed Carlo further explanation. When the children were asleep, she put on perfume and went down to the basement and knocked on his door. She waited. There was no reply. There was no light showing under the door. She turned to go upstairs. Then she stopped and turned back and opened the door to the hot tub. She rolled back the cover. She switched on the underwater lights and the bubbler. She took off her clothes and sank into the hot, faintly chlorinated water. Her perfume, which Carlo liked, mingled with it. The water bubbled around her. "Whayor's Daddy?" Rory would surely ask the next morning. One day she would have to say "Daddy's moved out." How would it be? Living as a single? She would have to get a job, she didn't know at what; perhaps she could get paid for being some kind of activist.

She got out of the hot tub and dripped on the slatted wooden floor. Wisps of steam rose from her body. She put on her terry-cloth robe. She held her sweater and jeans and bra and panties on one arm as she left the hot-tub room and walked out. Carlo was there outside his door.

Sara said, "Oh!" She pulled at the clothes on her arm to hide her underwear. "Hi," she said shyly.

83

He nodded curtly.

"Can I talk to you?" Sara asked.

"Have I done something wrong?" He was speaking in a small voice, like a bitter child, and she wanted above all to comfort him.

"No, Carlo, not at all."

He opened the door and gestured her in. He kept a tidy place, and the plant on the hook (where Zoe's portacot had been) was flourishing. "You're not making coffee," she said, "are you?"

He shook his head, he wouldn't help.

She sat down on the bed. She said, looking into the garden, "I just wanted you to know that my husband was only away for three days. Two nights." She blushed to hear herself.

"I don't care how long he was gone. You don't have to come down and explain."

"It's just funny. A child's sense of time."

He said nothing. Many seconds went by.

She said, suddenly, passionately, "But you gave me this look!"

Carlo slowly walked toward her. "Sara," he said, "go upstairs to your husband." But he sat down near her on the bed.

The air between them felt strangely heavy to Sara. "My husband's away again," she said. "This time I wanted you to know."

He nodded.

She just sat there waiting in the magnetized air. A whole minute passed, and she'd almost given up hope before he put his hand over hers and pressed lightly. She had never in her life been so relieved.

Now with his thumb, Carlo stroked her palm, and with his fingertips he played with hers. He went up and down each of her fingers, gently pressing and caressing. Her hand was passive and her heart was racing. He traced lines on her throat and circles on the nape of her neck, and she hung down her

84

head to let him. She felt like a heavy-headed peony, bursting and luxuriant. He kept giving her these tiny stroking touches, now on her shoulders and arms, now on her face, and still he hadn't even kissed her. All this gentle teasing was just lovely but she also liked it twisted and tough and he was just watching her suffer and melt, and gently running his fingertips over her cheekbones and nose and around her eyes and ears and only then very lightly touching her lips with the pads of his fingers.

Then at last, Carlo held her head between his hands and tilted her chin upward. First gently, then firmly, he brought his lips to hers; his mouth was fresh and soft. And Sara was pressing against him, squashing her breasts against his chest, pushing her mouth into his, thinking, Hard, baby, more, baby, oh.

They were unequally dressed, she realized after a while. While she was wearing only her thick terry-cloth bathrobe, Carlo had on a button-down shirt, a T-shirt, jeans, and presumably underwear. One tug at her robe belt and she'd be undressed, but he was wearing so much. Was she expected to remove his clothes? She could feel his chest under his shirts, but she doubted he could feel much but the vaguest body contours beneath her thick robe.

All at once, he pulled back and gave her a long look. She looked back at him. Slowly, deliberately, he pulled at the knot on her robe belt, giving her plenty of time to prevent him. She just breathed. The knot opened easily, and he pushed apart the two sides of her robe. Then, looking down at her body, he sighed before touching it.

They both undressed him minutes later. She would make the first move, pulling at a cloth, tugging at a button, and he would tactfully take off the garment. His skin looked golden; hers looked rosy-tan. When they were both naked, lying side by side, he said, "I thought of you like this from the day we first met."

"I thought you were cute but too young."

In response, he twisted her arm behind her, wrenching them both into a more passionate mode. They thrashed and wrestled while kissing. He pinned her arms above her head. She watched, as if helpless, as he stroked her breasts. Then he moved his hand down and she stopped watching.

Soon, she helped him get in her. For a while she lay absolutely still. "Sara?" he asked, concerned.

"I just want to memorize you," Sara said.

"Memorize this, signora." He pushed hard, then lay motionless in her arms. Many seconds went by. "Let me know when I can move."

"Now would be good."

"It's too soon," he teased.

"No—please."

"If you insist." He moved very slowly.

She tried to slow herself to his rhythm. She thought of the sun rising over the mountains, how the rays pass slowly over the hills. But she pushed back against him again and again.

"No!" he said, trying to make her be still.

"Yes," she insisted, past reason, "I will."

Carlo shuddered and shouted, "Oh, God!"

Sara said, "Carlo!" and wept.

PART II

PERRI

January 1987	January 1988	June 1988
* ———————————	* ————————	*

SARA * · * · · · · · · · · · · ·
conceiving Zoe   loving Carlo

PERRI * · * · · · · · ·
  meeting Fenley   returning from Utah

12

Perri wanted to be very to-
gether when she first met Fenley, so she didn't smoke grass
at midday, as she usually did. Doing without dope, she decided
in the elevator going up to his office, was just another reason
she was so nervous now. Being a marijuana addict certainly
complicated her life, she thought—not for the first time. Although a joint might have calmed her, Perri knew she had to
meet Fenley straight—clear-eyed and eloquent—to pursuade
him to let her work with him and begin a career in documentary
films.

Her friend Michael, a cameraman, had told her Tom Fenley
was just the person she wanted: an independent documentary
filmmaker who produced two or three films a year, usually on
social or political issues, often for public televison. He had a

wall full of citations and awards. Fenley's name on a project could help garner grants; hers alone couldn't bring in a dime. She needed a Fenley for her plan. Perri desperately wanted to make this film and get started in something that didn't depend on her looks. She knew that making documentary films was not the road to riches, but she had some savings and she didn't need much of an income living at Seventeen Morton Street. The intangibles of her project allured her: making *something from nothing*—which is the great joy of producing; the fun of group effort inspired by belief. Fenley was socially committed, idealistic. "A good man," said Michael, who usually shot his films. "Pitch him."

Perri left the elevator and found Suite 3030. She waited in the reception area. She had no notes with her, but she knew what she would say. Fenley's assistant, an earnest young woman, led her down the hall to a large corner office with splendid river views.

"Well, well," Fenley said, appreciatively, about Perri. "Michael's friend. Sit down." He was a narrow-faced, middle-aged man, with heavy-lidded gray eyes, a prim mouth, and tufts of ginger hair. "Michael tells me you have some idea. . . ?" He leaned back in his leather chair, waiting.

Perri said, "I want you to coproduce a film with me about the National Writers Union."

Fenley said, "Never heard of it."

"It's still small," she said. "These are the early years."

Fenley asked, "Who wants to watch a bunch of writers having meetings?"

"That's not what I had in mind," she said. "I had in mind an exciting film about purpose and confrontation. About books and society. About literature. About money. About people working for change against enormous odds."

He gave her a cynical look.

She continued rapidly. "On the one side, there are giant conglomerates and book chains. On the other, a group of writers working together for the first time. Union neophytes, powerless as individuals. The way I see it," she said, "the National Writers Union is the labor equivalent of David and Goliath." She felt her rhetoric redden her cheeks.

"What about PEN and the Authors Guild?" Fenley asked.

"They're literary organizations—but only the Union is fighting for the writer's *economic* rights. These huge new publishing conglomerates are making more profit than ever before. Yet most writers who publish a book make less in a year from their work than the ladies who clean up the offices at night."

"That's a good visual," Fenley said. "But with so little reading and so many writers, what can a writers' union really accomplish?"

"Ask the Screenwriters Guild! Ask the presidents of the writers' unions in Sweden and England and France! We could go to Paris and Stockholm and show what the unions have done there. It'd be fun."

"Oh really?" Fenley leaned back and looked at Perri appraisingly. Looked at her breasts.

She said, hurriedly, "I didn't mean *fun*."

"I've just come back from Malaysia. It's not a novelty for me to shoot abroad. And it usually isn't much fun."

"But it might be interesting to meet some of the writers." Perri mentioned several American authors who were union members. "You know how people like to see celebrities."

"That's unfortunately true. But it sounds like you just want to make some promotional film. Where's the tension? The dynamic?"

"It's a debate. One side and the other. Footage of internationally known novelists who can't afford to buy a car. And interviews with those who oppose the idea of a union. Conservatives like Hanson Hall. We show both sides of the story."

"Good," Fenley said. "Because that's the only way we could ever get funding."

"We'd want an interview with the head of some giant publishing conglomorate."

"Like Asa Pons," Fenley said. Asa Pons owned a book chain, two publishing houses, ten magazines, a recording company, four homes, and five Picassos.

"That's the one," said Perri. "We ask him who should be making the profits from writing: writers or publishers? We ask him about the blockbuster syndrome—and how it's affected the books our authors write. We demand that he talk about decisions that he made just for business reasons."

"Asa Pons never gives interviews."

"Then that becomes part of the story. We stake him out with our camera crew, catch him unawares."

"What if we never get him?"

"We talk to his secretary, his chauffeur, his masseur. It could be an ongoing motif—quest and frustration. Meanwhile, we're revealing his sumptuous lifestyle."

Fenley chuckled. "You have some good ideas. Why are you interested in this? You're much too pretty and well dressed to be a writer."

Perri said, "You don't have to be an author to see how unfair it all is. My best friend is a fabulous writer. She's had three novels published and won several awards. Yet she earns maybe nine thousand a year and gets pushed around by everyone—editors, agents, magazines. The Writers Union could make a difference to people like Ann . . . if it got stronger. It would empower her, help her make more money and get some respect."

"As easy as that?" Fenley asked.

"Of course not. But where there's a struggle, there's a story, and where there's a story, there's a film."

"Could be," Fenley allowed. He tapped his pencil on his desk. "Michael says you don't have much film experience."

Perri said, "It's true, I don't. I've been working at Rafferty

Productions since November." She was deliberately vague about her job, which was mainly scheduling shoots. Before that she had worked as a deejay at Heartbreak, spinning records and dancing. And before that for ten years she had modeled.

"And now you want to be on top. Coproducer."

"The film *is* my idea," she began. Then she halted, smiled, and said—winningly, she hoped—"Besides, what else can I do? I can't shoot film or take sound or cut picture, and I'm too old to be a gofer. But I'm good on the phone and I'm very good with money and arrangements. I've produced other things." She told him she had once produced a models' anti-hunger dance-a-thon that had raised eighteen thousand dollars. "I work hard and I learn fast. I'd learn a lot from you."

Fenley said, "I suppose I could tell you what steps to take first. To raise money."

Perri tried to hide her elation.

"You're going to be busy," he said. "Researching. Writing. Fund-raising."

"I know." Perri was grinning away. She would interview her friend Ann—and Jed Spielman. She'd create portraits of people with passion! She said to Fenley, "It will be a stirring film! Informative. Inspirational."

"More importantly," Fenley said, "it might even be fundable. We'll give it a try. I know a few foundation people. But it's not going to be easy."

Perri said, "My labor, your resume. My gamble, your guidance."

"Well," Fenley said, "it seems I have nothing to lose. When could you start?"

"Next week? Tomorrow?"

"Monday's fine. All the other rooms along the hall are being used for editing, so you'll have to work in here with me. I'll move another desk in."

"No problem," Perri said. She looked out the window at a barge coming down the Hudson. "I'll just have to get used to the view."

"Me too," said Fenley, meaning Perri.

She put on her jacket and stood up to leave. "By the way," she said, "there are lots of good-looking writers. Ann Beattie. Jayne Ann Phillips. Louise Erdrich."

"Never heard of them," Fenley said.

As soon as Perri got outside, she took a joint out of her pocket and lit up, although it was a crowded midtown street. As long as she didn't meet eyes or break stride, Perri felt fine smoking anywhere. Two blocks later, she was enjoying the street far too much to go down the dark steps to the subway. Anyway, riding high was always a drag. That was when you were likely to see menacing teens or a puddle of vomit or a dignified drunk carefully pissing against the station wall.

Perri kept on walking down Seventh Avenue, striding along with her burning joint, when she noticed, coming right toward her, two policemen, ten feet away. She pinched out the joint with her fingertips and dropped it in her pocket. She kept on walking. She didn't turn to see what they would do when they smelled it. They didn't stop her. They never stopped her. Nobody gets in my way, she thought, when I really get going. Fenley's agreed! Although it was a raw and windy afternoon in March, Perri walked all the way home. Her jubilance kept growing; her cheeks felt tight and red. When she got to Seventeen Morton, she rang Sara's bell.

"Perri," Sara said at the door. "I was just working." She was hooking a rug with a snowflake design, a commission.

"Time for a tea break," said Perri. "I'll put on the kettle."

"How did it go?" asked Sara, following her sister into the kitchen. She was four months pregnant with Zoe. "Were you wearing the right clothes after all?" Sara had approved Perri's outfit.

"Nah, too stylish. I mean, Fenley was in a brown nylon turtleneck. But, Sara—he said yes!"

"Wonderful! Something stronger than tea?"

"I'll make myself a celebration joint," said Perri, reaching for her bag. "Unless you mind terribly." Sara didn't smoke when she was pregnant or nursing.

"Not a bit," Sara said. "Go ahead."

Perri rolled herself a joint. Since she was already high, she really got into the mechanics of the process. She carefully creased a single sheet of white cigarette paper. (She bought her cigarette papers at several stores, so no one would know her rate of consumption.) She poured a gentle trickle of dope from the film can where she kept it into the fold of the paper. She tamped the marijuana back and forth and admired the thick even line she was producing.

Sara said, pouring tea into mugs, "I think you just do that stuff because you like to roll it."

"Hell no—it satisfies so many ways." Perri enjoyed expounding on this subject. "First, there's that hit to the back of the throat, the rush as it bites into your lungs. For an ex-tobacco smoker, it's a blast from the past . . . *smoke*, wonderful smoke. . . ."

Sara said, "Listen." There were voices in the outside hall, and a laugh.

Perri said, "Lucy and Paul."

Sara nodded. "It's Tuesday." Paul came to Lucy's every Tuesday. Sometimes he came Thursdays as well. "I'm glad she has someone," Sara said. "He seems very kind."

"So much older," Perri said. "And married."

"So he and Lucy will never get married. Lucky them! They'll remain lovers and never just be man and wife."

"Aren't we bitter today," Perri said. "Gordon still giving

you a hard time about the baby?" She finally sealed the joint she had been working on.

Sara nodded. "When people congratulate him, he just winces. And when we're alone, he treats me like a criminal."

"That bastard! I'm going to speak to him, give him a piece of my mind . . ."

"Perri, it would only make things worse. You're not exactly soul mates to begin with . . ."

"But to treat you that way! His wife of twelve years! When you warned him in advance. But, no, he had to have his way . . . You've heard of wife-rape, haven't you?"

Sara gave a small smile. "I wouldn't go that far," she said. "But I gave him a chance to cease and desist and he certainly didn't." She shook her head. "I thought our problems would be over once we decided to keep this baby, but now it seems they've just begun."

"You can't tell yet," said Perri.

Sara said, "Oh yes I can." She turned her face away.

Perri slipped the beautifully rolled joint into her pocket for later. With Sara upset, it was not, after all, a great time to get high. (High again, she reminded herself—she'd *had* her "celebration joint" out in the street.) She put her arm around Sara and said, for beginners, "If it's a girl, he'll come around. You'll see."

PERRI HAD ALWAYS THOUGHT
that documentary films were made one step at a time. She had
taken a film course a few years before and came away believing
that the filmmaking process was well defined and well ordered.
You got the idea, you wrote it up, you raised the money, you
shot the film, and you edited—created a coherent whole by
choosing and moving pieces of film and sound track to tell the
truest story best.

By September, after working at Fenley's for six months,
she saw that these steps could be reversed and merged. Sometimes your idea was refined only after shooting. Sometimes
only cutting revealed what you still had to shoot. Sometimes
you raised your money only at the end. Sometimes you never
did.

Luxurious elevator interior. Lighted buttons indicate that we are nearing the penthouse. Doors open on a marble lobby. The handheld camera follows coproducer Perri Jennings as she goes to the reception desk.

Receptionist: "I'll tell his personal assistant."

She returns with a stern, middle-aged woman.

Assistant: "I've told you three times on the phone now, Mr. Pons is a very busy man—too busy to see you. And turn that thing off."

She approaches the camera. We hear a click, and the film goes black.

Perri's voice: "What's he frightened of, anyway? We're just going to ask him about a few company policies."

Assistant: "He doesn't like publicity, and he doesn't have to submit to your questions. Or your camera."

The picture comes on again. The assistant looks angry.

Assistant: "I said turn off the camera. You're making a nuisance of yourself, and if you don't leave right now I'm going to call the police."

Perri: "Call them."

Voice of coproducer Tom Fenley: "Just a minute, Perri. Michael, cut."

[From *Birth of a Union* (working title), raw footage, Fenley Films.]

Perri and Fenley had been lucky with funding, and by August they had already raised half their budget, enough to give themselves a tiny salary. Perri had had to stop smoking at midday; she hated doing office work stoned. That's what it felt like—office work, not filmmaking, all the writing and typing and calling she was doing to get grants. Twice her name, but not Fenley's, had been omitted from the grant citation—mere oversights, Fenley insisted, but she wondered. It was not beyond Fenley to take credit for the work of others. And since the Stockholm shoot, things had not been good between them. She didn't like sharing an office with him or listening to his telephone calls and having him listen to hers.

But she loved the large corner office they shared. In the afternoon, so much light poured into the room that Fenley always pulled down all four sets of fat, old-fashioned venetian blinds. Whenever he went out, Perri would hoist up the blinds again, hungry for the river and the sky. Fenley's earnest assistant, Nancy, worked in a small office next door.

On this sunny Thursday in September, Fenley was in Washington, trying to raise money for the film, so the room was full of light. Perri, for a change, was not sitting on her metal chair at her metal desk making dreary telephone calls. Instead, she sat in Fenley's leather chair, at Fenley's teak desk, and looked out at the river. She thought about the film they were making. You could lose track of the film for the funding: she had spent more time on grant applications than on the film itself.

Now she tried to think through a problem. In her talks with Union writers, Perri had learned that the New York chapter (which comprised half the members nationally) had soon become divided. Two coups were central to its history: one that brought in and another that overthrew a group of mid-list authors considered the elitists. This group wanted to get the support of well-known authors so all writers would receive a better deal from publishers. It also favored centralization of union power. The other group sought to organize all people working as writers—including publicists and business writers—and form ties with other labor unions. It wanted a broad-based organization with strong local chapters.

To Perri, the two factions seemed alike enough in their general goal of helping writers—but the schism had crippled the infant union, and Perri was trying to decide if it should be part of the film. It was certainly part of the story, but it wasn't the story she wanted to tell. After all, she wanted to help the Union: that was why she was making the film in the first place. Should they document the petty infighting and personality wars she was learning about? Fenley would probably ask what exactly they would shoot, and she would say interviews with the people involved and he would say more talking heads. Yet wasn't internal conflict an interesting issue to explore? It certainly was in government, and marriage. . . .

Perri lifted the telephone receiver and tried to call Sara at the hospital, but the line was busy for the second time. Sara and Gordon had their girl after all, but clearly Gordon was still sulking. What a selfish, stodgy, practical bore! Perri never understood what Sara saw in him. Reading the Sunday *Times* while Sara was in labor! And Sara. Taking it. Graciously. And calling the baby that terrible name. Zoe. People would always be mispronouncing it. Just like Sara to give her American baby a name that needed an accent mark. Pretentious—or was it precious? "Roland" and "Rory." I mean, really.

A button on the telephone began to flash, and Perri pressed it. "Hello? Oh, hi, Larry."

Larry was the film editor on the project. He had worked with Fenley on five other documentaries. "I've just finished synching the Stockholm stuff," he said, "if you want to have a look."

"I sure do." She replaced the receiver and went down the long corridor to the editing room.

"'Allo Perri," said Claudine, Larry's assistant. "Ee looks vairry good."

Claudine was a French lawyer, a fact that continually astonished Perri, especially when Claudine revealed that in France she could make more money in two hours than she did in a week on documentaries in New York. "But I want to starrt, to learn about feelm," she'd explained.

Claudine wasn't exactly pretty but she was piquante and provocative. Her figure was sensational, and when she came into a room, men always took notice. She wore short, tight pants to work, often with polka dots. Today she was wearing leopard-spotted stretch pants and a shrunken black T-shirt. The look of a street slut, the mind of a lawyer, and here she was labeling cans and filing trims.

What was it about documentaries that attracted such high-level people? Nancy had a Ph.D. from Brown, and she earned a pittance each week answering the phone and typing bills for Fenley. Was it the fun of making things with other people? The knowledge you were working for a cause and a film?

The editing room certainly wasn't glamorous. Metal shelves held old cans of film and bulging file folders. Back issues of *Mother Jones* and *Millimeter* were stacked on the floor. The Formica tables were scarred, and the rewinds were battered. Even the flatbed film-editing machine, a high-tech affair at one end of the room, had bits of blue and yellow tape stuck onto it and old Styrofoam coffee cups on the monitor.

"The stuff outside the hotel is the best," Larry said, without turning from the machine. "Really nice light."

"I remember," Perri said. "It was a golden afternoon."

"Oh, God, she's getting rhapsodic," Larry said, still with his back to her.

Perri said, "I'm still at the honeymoon stage." She found she was grinning. "You'll have to bear with me."

"'oneymoon?" Claudine asked. "Did you get married?"

"No, no, I meant about film, now that I'm finally seeing footage. Just a joke. Figure of speech."

"Turn off the light," Larry said to Claudine. He sat on his chair facing the editing machine, which enclosed him on almost three sides. Perri pulled up a metal stool and sat in back of him and to his right. Claudine grabbed a yellow legal pad and turned off the light.

There was Pia Dahlburg again, a woman of forty, leaning on her elbows and gazing dreamily at a computer terminal. Then, off-mike, Fenley's flat-sounding voice: "Good, fine, now could you turn to face me?" Dahlburg moved her head slowly until her large blue eyes stared out from the screen.

Now Fenley instructed: "Okay, you're inspired, go back to your work." She gave a slight smile and a nod and faced the computer again. "Write something," said Fenley. She typed a sentence on the keyboard.

"This all seems so phony," Perri said.

"It won't," Larry said. "Not with the right voice-over."

The camera shifted angles and Fenley directed Pia through the entire sequence again. Larry turned down the sound, so Fenley's voice couldn't be heard, and over the picture of Dahlburg writing at her computer first "stuck," and then "inspired," Larry intoned: "Pia Dahlburg writes essays for the Swedish review *Bleak and Black*. She is also a lawyer for the Swedish Writers Union."

He stopped the machine and looked at Perri.

"I see what you mean," she said. He was good.

"You need this sort of visual stuff for those obligatory introductions."

"You improvise excellent narration," said Perri. "But I was hoping we could do the film without narration."

"I don't think so—it's too informational. But you and Fenley will have to decide."

Pia Dahlburg now walked up a small hill behind her house. Perri narrated, "At first, it was an uphill fight . . ."

Larry said, "No, no. You don't want to be on the nose."

Rebuked, Perri felt herself blush in the dark.

"On ze nose?" asked Claudine. *"Sur le nez?"*

"You can't be too literal," Larry said.

Pia now was speaking softly, explaining the legalities in a recent union action. In Stockholm, Perri had thought Pia somewhat soporific, but on film her low-key presence worked well. Even her slight hesitations were good: Perri saw Claudine leaning forward, involved.

Their second interview had been with Anders Langstrom. A booming, jovial man in person, on film he seemed outsized, hyper, insincere. Perri said, "I didn't remember him this way—so manic."

"He calms down later," Larry said. "Watch." And then the outside footage came on. In the late afternoon, Anders Langstrom had taken them to a shabby street. They had filmed him outside a dilapidated building. Langstrom said, "In this house, Dan Andersson died at the age of thirty-two. Andersson was a brilliant working-class poet and storyteller who is much admired today because of the way he used words. During his lifetime, six of his books were published—and after his death many more—but he always endured the most bitter poverty. He died from asphixiation here in this cheap hotel room, after his room had been fumigated for rats and roaches—and not properly aired." The camera followed Langstrom's finger pointing to a window. Then the camera moved in on Langstrom's face. "Today, Dan Andersson would have had a better life—and we can thank our Union for that."

The camera pulled back to show Langstrom and the building in a wide shot. "Beautiful light," Larry said. "Michael's great in the late afternoon." Perri saw, at the edge of the frame, a tall blond man wearing a gray sweater. Then the camera-roll ran out.

"Could I see that shot again?" she asked.

Larry ran the film for her again. "There's a better shot of this at the top of the roll."

"Mmm." It was Sven all right.

After the interview with Langstrom, while Fenley and Michael packed the equipment, Perri walked Langstrom and the Swedish soundman out to the main street. (If Fenley granted her any role at all on this shoot, it was social coordinator.) Perri thanked them both and said good-bye. When she returned, Fenley and Michael were still wrapping up. Perri was slowly approaching them when the tall blond man came over to her and asked about the film. He worked on children's programming for Swedish television, and their similar jobs somehow dignified the pickup. Perri liked his looks and agreed to meet him after dinner for a drink.

It seemed wise to hide her date from the others, so, two hours later, pretending she was sleepy, Perri left the restaurant where they were eating and went back to her hotel room alone. She took a shower and put on fresh clothes. She met Sven at a café and went home with him to his airy apartment. After a while, they went to the bedroom. His neck smelled like cedar. "How do you say this in Swedish?" she asked, of various parts of their bodies.

When things began to get serious, she said, "Sven, why don't you put something on?"

"Something?" he said.

"You know. On this." It was so smooth.

"I don't have any somethings."

She drew back from him.

He said, "I could get some, if it is important to you."

"Of course it's important."

He said, "Maybe people have to in New York . . ."

"All the more reason for you."

"All the more reason for what?"

"To go out and get some. If you want to go on."

"Of course I want to go on."

"Then go. It's better to be safe. I'll stay right here."

This idea of her waiting there in his bed seemed to please him. Sven put on his shirt and pants. He said, "I'll be back in one quarter hour."

Perri heard him leave the apartment. She listened to the background sounds. New York at night was a muted roar, Stockholm was a far-off murmur. She yawned. It had been a long day.

The next thing she knew it was light out and Sven was asleep beside her. She groped for her watch. Eight-fifteen! She and the crew were catching a noon flight to London. She jumped out of bed and began to get dressed. Sven opened his eyes. He was one good-looking Swede.

"Are you leaving?" he asked.

"I must. I'm terribly late. I'm so sorry. Why didn't you wake me last night?" She eased her head through her sweater.

Sven said, "I tried. You just went like this." He gave a little sigh and drooped. "You are a thick sleeper."

"A deep sleeper. Yes. When I was young, I shared a room with my little sister, Lucy. She used to cry in the night, and I trained myself to sleep through anything."

"I noticed," Sven said.

She said, "Hey, I'm sorry. Next time I'm in Stockholm? Or you're in New York?" She was dressed now. He sat up and put on a robe. They exchanged business cards, of all things, and she left.

Back at the hotel, there was a message for her in Fenley's large scrawl. "We can make an earlier flight, if you get back in time. Where are you? We're having breakfast in the dining room." They were finishing their coffee when she arrived.

"Hello," she said. "I got up early and went for a walk."

A look passed between the two men. Ridiculous! thought Perri: all for a little making out.

But after that, it was harder to feign outrage at Fenley's dirty jokes and suggestive remarks—which suddenly acquired a bitter edge. He didn't mind her (implied) rejection of his (implied) advances—as long as she rejected everyone. Never mind. She didn't have to get on perfectly with Fenley. She liked Claudine, and Larry seemed very smart. She would learn a lot from him. She would try to get him on her side.

Now Larry had almost finished rewinding the film on the machine. Pia Dahlburg typed backward. "I wonder what she's writing?" asked Larry.

" 'I'm nervous about all of this.' "

After a few seconds, Larry said, "I'm sure it will work out okay." Claudine turned on the light.

"*I'm* not nervous," said Perri, blinking in the sudden brightness. "I was telling you what she typed—I asked her later. *Should* I be nervous?—she asked nervously."

"No, no, I misunderstood." Larry stood up. To her surprise, she saw that he was wearing an earring. He wasn't at all the earring type; he wore white shirts and chinos. Yet he had pierced his skin, mutilated his flesh, so he could wear a gold ring in his ear. He wanted to be looked at. Perri began looking at him.

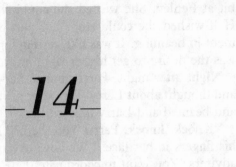

_**14**_

CONTRARY TO THE *LOUCHE* REP-
utation she cultivated, especially with her sisters, Perri did not
go after every man she wanted. She had her standards. She
would not date the boyfriends or recent ex-boyfriends of her
friends, nor the friends of present boyfriends. She tried not
to sleep with married men and never slept with fathers-to-be.

Perri had no taboos about colleagues or live-ins, however,
so although she knew that she and Larry were going to be
working on this film for months, and that he was living with
a high-school teacher named Maude, she began eyeing him.
Soon, she was beaming at him. That was her word for it,
"beaming." Perri sometimes felt she sent out this current, and
she could no more control it, fake it or stop it, than decide
whether or not it would rain. She wished she could beam a

bit at Fenley. She wished she could stop beaming at Larry. Half-wished she could stop. For part of beaming was enjoyment in beaming. It was like getting high. The first symptom was the desire to get higher right away.

Night after night, Perri smoked her midnight joint in bed and thought about Larry. Day after day, she came to the office and beamed and Larry ignored her.

"Knock, knock. Perri? You there?" It was Fenley, waving his fingers in her face. "We have to have a meeting with our advisers. You want to coordinate that?"

It meant phone calls back and forth for days. Perri wrinkled her nose. "Couldn't Nancy . . . ?"

Fenley said, "Remember, there's no secretary in our budget."

"How could I forget?" She herself had been making the transcripts from the rough footage all week. She opened her desk drawer to get out the adviser's file.

"And you should make follow-up calls to every foundation we haven't heard from."

"Isn't that a waste of time? I mean, wouldn't they give us a call if they were interested in the idea?"

"Usually. But you never can tell. Maybe they lost our last letter. Maybe the person handling our file got sick. It's worth finding out."

Worth finding out, Perri thought, because *I'm* doing the work. She pulled the phone to her. "The exciting world of filmmaking," she muttered.

He jeered, "You thought it was all lights, camera, action?"

"I thought it was more than just desk work."

Fenley said, "You got your Europe shoot. Your Stockholm adventure."

"My what?"

"Never mind. Now you're learning some important skills. Getting information. Writing proposals. Developing a relationship with foundation people. After this," and here he smiled condescendingly, "you can always get a job fund-raising."

Perri stuck out her tongue at him.

"Is that a come-on?" Fenley asked.

"You wish," Perri said.

A long private drive on a luxurious estate. We approach a magnificent stone-and-cedar house.

Narrator (Tom Fenley), voice-over: "This is one of the country homes of Asa Pons, the millionaire publisher many writers call 'Scrooge.' "

Long shot of a woman walking up the front path between manicured lawns. She approaches the front door.

CUT TO: Her hand on the brass knocker. CUT TO: Her face. It is Perri Jennings. Camera pans to door. When it opens, camera opens up for a better exposure on the interior. We see a uniformed maid.

Maid: May I help you?

Perri: Is Mr. Pons at home?

Maid: He is unavailable.

Perri: And Mrs. Pons?

Maid, nervously, looking over her shoulder: Here she is now.

A good-looking woman of fifty comes to the door. She wears cashmere, pearls.

Mrs. Pons to Perri: How may I help you?

Perri (voice-over): We want to interview your husband.

Mrs. Pons: My husband never gives interviews.

Perri (voice-over): Perhaps we could have a few words with you.

Camera pans to Perri: Did you know that whenever the Writers Union audits the books at your husband's publishing houses, it finds thousands of dollars that should have been paid to writers?

CUT TO Mrs. Pons: I don't know anything about that.

Perri (voice-over): Did you know that half the books he publishes were bought for $5,000 or less?

Mrs. Pons: Asa's a very fine businessman.

Perri (voice-over): Is it good business to cheat writers out of the meager money they make?

Mrs. Pons: I'm sorry, this interview is over.
Perri (voice-over): Wait a minute! Imagine spending years writing a novel and finally getting it published. For *five thousand dollars.* And getting cheated on royalties.
The door closes on Perri.
[From *Tilting at Windmills: The National Writers Union* (working title), sample reel, Fenley Films.]

Claudine, in skimpy polka-dot pants, came into the corner office to say that Larry was ready for them. "Zis will be fun," she said to Fenley flirtatiously.

Little minx! thought Perri. They were about to screen their "selects."

For the past three days, they had been screening all the rough footage to make reels of selected material. Fenley and Perri would sit in the editing room behind Larry and run what they had and decide what should be selected. Sometimes a shot was chosen because of the content. Sometimes because of the color. Sometimes because it would make a good transition. Fenley would say, "Good, this is good, starting from 'workers' self-respect.' All of this, and this . . . through 'great goal' . . . and out." Larry marked up the "dailies" reels so that later Claudine could pull out the selected takes. Sometimes Perri suggested something, and Fenley would sigh and say to Larry, "All right, mark that too."

Perri felt a curious constraint about giving Larry any direct order. He and Fenley had a long history together and knew how the other worked best, and the filmmaking process was still new to her. Also, she didn't want Larry to think of her as his boss. She liked her men to boss her.

Fenley always took the seat to Larry's left, leaving Perri the right—not his earring side. Worse, she never got Larry's gaze. He always turned to face Fenley. The men addressed each other exclusively, and sometimes Perri had to sneeze to get their attention. She had an unobtrusive way of tickling her sinuses while pinching her nose. She sneezed several delicate times in a row, like a cat. "God bless you," Fenley said, turning to face her. He added, as she continued to sneeze, "God bless you, God bless you."

Larry said nothing.

On the second day, Perri said to Fenley, "Maybe Nancy would like to screen with us."

"If she has the time," Fenley said, displeased. He liked his assistant to stick to the paperwork.

Perri sensed this, but she went ahead and asked Nancy anyway. Nancy was delighted. Her intelligence had been underused at Fenley's. When they screened, Nancy was talkative and enthusiastic. Soon, she was calling out, "Use this," and "Cut it here."

Fenley said, "Thank you. I'll make those decisions."

Perri's ears burned for Nancy. Perri said, "We all have some say here."

Larry said, "Well, do I mark it or what?"

"Mark it," Perri said.

"We can't mark *everything*," Fenley said. "The whole idea is to select."

The third day Perri didn't suggest that Nancy join them again. She and Fenley and Larry were all talkative people. One more lively voice made for chaos. She was glad that Claudine—usually a real chatterbox—kept quiet while they were screening.

Now, in the corner office with the marvelous views and light, Perri stood up to follow Claudine. Fenley's eyes were on Perri. He let her walk ahead of him down the hall to the editing room. Whenever she moved, he watched. But Perri was used to being watched. The only one who didn't watch was Larry.

As usual, he did not turn to say hello when she entered the long, windowless editing room where he worked.

"Awright, gang," Larry said when they were seated.

Perri thought it was cute that despite his Dartmouth education, he had kept a Brooklyn accent. She knew she would think it was cute however he spoke. You're a goner, she told herself, highly pleased at the idea. She always liked it when she fell for someone inappropriate. She was pleased to think that she alone perceived a person's true charms. She was proud that she had never been in love with a very handsome man.

Larry said, "Today we're going to screen the selects to see if some shape suggests itself. Some dramatic skeleton to the film."

"Also," Fenley said, "to see what we need most from the New York shoots."

Perri sat prepared to take notes, a yellow legal pad resting on her lap. She took off her outer sweater, aware of Fenley's eyes. The editing room was always so hot. Then Claudine turned off the light and they all looked at the footage. Sometimes Perri just looked at Larry's profile, which wasn't special. Despite experience to the contrary, Perri thought that Larry's rather ordinary looks gave her some measure of safety.

"What we have to find is the story," Larry said as he changed reels. "Scenes of the conflict, the issue."

"Maybe we should go from the known to the unknown," Perri said. "I mean, everybody knows about how some authors get million-dollar contracts, but the struggles of the ordinary writer are not common knowledge. So we could start with some clips of blockbuster authors on like 'The Today Show' and go on to Alice Bright of Hoboken."

"That's not a bad idea," said Larry, and Perri felt a surge of happiness.

Fenley said, "I don't like it."

Perri said, "Maybe we should start at the beginning. With the video tape of the *Nation* conference when there was that unanimous resolution to start the National Writers Union, and everybody stood up and cheered . . ."

"Too obvious," said Fenley.

Larry said, "The tape's prolly not good enough."

Prolly! Perri was enchanted. She said, "There's going to be some action at the *Village Voice* on Friday. Maybe we should shoot that."

"You didn't tell me," Fenley said.

"I found out last night."

"What's it all about?"

"The rights of free-lancers. It's pathetic how little they make. The Union has organized a group of them, and they're meeting with the publisher next Friday."

Fenley said, "I wouldn't say that was much action. A meeting."

Perri said, "Well, it isn't *Harlan County, USA*, where miners on strike are getting shot at, but what do you want? We're talking about writers!"

"What else is the Union doing?" Fenley asked.

Perri said, "They're working on a model contract. They've gotten insurance for writers. They're creating a data bank of job listings."

Fenley said, "Yawn."

"They're very good on grievances. They write letters to publishers and get back thousands of dollars for writers wronged—especially genre writers." Fenley looked bored, so Perri said, "You'll like this. They're filing a class-action suit against a porno magazine called *Different Strokes*, which has a history of cheating writers."

"Really? Now, there's a possible segment."

"You're kidding," Perri said.

"Not at all. We have one of the porno writers reading from his work—or better yet *her* work, especially if she's pretty—then we interview the editor in the office, have the camera linger on choice magazine covers . . ."

"Really!" Perri said, disgusted.

Nancy knocked on the door. "I'm going out—does anybody want any lunch?"

It was two-thirty. Perri was astonished at how late it was.

113

Fenley said, "I'll have the usual." He always had a vanilla yoghurt as he went over bills and proposals.

Claudine said, "I have to go to the bank."

Perri stood up and said, "Thanks, Nancy—but I think I'll go out to the deli and gorge on a hot turkey sandwich."

That just left Larry. She thought he might say, *I'll come with you, Perri,* but he didn't. He said to Claudine, "Wouldja do me a favor?"

Perri was already leaving the editing room, so she didn't get to hear what the favor was. But as Perri walked down the hall, she replayed Larry's voice asking "Wouldja do me a favor?"

"Yes?" Perri would say.

"Take off all your clothes."

But he wouldn't say that.

"Wouldja do me a favor?"

"Yes, Larry?"

"Stop laying this sex trip on me."

Now that was more like it. And Perri would say, "What sex trip?"

And he would say, "You know what I mean."

And she would be silent.

And he would say, "I'm warning you, Perri. I just might call your bluff."

And she would say, "I was hoping you would."

And then there would be no more words, they would move toward each other. Beyond that she could never imagine— aside from melting fury and ecstatic relief.

_15_

P<small>ERRI</small> <small>MET</small> <small>LARRY'S</small> <small>GIRL</small>
friend when Maude came to the office to Xerox some things
for her class. Unlike the romantic image her name evoked,
Maude was a sturdy, short, no-nonsense woman with straight
brown hair and a briefcase.

Larry and Claudine were busy putting together a sample
reel of the Europe footage for a Smythe Fund screening the
next day. Fenley and Nancy were working on the Spanish
narration for Fenley's last film, about global urban migration.
Perri, busy only with the never-ending follow-up letters, was
glad to leave her chores and make coffee for herself and Maude.

No one ever washed the coffee cups, so Perri had to hunt
down some sticky ones and take them to the ladies room by
the elevator. She squirted liquid hand soap inside them,

scrubbed them with wet paper towels, rinsed them and turned them upside down on the rim of the sink. Then she washed her own face and hands. There was grime everywhere in the office. She patted her face dry with a paper towel. Someone came out of a stall; a woman's face watched hers in the mirror. It was Maude.

Perri said, "It just gets so dirty in there. And so hot." This was to explain the skimpy T-shirt she was wearing. Before Maude arrived, Perri had taken off two sweaters in the editing room, one by one, showily.

Maude said, "Larry often complains about the heat. When he's alone in there, he sometimes works without a shirt."

Perri found this interesting. What would Larry's chest be like? Skinny, she supposed. He wasn't the body-building type. Oh, she would press his naked chest against her own . . .

Maude brushed her hair and continued to watch Perri.

Mirrors were funny, Perri thought. People felt they could examine you in them as if you weren't there. The mirror made you flat, two-dimensional, like a photograph. You were somehow no longer present, no longer real, you couldn't protest the invasion. Perri gathered up the cups and said, "See you in there."

They drank their coffee by the Xerox machine. Perri didn't learn a great deal from her conversation with Maude. Larry apparently liked working on the film. He had won a Cine Gold Eagle for another union film. The others in his M–L group approved of the idea. "M–L group?" Perri asked, bewildered.

Maude said, "Mmm" and seemed uncomfortable.

"What's that?" Perri asked.

"You'd better ask him," Maud said. Then she stood up and went to the phone.

Perri was intrigued, but just then Fenley called her into the office, and for the next two hours she did phone chores for the film. She heard Larry and Maude leave. He shouted, "'Night everybody!" down the hall.

116

What was it with Larry? Why wasn't he interested in her? That Maude was a frump did not make Larry less attractive —it only added to the mystery of the man and his seeming lack of interest in Perri.

If Larry liked anybody at the office, it was his assistant, Claudine. He kidded around with her as he never did with Perri. Perri had two explanations for this and believed them alternately: a) Larry didn't kid around with her because he didn't like her; or b) Larry didn't kid around with her because he liked her *too much for that*.

Claudine, Perri saw, flirted most with Fenley. Fenley could help her get her green card, help her get a start producing films. Or perhaps she found Fenley attractive—Fenley! There was no accounting for taste. Then again Claudine was flirtatious with all men. Watching her kiss Larry and Fenley hello and good-bye on both cheeks, Perri realized how stiffly she herself dealt with her colleagues. She neither kissed nor patted: at most, on being introduced, Perri shook hands.

She wished she and Larry shared a history of casual touching and that each day she could at least look forward to a touch or two on arrival and parting. Any of that was impossible now. If she touched him at all, she would probably do something awful, like pressing her lips to the inside of his elbow while they were screening footage.

The next morning, as Perri slid behind her desk, Fenley asked, "Hot night on the town?"

"Excuse me?"

"You're wearing yesterday's clothes."

"So I am," Perri agreed, but she wasn't going to tell him anything more. The night before, she'd had dinner at her friend Ann's house and had slept on the sofa there, totally zonked on Hawaiian sensimilla. "What time is the Smythe Fund screening?"

"They called to postpone till next week."

"Any reason?"

" 'Overscheduling.' Not a good sign."

"Hello?" A repairman in gray workclothes was at the open doorway. "I'm here to fix the Steenbeck." The editing machine had been jamming.

"It's just down the hall," said Fenley.

Perri stood up. "I'll show him the way."

In the editing room, Larry was on the phone, and Claudine, in zebra pants, was going through the log. "I'll get back to you later," Larry said and hung up. "You're new," he said to the repairman accusingly. "Where's Buzzy?"

"Buzzy's at a funeral."

"Oh. Too bad, 'cause he knows this machine. Something's wrong with a belt again."

Perri could find no reason to stay in the editing room, so she drifted back to her desk. But half an hour later, she was back in Larry's room. The machine was partially dismantled and was being scrutinized by Larry and the repairman. The repairman looked up when she entered.

"Claudine," Perri said, "did I leave a purple file folder here? I had it last about two weeks ago."

"I meuved some folders to ze top shelf, over zair."

"I see it." Perri stood on a chair to get it.

The repairman watched her with interest. Then he turned to look at Claudine, who was tucking in her T-shirt. He shook his head as if overcome. "How can you get any *work* done?" he asked Larry. "Near such women?"

Perri grinned and looked down at Larry to see what he would say. But it was Claudine who answered the repairman: "Ze question is," she said roguishly, "'ow can we get any work done near such a man!"

Larry did not look up from his machine, but he seemed to be smiling. Perri gazed at Claudine with unwilling admiration. Clever, quick, flirtatious Claudine!

At intervals throughout that day, Perri found herself playing and revising the repairman incident. In one version Larry

118

answered the repairman, muttering, "I can't, they're driving me crazy." In another, Claudine was gone and it was just Perri and Larry and the repairman. The repairman asked Larry, "How can you get any work done? With her?" Larry swallowed and was silent, torn between his feelings for her and his absurd (but endearing) pride. Perri replied to the repairman, "Larry's very good about hiding his passion for me."

For some reason, this last version proved the most appealing, and it was this one she settled on, as if even in fantasy she had to have the last word, and to suffer. She was staring at the river when someone began talking behind her. She jumped from a daydream of Larry to the sound of his voice.

"The machine's fixed," he said to Fenley. "Since we have a few more days, I'm going to cut some sequences for the Smythe Fund."

"Good idea," Fenley said, standing up. "I have to go to a board meeting now." Fenley was an officer in a charitable organization. "Which sequences?"

"The stuff in Stockholm. The London pub."

"Sure, go ahead." Fenley walked to the office door.

"I'll work with you," Perri said to Larry. "I mean, I'd like to watch, if that's all right. Get a sense of the process."

There was a long pause before Larry said, "Sure. But you'll find it very boring."

Fenley put his head in through the doorway and told Perri, "Don't forget to get to the post office before six."

Perri felt her teeth clench: He treats me more like his secretary than like his colleague.

"Okay?" asked Fenley.

"Okay," she said at last.

"See you at Nino's tonight," he said to Larry. Larry and Fenley were part of the same social/political set and had many friends in common. Perri thought they went out of their way to remind her of this.

After Fenley left, Perri followed Larry down the hall to the editing room. She pretended she was following him to an empty room at a party. Larry sat at the machine and asked Claudine to get him the Stockholm footage. Perri sat in Fenley's usual chair so she could glance at Larry's earring as he worked. He moved the film back and forth many times. He marked it up. He pulled long strips of film and soundtrack out and cut them with a splicer, and rested them in loops around his neck. With the same splicer (it amused Perri that "to splice" meant "to cut" and "to join"), Larry taped these pieces to the film and track on the left side of the machine. Perri felt she could watch him for hours: his small, neat hands moving quickly, his white neck draped with acetate necklaces of film.

After a while, Claudine left the room, and Perri and Larry were alone. Perri tried to remember what she wanted to ask him, besides how he liked to make love. Oh, yes! "Larry," she said. "What's an M–L group?"

"How did that come up?" he asked.

"Maude said something, I forget."

"Marxist–Leninist," he said. "It's a discussion group. About the issues of the day. Within a Marxist context."

"Does that mean you're a Commie?" Perri asked. She grinned in flirtatious disbelief. "The real thing?"

Larry turned to face her. "Perri," he said, "why don't you get off my case?"

"I'm not, I'm not *on* your case." Tears came to her eyes. She stood up. "But you're right," she said, "it *is* pretty boring in here."

Perri hurried down the hall to her office. She closed the door behind her—unnecessarily. No one was following. Tears were running down her cheeks as she stared at the river. Then she found herself scrabbling through her handbag to take out her fixings. Soon she was rolling a joint to smoke in the ladies room. It was already five o'clock; she didn't expect any more calls.

Perri unlocked the ladies room door, and made sure she was alone. After she opened the window, she lit the joint, then held her hand outside. She still had about a third of it to go, the best third, when she heard a key in the lock—her warning signal. She dropped the joint, letting it fall thirty stories down an air shaft, and went to the mirror.

"Hi, Perri," Nancy said, walking in.

"Hiya." Perri pretended she was taking something out of her eye.

"God, the smell in here!"

"What smell?"

"Of marijuana! Can't you smell it?"

"I have a cold," Perri said. "I can't smell much of anything." She put her bag on her shoulder. "See you in there."

Stupid junkie! Perri scolded herself. Running these risks! And lying to Nancy, a woman you like! You should have offered her some! It would be fun to get high with a friend from the office. It would be fun to get high with Larry. No it wouldn't. If you're uptight with him straight you'd be miserable stoned.

Passing the cutting room, she heard him joking with Claudine.

Perri sat at her desk and stared at the lights across the river. She thought, What a miserable chain of desire. Larry wants Claudine. Claudine wants Fenley. Fenley wants me. And I want Larry. Perri saw a star and wished on it. Just one single night with him. One. All the way home, she thought about Larry and how her hands and mouth would move on him. Inside her apartment, she put down her bag, and looked around her living room as if she were Larry. What would he feel coming here? Definitely decadent. That had to be her appeal. Her doorbell rang before she'd taken off her watch and shoes. Larry? Ridiculous: It was Lucy.

"Lucy, come in, how nice! I just got home, I'm getting out of these clothes." Lucy followed Perri into her luxurious and gloomy gray bedroom. Lucy sat in a built-in windowseat up-holstered in gray carpeting and watched her sister undress. Perri wore a matching bra and panty set of shimming ivory with brown lace insets. In terms of support, the brassiere was superfluous, but not in terms of aesthetics.

"Such good underwear for work," Lucy remarked.

"You never know what may happen," Perri said.

"Is anything happening? In your life?"

"Not at the moment," Perri said. "The only man I want I've never even kissed."

"Who's that?"

Perri wrapped her blue silk robe around her slender body and said, "I might have mentioned Larry? My editor on the film?"

"I think so."

Perri said, "I love the phrase 'my editor.' It makes him seem more mine. In point of fact, most of the time I think he doesn't like me."

"That's probably his appeal."

"You think? No, Lucy, this is an interesting guy. Very smart. Very radical. A Marxist, maybe even a Communist."

Lucy said, "If he's a Communist today, how could he possibly be smart?"

"He is, he just is. He knows what he's doing. He sees to the heart of things. Really. He's just great." Perri went on about Larry for a while.

Lucy said, "I haven't seen you this obsessed in years."

"It's true. Some days, I think about Larry all day." Perri felt her eyes were wet. She repeated, "All day."

Lucy replied, "Well, you can't be thinking of him *all* day."

"Most of the time. The times my mind is *mine*—then it's his."

Lucy asked, "What percent of your 'discretionary thought' do you give him?"

122

Perri smiled. "Lucy, you're so funny. Such a scientist. What percent? I don't know. Seventy, eighty. Is that possible?"

"Sure. You should read *Love and Limerence* by Dorothy Tennov. She's examined the whole phenomenon of falling in love or obsessing."

Perri wrinkled her nose. " 'Limerence'? I hate books with jargon."

Lucy said, "I know what you mean. But don't let that put you off. New ideas sometimes mandate new words."

"Okay, okay, Professor Jennings."

They sat in the living room. Perri lit a joint and held it out to share.

"Not for me," Lucy said. "You're doing too much of that."

"I'm an addict," Perri said, inhaling. "You know that. But at least I don't do it at work. Much." She tapped the ash off the joint and said, "Do you know what really gets me about Larry?"

Perri had been off the subject for all of a minute. Lucy smiled and said, "No, Perri. What really gets you about Larry?"

Perri wailed, "I can't even invent the right fantasy for us! I mean, he resents me in so many ways—professionally, politically, personally—that even in a daydream I can't overcome his hostility!"

"Tennov talks about the nature of the daydream or reverie, how it has to be emotionally plausible."

"She's absolutely right." Perri told her sister about her repairman fantasies. "I sometimes feel that in my daydreaming I'm sort of like a novelist."

"How do you mean?"

"We both pretend. We say 'what if?' We make up dialogue and detail. We insist our characters act plausibly. We delay climax exquisitely."

123

Lucy smiled. "And you both reveal the deep truths, I suppose."

"Perhaps."

"Aren't you being a little grandiose? About fantasies?"

"Well, I live in fantasies now."

"Not entirely. You're also working away at a challenging job. Don't forget that."

"But it's all intertwined—making the film and being with Larry. We have to see each other, whether or not we would choose to. Oh, Lucy. I keep thinking of classic film comedy. Boy meets girl. Boy hates girl—or girl hates boy. Then one day this hate turns to love. I can't help hoping Larry and I will end up in some passionate romance. But meanwhile it's just miserable."

"It's misery you've chosen, Perri."

"That may be true. But I'm in too deep to get out now. And once in a while there's this weird, um, *sex flash* between us. Then days and days of hostility. How do these absurd infatuations end? According to that woman?"

"Tennov? She says they end three ways: by absence, by consummation, or by extinction. If you never saw Larry at all, after several weeks or months you'd probably stop obsessing. And if you slept with him, you'd probably be fine."

"What's extinction?"

"The absolute conviction that Larry didn't like you. The way it is now, every so often, you feel he really does. And this constant doubt about the other's feelings prolongs a crush more than any other factor. If he always responded one way or the other, you'd know what to do. But the uncertainty drives you crazy with desire."

"Yes. That must be it. When we have those *moments* I'm flooded with joy. Then he's cranky and rude for a week."

Lucy said, as their mother once had, "Why don't you go out with some nice, cheerful man?"

They wrinkled their noses at each other.

124

16

FENLEY WAS AWAY IN EUROPE for the week, presenting one of his films at a festival in Prague, when Perri got the call from Hanson Hall's office.

Hanson Hall was the most recognizable book publisher in New York, a witty conservative who hosted the television series "Making Books." He felt that the Writers Union was a ludicrous endeavor and had agreed to argue that position for the film. Perri felt Hall's would be a lively counterview, and if he was properly questioned, what he said could provide Larry with needed transitions. Fenley had planned to interview him in two weeks, after he returned from Europe.

But an English-accented secretary informed Perri that Mr. Hall's schedule had changed. The shoot in two weeks would have to be canceled. Hall could be interviewed the coming

Thursday, for half an hour—or else in three months. Perri swallowed. "Thursday," she said. "Twelve o'clock. We'll get there at ten, to set up."

Fenley called Perri from Prague that afternoon, and she told him what had happened. He said, "You can't do it—you've never directed a shoot in your life."

"So what? I know the routine. It's not so mysterious. Anyway, we don't have any choice. We need footage of him now, not in January."

Fenley said, "And you think you can handle Hanson Hall? He's very shrewd, very slippery."

"I'm not trying to entrap him," said Perri. "I'm giving him a chance to sound off. He loves to talk. And he's funny. We'll be fine."

"Well, okay, if you're sure. Is Larry there?"

Perri buzzed the editing room and hung up. She herself had not spoken to Larry since their M–L fight on Friday.

Perri stared out the window. It was a white, foggy Tuesday, and she could barely see the river. Why was this project so hard? Instead of working as a team with Fenley and Larry, she had somehow become their enemy. Bad enough to have an enemy at work, worse luck to have two—one of whom you secretly adored.

Larry, in a red shirt she had never seen before, walked into the office and sat down on the couch. "Hello," he said. "Wanta see the pub scene?"

"Sure."

"Good, I'll have it ready in an hour." He looked out at the fog. "Spoke to Fenley about the shoot with Hanson Hall."

Perri nodded.

Larry said, "He thinks I should go along with you on Thursday."

"What? Why?"

"To make sure things are going smoothly."

"I've worked with a crew before."

"And to make sure we get what we need."

"Don't you trust me?"

"Perri, come off your high horse. I'm not going to take over, I'm going to help. If you need it. I've gone on a hundred shoots. I know what this film is about. It makes perfect sense for me to be there."

Perri thought a moment. Then she said, surprised, "It's true. You're right."

"Of course I am," he said. "What time's the interview?"

"Twelve. The call is for ten."

"Make it nine-thirty. I'll arrive at eleven."

"Such a long setup for such a simple shoot?"

"Shoots are never simple," said Larry. "There's always some last-minute twist . . ."

He stood up. "Screening's in an hour, don't forget. I think you'll like it." He strolled off down the hall.

Perri gazed after him. How nice he could be. Had Fenley put him up to it for the good of the production? Had Larry been told to butter her up? She thought, I'll take whatever he can give—butter, cream, flesh. She grinned. This was ridiculous, no way to go about making a film. Her priorities, she knew, were all wrong. She felt if she could just figure out what to wear for the Hanson Hall shoot, everything else would fall into place: Hanson Hall would shower her with eloquence and Larry Mercator would shower her with love.

For inspiration on the clothing question, Perri smoked a joint in the john, her hand out the window between tokes. She had a lot to do by Thursday, yes indeedy. She squirted eyedrops into her bloodshot eyes. She smiled as she thought of her outfit: tweed pants, silk shirt, suede jacket.

Back at the office, she sat at her desk, turned on the computer, and made a long, detailed list of the things she had to do. She shifted items around. Her phone rang, Larry was ready to screen.

Perri sat on Larry's earring side. Today, he wore a gold

stud, ho-ho. This dope-smoking at work was all wrong. She smothered a giggle. Claudine turned off the light and Perri watched the pub stuff from London—not rough and rambly as in dailies, but shaped and sharpened, angled. The scene was extremely convivial, with Haney and Frim, artists and friends, speaking with spirit. The film went to black.

"More, more," said Perri. "It's great. Can I see it again?"

"Sure." Larry began rolling it back.

"How long was that?"

"Two minutes, forty seconds. We can trim some later if you want."

She watched it again. This time, she noticed one or two places the rhythm was off, and a funny aftertaste about Frim—something disconcerting had happened so fast she couldn't quite tell if . . . "Larry? Could you go back to Frim's final speech and play it at slow speed."

"No problem."

She watched intently. In that underwater growl that human speech becomes when slowed, Frim made one last joke. Then he threw back his head and laughed. Larry had cut from Frim's open mouth to a barmaid filling a glass.

Perri said to Larry, "I think you should extend the Frim shot. So that he closes his mouth."

"Oh, yeah? Why?"

"Well, with his mouth open, it makes him seem dumb. Impolite. And that's not at all how he is."

Larry sighed. "Okay, I can put back a few frames, but remember, this isn't the fine-cut."

She had heard Fenley make suggestions similar to hers without Larry objecting, but she said only, "Okay. It's just a detail. The scene as a whole works real well."

"Good idea to shoot them in that pub."

She said, "That was my location. Fenley wanted to shoot them in the editorial offices of Peckham and Spack, but I found out where they went for a pint . . ."

"You have a pretty good film sense."

"Well, thank you. Where can I faint?"

Larry said, "Put your head between your knees."

And suddenly there was that shimmer between them, that erotic tension—had he said head and knees?

He stood up. "Gotta make a phone call," he said, and that was all she saw of him that day.

Slow pan on a gleaming white Rolls Royce parked outside Le Cirque. The uniformed chauffeur suddenly leaps out to open the door for a prosperous-looking, middle-aged man who is leaving the restaurant. In the middle distance—the camera is somewhat concealed—we see Perri Jennings rush over to him.

Perri: Mr. Pons?

Asa Pons: Do I know you?

Perri: My name is Perri Jennings and I'm making a film about the publishing industry and I wonder if you would—

He gives her a stony look, shakes his head, gets into the car, and sits staring ahead until the chauffeur enters. They drive away quickly. From the curb, Perri stares after them.

[From *Tilting at Windmills: The National Writers Union* (working title), rough cut, Fenley Films.]

Perri was all set to watch Hanson Hall's show. She had a legal pad on her lap, a pencil behind her ear, and a joint in her mouth. Sara was with her.

Sara said, "I think you're doing too much of that stuff."

"I can take it," said Perri. "It doesn't do that much for me anymore."

"Why bother, then?" asked Sara. "Feeding cannabinol into your brain, where it accumulates . . . ?"

Perri smiled. "It feels good. It relaxes me."

"What about what it does to your eyes?"

"Sara, stop nagging me!"

Sara said, "I don't nag, I hector."

"Whatever. Stop it." Perri reached into her bag and took

out a pair of black harlequin sunglasses. She put them on. "See, if the eyedrops don't work, I use these."

"Very vamp," said Sara.

"That's me. The vamp who never gets laid."

"Since this Larry thing, you've been so obsessed you've passed up other possibilities . . ."

"*Moi?* Obsessed?"

The theme music to "Making Books" came on and Perri and Sara settled down to watch. The camera moved in on Hanson Hall's face. The topic for the show was libel law and book publishing. His guests were Jilly Jackson, a female novelist of thirty-five who had written a book about a brilliant, perverse designer of Portuguese descent; and a spokesman for Royale Blue, the brilliant, perverse designer of Portuguese descent who had brought suit against her. (The case had been settled out of court for an undisclosed amount.) Hanson Hall presided over the angry debate that ensued from his questions. He seemed amused, removed, above it all, aristocratic. He had a funny mannerism of blinking, then widening his eyes in disbelief when he heard anything he considered dubious. Perri made note of this.

"He's not such an ogre," Sara said when the show was over. "You'll do fine."

"What if he throws one of his fancy French phrases at me?"

"Say, 'What does that mean, *exactly*?' As if the nuance escapes you."

"Clever Sara," said Perri. "You are."

"So clever my husband's walked out on me."

"It's a ploy. He'll be back. If you want him."

"I don't know anymore."

Perri's doorbell rang. She went to the door. Carlo was there, with Zoe in his arms. "She is hungry," he said.

Sara said, "So early!"

Perri said "Hi" to the young man who was Sara's au pair.

The baby cried. "She wants mommy," said Carlo, passing

Zoe to Sara. He looked hard at Sara, but she was busy rubbing her mouth against Zoe's cheeks.

"Shoosh, my little, shoosh . . ." Sara crooned. She stood up. "I'm exhausted, Perri. I'm going to feed her in bed." Carlo preceded them down the stairs.

Perri said, "Good night," glad to see them all go. She wanted to think about the the questions she would ask Hanson Hall.

Perri was right about the setup. By eleven o'clock on Thursday, the crew had finished lighting the room for the Hanson Hall interview, and there was nothing left for anyone to do. They were waiting. Filmmaking, Perri felt, was a waiting game. You waited for your money and you waited for your subjects and you waited for your shots. Nancy was sent out to get coffee, and now they were waiting for that too.

At times like these Perri wished she still smoked cigarettes: she looked hungrily at Michael's shirt pocket, hoping to see a rectangular bulge. But Michael had given up tobacco six months before, the sound recordist didn't smoke, and Ivy, Michael's assistant, smoked a cigarette too bland to bother with.

Perri sat down at the conference table and tried to persuade herself that she craved several deep breaths, not a cigarette. If you breathed just right, you could feel the incoming air rush down your nostrils and bite into your lungs in that Marlboro manner she loved. Sometimes Perri thought she smoked so much dope not to get high but to feed her chest smoke.

Larry walked into the room, wearing a sports jacket and no earring. Seeing him so straight was like seeing him in drag. "Everything under control?" he asked Perri.

"So you see. We're just lounging around." But her heart wasn't languid. She showed him her list of questions. "Do me a favor." She pointed to three starred items. "Make sure I get answers to these. When I finish the interview, I'll ask if we have what we need, and you tell me yes or no."

"Sure. Good idea."

"I'm worried about him deflecting me, getting me off on his own side issues," said Perri.

"He can do that," Larry said. "I'll be listening carefully. And remember. Get him to answer in complete sentences."

"Of course." She had been on enough shoots with Fenley to know his ways. In editing, he liked to cut out the interviewer's questions. For this reason, the answers had to hold up on their own.

Nancy came in with the coffee. She did a take when she saw Larry. "You're here?"

"Yeah, why not?"

"I thought you were chained to that editing machine," Nancy said. "Just kidding. You can share my coffee, if you like it black and sweet."

"Sure," he said, smiling.

Perri watched in dismay. Was *Nancy* also interested in Larry? Were there rivals everywhere for the attentions of this irritable leftist? Ivy, at least, wasn't flirting with him. But Ivy was gay, Perri thought, or neuter. Ivy yawned. Perri looked at her watch. She had to choke back the impulse to make general party conversation, to entertain the people she had hired. Fenley, she remembered, never felt he had to be host on his shoots.

Michael said, "Would you like to look through the lens?"

"Sure."

The sound recordist sat in for Hanson Hall, and Perri looked through the camera for the composition of the shot. "You'll be changing focal lengths so we can cut . . ."

"Uh-huh."

"Well, I had this idea." She told Michael something and he grinned and said, "Sure, that sounds like fun."

Perri rearranged some books that would be in the shot, although she knew it was unlikely anyone would be able to make out the titles on the shelf.

Finally, Hanson Hall came into the room. His face was so familiar Perri felt like saying, "Why, *hello*." Then she remembered that they had never met, and she introduced herself. Her voice shook; she found she was nervous. As with other celebrities seen at last in the flesh, Hanson Hall seemed hyperreal, super 3-D.

Ivy turned the lights on Hanson Hall and now he seemed more vivid and intense than ever. The sound recordist clipped a microphone to Hanson Hall's suit jacket and stepped to one side. Hall said, in his familiar drawl, "Did Alison tell you? I can only spare half an hour? I have to speak at this luncheon . . ."

The sound recordist took a reading while Hall talked.

"We should start, then," Perri said. "Ready?" she asked the crew.

In a moment, Michael said, "Rolling."

This was it. She was directing the shoot. She had to begin the interview; she had to ask the first question. And she was paralyzed. The silent seconds passed. Everyone was waiting. Larry was waiting. Hanson Hall was waiting. Perri swallowed. Then she found her voice, a tremulous croak, and began. "Mr. Hall, what is your own publishing background?"

"I've worked in publishing for over thirty years. I started out as an editorial assistant, became an editor, and now I'm president of Quantum House, which publishes almost two hundred books a year. I also have a television series about the publishing industry. And I'm the author of six books myself. So I know the business in breadth and in depth, if you'll excuse the assonance."

"Excused," Perri said, at loss for another response. (Wasn't assonance similar vowel sounds and shouldn't she let him know she knew?) She went on to her next question. "Do you think the Writers Union is a viable organization?"

"Certainly not! It hasn't got a chance!"

She said, "Cut" to Michael and then turned to Hanson Hall. "Mr. Hall, I'm sorry, could you do that again, speaking in a complete sentence?"

"What do you mean?"

"Well, when we make the film, we're going to cut out my questions, so your answers have to be complete in themselves. So instead of saying, 'Certainly not! It hasn't got a chance,' say 'The Writers Union hasn't got a chance.' Okay? Michael?"

The camera was rolling again, and Hanson Hall said, woodenly, "The Writers Union hasn't got a chance."

He stared at her coldly.

"Why doesn't the Writers Union have a chance?" Perri asked.

"Because it's ill conceived and ill designed and wholly inappropriate."

"Could you say that again, naming the Writers Union?"

"Come on!" He was getting angry, on her film and on her time. "I've never had this problem before! I've been interviewed dozens of times, hundreds of times, and it's always gone smoothly."

"I'm sorry, but for the kind of film we're making, we need complete statements."

Hall shook his head in frustration. "All right, where were we?"

She asked the question again.

"The question was," he repeated, "why doesn't the Writers Union have a chance. And the answer is because it's ill conceived and ill designed and wholly inappropriate." He developed this theme at some length; Perri prodded him by nodding. She ran a pencil line through two questions she would no longer need to ask. He used two French phrases, made a joke, and came to the end of his speech.

Perri said, "But don't you think today's writer faces a uniquely discouraging situation?"

"Not at all. It was just as bad twenty, thirty years ago."

"I'm sorry, Mr. Hall, could you do that again in a way that's complete in itself?"

"I don't think I can take this," he said.

"Please," said Perri. "We really need your voice in this film. But we don't want mine in it."

He shook his head in resignation. "All right. Let me see. The question was whether today's writer has it especially hard." Perri wished he hadn't construed her instructions to mean he must now repeat her every question, but she didn't dare alienate him further. Hall went on, "Writers have always had it hard. Read George Gissing's *New Grub Street*. One doesn't go into writing for the money—and besides, no Writers Union can change the law of supply and demand."

"Would you expand on that somewhat?"

"The question was, would I expand upon the law of supply and demand? Well, it's really very simple. Many people write. Few people buy. The market takes over and what will sell best gets published—with a few exceptions. What's the Writers Union going to do—call a strike against mediocrity? Even if the nation's top five hundred writers went on strike, the next fifty thousand would fight among themselves to replace them. It's a literary jungle, dog eat dog. How does the Writers Union plan to change that?"

"By unifying writers. After all, they're all workers, all being exploited so that someone else makes a profit . . ."

Hanson Hall laughed. "Marxist twaddle," he said. "You can't really believe writing or publishing works that way." He pulled his "incredulous" face: eyebrows drawn back, mouth pursed forward.

Perri said, "I'm curious about how you justify the pay-scale at Quantum. At a time of huge profits for publishers, you are paying less than ten thousand dollars for ninety percent of the books you publish—books that take a year or two or three to write. How can an author survive on that kind of pay?"

"The question was . . . let me see, just what was the question? How authors survive? Or why we don't pay them more? Authors survive by teaching and getting grants and wheedling and borrowing and, if they're very lucky, by publishing. It's never been prudent financially to become an artist."

"The artist's life has other consolations," Hall continued. "If the question is why don't publishers pay writers more, the answer is"—and he grinned gleefully—"because we don't have to. It's a question of power. Publishers have it; writers don't. Can a few hundred scribblers who call themselves the National Writers Union make any difference to the industry? That's about as plausible as the stork theory of human reproduction!" His grin lingered on his face.

After a few seconds, Perri said, "Cut."

She asked Larry, "Are we okay? Did we cover those questions."

He nodded.

Hanson Hall stood up and unclipped his microphone from his jacket. Ivy began turning off the lights. An assistant came to take Hanson Hall to his next appointment. Larger than life, he walked out of the room and down the hall to his office.

Perri closed the door behind him. As the crew began packing up, no one said a word. Then, in that fragile moment that follows a performance, Larry said to Perri, "You might want to listen to it first before printing it."

"What?" The silence in the room intensified.

Larry said, "You might not think it's worth printing."

"That bad?" Perri felt her face redden with shame. "I don't understand. I was shy and he was mean—but we got what we needed, right? I mean, Larry, I *asked* you!"

"Relax," Larry said. He smiled. "It was fine. I was just kidding."

"Kidding!"

"Yeah, a joke, you know, laugh?"

"Not funny," she said. "On my first shoot, not fucking funny."

"Whoa," he said, "touchy. I didn't mean to rattle you."

"Like hell," Perri said. "Go back to your dark room where you belong."

_17_

THE NEXT DAY, PERRI ARRIVED
at the office to find three red carnations jammed into a Coke
bottle on her desk. An envelope lay against the bottle. The
note inside said, "Sorry, Larry." Perri felt her face turn red.

Nancy came in with the mail and said, of the flowers, "Secret admirer?"

"Neither," said Perri, forcing a smile. "Just Larry. Apol-
ogizing for yesterday."

Nancy said, "I thought that was awful what he did." She
paused, then added, "But it was also awful what you said."

"Maybe."

"What is it with you two? You get so tense around each
other."

Before Perri could reply, the phone rang, and Nancy went

138

back to her office to answer it. Perri stared at the carnations, a species she didn't much like. Men think you'll forgive them anything if they bring you a couple of flowers. Perri felt embarrassed that Nancy had noticed how uncomfortable she and Larry were together. On the other hand, if they were similarly weird around each other, maybe he was crazy for her, too. On the third hand, perhaps *Nancy* had a crush on Larry and was not an impartial observer . . . Perri went through the mail and did some clerical chores. When Perri finally looked into the editing room, Claudine said Larry was at the lab. Then Perri left for the day to do some research.

So it wasn't until the next morning that she saw him at all. "How are ya?" he said bright and early in her office.

"Okay. Thanks for the carnations." Perri had brought in a narrow chrome vase for them.

Larry said, "I didn't mean to make you angry after the shoot. Really."

"It's just—at that moment, I believed you, I thought the interview had gone terribly."

"Well, come look at it. It's all sunk up."

This meant the picture and soundtrack had been synchronized and were ready for viewing. "Why isn't it 'synched'?" she asked, following him.

"I'm not an English major anymore. Just a humble film technician."

"You don't believe that," Perri said, sitting down by the machine.

"Not for one second," he said with a grin.

"You probably feel you 'write' the documentary here in the editing room."

"Something like that." He sat down. To Perri's intense disappointment, he wasn't wearing his earring.

Claudine turned off the light and Hanson Hall's face filled the screen. Waiting, he frowned slightly, and off-camera, off-mike, Perri asked the first question. Listening now, she could hear her own voice quaver. But of course that would be cut. The real thing was Hall's response, and he was good. The man could talk, his voice had zest. After a while, he pulled his "incredulous" expression, and Michael zoomed out with the camera at the exact moment Hanson Hall's eyes popped. Perri laughed aloud.

"Great zoom," Larry said.

"Yeah," said Perri. "I asked him to try it."

"Good idea," Larry said, and he rubbed her bare wrist twice, up-down, up-down. It seemed all motion stopped within her. Then he put his hand on the machine again. She sat there numb, unable to assess the footage. Her skin was alive to the man at her side, and her mind was a mush. He had touched her at last! He was sitting right next to her in the dark!

"Could I see it again?" Perri asked when they reached the end of the footage.

"Sure," Larry said. "I'll wind it back for you and take a break."

This was not what Perri had in mind. She wanted to be with him in the dark. She said, "I thought I'd get stoned and look at it." He said nothing. She went on, "Care to join me?"

"Now? Here? No thanks."

"Well. See you in a bit," Perri said, feeling foolish. God, he must think she was an addict, getting stoned at eleven o'clock on a weekday morning for a second look at the dailies. She went into the ladies room, rolled a joint, opened the window, lit up. The smoke felt so good going down. She should never have asked him to join her. Now she was exposed as the user she was. And all because she had hoped to touch his hand while passing the joint. She had given him yet another chance to turn her down, another reason to despise her. But maybe that wasn't so. He had bought her flowers. He had touched her wrist. Perhaps in another three months he would touch her wrist again.

In high spirits, Perri returned to the editing room and was

only slightly deflated to find Larry in the far corner on the phone. She looked at the footage alone and took a few notes. She saw two useful bits that would make good transitions and one contemptuous response that was so entertaining it had to go in. She'd done okay. She hadn't let Fenley down. She rewound the footage and looked at it a third time.

When she was finished, Larry and Claudine were gone, presumably to lunch. So Perri had lunch with Nancy at the local health food restaurant. Nancy kept turning the conversation to Larry, Perri's favorite subject in the world. Perri wasn't really bothered by Nancy's interest in Larry until it occurred to her that Nancy was more in the Maude mode than Perri; if he had a "type," then Nancy had the edge. How amazing to find this wholesome and earnest young woman her rival! Perri had once heard Gordon say that although he had never been in a fight in his life, on meeting a man, he always gauged his height and weight to see if he could "take" him. When Perri met a woman, she always assessed her sexual power and compared it to her own. Even before her years as a model Perri had been a competitive beauty.

The next morning, she got a call from the Smythe Fund, rescheduling the canceled screening for Friday, the day Fenley would return to work. When she spoke to Larry about it, he told her he wanted to prepare a new version for them, using the new footage. He said, "I'd like to work on it today and tomorrow. Late if I have to."

Perri said, "Sure. I'll work with you."

"Supervise every cut?" he asked bitterly.

"I don't want any surprises," she said. "Especially at a funder's screening."

"Not even happy surprises?"

"Look, Larry, I just want control of my film!"

"Yours and *Fenley's*," he said, "and I'm involved too. I need some space here!"

Perri stared at him.

He went on, "Tell you what. Why don't you let me work on it alone today and tomorrow, then come in tomorrow night and the two of us will go over it together. How does that sound?"

Nighttime at the office. Dim lights. Claudine and Nancy gone home. Fenley away. Just she and Larry alone together at last. Outside the window, ten thousand lights and two rivers. Inside, a man and a woman, coworkers, a team, combining their talents, uniting their bodies . . .

"That sounds good," Perri said.

A rebellious-looking fifteen-year-old boy, Ronald Pons (Asa Pons's son), sits on a rock in Central Park. Black T-shirt; denim vest; moussed, spikey hair: very short on top, very long at the bottom.

Ronald: My dad's always been a maniac for privacy. He says journalists can't to be trusted. Especially filmmakers. He says they can make you look stupid no matter what you say. Is that true?

Camera pans to reveal Perri sitting near him on the rock.

Perri, smiling: Sometimes. What else does your dad say? Like, about writers?

Ronald (voice-over a montage of some of the writers interviewed in the film): He says they're like children. Always needing feeding, one way or another. And they have to be the center of attention! I don't think he likes them too much.

Ronald (synch sound): He'd probably like to do without them altogether!

[From *Going After Goliath: The National Writers Union* (working title), fine cut, Fenley Films.]

"So since I have to work tonight, I took today off," Perri told Sara at eleven o'clock in the morning. They were at Perri's gray-tiled kitchen bar, sitting on chrome and leather swivel stools. Zoe was asleep on the industrial carpeting. Perri said, "I'm so thrilled about tonight. My love and I alone at last!"

"You are so crazy," said Sara. "It doesn't even sound as if he likes you."

"He's just defensive."

"You're just obsessive. You are."

"Yawn, yawn. Any news?"

"Well, yes in fact," said Sara.

"About Gordon?"

"No—I haven't heard from Gordon. I could always call him at the office, but . . ." She shook her head.

"But what?"

Sara said, "I think I'm in love."

"Of course, I forgot, the new person in your life! The one you wouldn't tell me anything about. Sara! Is that why Gordon left?"

"Gordon left because I threw the tax things out the window, as I told you. He doesn't know I'm in love. It's just begun."

"So who is the man? It *is* a man?"

"No, it's a koala bear." Sara paused. "Actually, Perri, keep this secret. It's rather awkward."

"Your true love?"

Sara nodded. "It's Carlo, my au pair."

"I see," Perri said, after a pause. "He's very nice looking."

"He's much more than that!" Sara said heatedly. "He's got energy and joy and intelligence and verve . . ."

"Okay, okay," Perri said. "That's great. How old is he?"

"I knew you'd ask that, I just knew it. He's not even so young—he's almost thirty."

"Twenty-seven?"

"Twenty-nine."

"Eight years younger than you."

"A *mere* eight years younger," Sara said.

"Very fashionable. Does he know how you feel about him?"

Sara smiled and nodded.

Perri asked, "Does he feel like that about you?"

Sara smiled and nodded.

Perri said, "Aren't you smug! I suppose you've been fucking your brains out."

"You are always incredibly crude."

"Don't get starry-eyed with me, Sara darling. I know the look of a woman well fucked."

"You spend too long at the mirror."

"Ha ha. And he's good?"

Sara stared into the middle distance.

"Sara, don't just sit there looking beatific. What's it like, you and Carlo?"

"Don't mock and don't laugh or I won't say anything at all."

"You came up to talk," Perri said, "and you know my basic fix on life." She poured them each more coffee and said, "But I'll be good. Tell me."

"Well, one thing is I love the self he sees in me, the reflection I see when I look in his eyes."

"And what's that?"

"Oh, this strong and lovely woman, warm and good. This sensual, serene American, this lady with a loom . . . And he's right there to stir me up, my handsome young Italian in the basement. Part of the thrill is it's all so domestic. He feels me up in the kitchen. He gives me hot looks while feeding the boys. His bed is a wall away from the washer and dryer. I should be ashamed of myself, and I am, and that's part of the excitement. It's so weirdly passionate and familial. Peculiarly romantic."

"And then there's his body," Perri prompted.

"Bodies aren't that important," Sara said. "He could be twenty pounds heavier or lighter than he is and I wouldn't care." She smiled. "As it is, I just have to make do with the fact that he's perfect."

"Larry's too skinny," Perri said proudly, "kinda runty. But his earring makes up for it."

"What is this earring mystique?"

"The incongruity, I think. Everything else in the vicinity —the ear, the hair, jaw—looks supermasculine by contrast. An earring on a man is like a fedora on a woman. It makes you think masculine, feminine, *sex*."

"It makes *you* think sex," Sara said. "Anything does."

Perri persisted, "Earrings are kinky as well. The idea of piercing your flesh for adornment! If you're a guy! Like a harlot."

"And you appreciate all this?"

"And identify. Yes."

"Larry must have some other attractions."

"He insults me a lot." Perri smiled dreamily.

"Carlo admires me," Sara said tenderly.

Perri said, "Look at us, sitting here, sisters in love."

Perri ate again, equivocally, at five. She wanted to have enough in her stomach to work until midnight if she had to but not so much that she couldn't join Larry somewhere for dinner if he suggested it. At five-thirty, she took a shower and made herself extremely clean and smooth and fragrant. At six she stared into her underwear drawer.

Now, there was no reason to think he might see them that night, Perri told herself, none at all. Yet she spent some time deciding which underpants to wear. You couldn't wear anything really sexy on a first date, or the guy would know you'd been planning for sex all along and think less of you for it— and this wasn't even a first date! So she couldn't wear her favorites, which had a translucent, lacey panel in the front, nor the ones cut so high you saw a bit of flesh at each side, or anything in black or red. And she didn't want to be too drab (he had Maude for that), so it was no to the plain cotton exercise panties, although she'd once gone out with someone who adored white cotton panties, they reminded him of the girls of his youth. The various novelty undies that Tony had bought her were clearly out of the question and her pink silk

145

bikinis were getting kind of tatty. She finally decided on a pale
blue cotton pair with embroidered flowers at each hip. Country girl. White lace brassiere. A thin silver necklace with tiny
blue stones she had borrowed the week before from Sara.

She smiled at her reflection. Reluctantly, she put on pants
and sweater. She guessed she still had several years to look
best seminude. She applied makeup. This year, for the first
time in her life, she was wearing fire-truck-red lipstick. It made
her feel blonder.

A service elevator took her up to the office. The place felt
strange at night. She wondered what Larry would be doing
when she arrived. Would he be at his machine or making calls
or pacing back and forth waiting for her? Perhaps this was the
night to start touching on greeting, her hand on his arm,
comrades. She put her key in the lock to the suite, then tiptoed
down the hall. She wanted to peep in at him.

But she didn't see Larry at all. She did see Claudine, standing up, filing trims. Perri shrank back from the door. Why
was Claudine still at work? Maybe she was going to leave soon.
Hadn't Larry said, "Just the two of us"? Perri felt immobi-
lized, but she couldn't stay where she was in the corridor.
When Larry came back from the bathroom, or wherever he
was, he would think it was odd to see Perri frozen by the
doorway. She walked into the editing room.

"Ah, Perri, *bonsoir*! I think you're going to like this."

"Where's Larry?"

"'e 'ad to leave. 'e told me to make any changes you want."

"He had to *leave*?" Perri felt the blood drain from her head.
She thought she might black out from disappointment. She
gasped, "What happened?"

Claudine shrugged. "'alf an hour ago, 'e said 'e 'ad to leave.
'e'll come in early tomorrow and look at any changes we've
made. Make sure they work. Eet will be fine. You'll see."

Perri saw all right. Larry had said "just the two of us" (*had* he said it?) just to buy himself some space. The last thing on earth Larry wanted was "just the two of us."

"Perri?" Claudine was saying. "You look white. You okay?"

"Just a cramp," Perri said. She felt like she'd been kicked in the stomach.

18

F<small>RIDAY MORNING, FENLEY WAS</small> back in his leather chair, looking very fit. His film had won a prize in Berlin and he had been to dinner with Bernardo Bertolucci.

"Fifteen of you sitting around a large table in a restaurant?" Perri suggested.

"Yes, as a matter of fact," he replied, annoyed.

Perri said quickly, "I love that European bonhomie."

"Let's look at the film before the Smythe people come."

"Good idea."

"Larry's ready," Fenley said. "You two getting on okay?"

"Up and down. What does he say?"

"Nothing much." Fenley stood up. "After you." Once

more, Perri went down the hall in front of him feeling his eyes on her butt. Would she miss it when her ass wasn't worth watching? You bet she would. Today, she was wearing her dignified clothes, for the foundation people, but next week she going to dress so hot and be so cold to Larry he would be so sorry . . . Of course, if she dressed hot for Larry, Fenley might think it was for him. Ugh—Fenley in bed. It came to her then that maybe Larry thought, "Ugh—Perri in bed." The parallel appalled her.

So she was quite unprepared for Larry's friendly smile and look of unalloyed appreciation. "Nice suit!" he said. "You look terrific. Sorry I missed you last night—I had to go check a print. Trouble at the lab . . ."

"Check a print?" she repeated as she sat down.

"On *Robeson*." The year before, Larry had produced a half-hour short on the singer Paul Robeson. "It's going to be shown in Park City on the twelfth and they need a print now."

"Where's Park City?"

"Utah."

"The USA Film Festival," Fenley said. "Sponsored by Sundance. It's one of the best."

Larry said, "Especially if you ski."

Perri said, "I love to ski."

"Then you should go sometime. You'd really like it."

Fenley asked, "Are we going to screen or are we going to schmooze?"

They looked at the film together and made two minor rearrangements before the executive director of the Smythe Fund and his assistant arrived for their screening. Perri sat at the side of the room and took notes on their reactions. She was overwhelmingly relieved. It was all clear to her now. Larry didn't hate her at all. He just was busy. He had things to do. He was worried about fooling around—especially with a colleague. But he was attracted, all right—she wasn't inventing the sexual crackle between them. If she could be with him away from the office, away from New York, she was sure she could get him.

She said to Larry later in the day, "Does Maude ski?"

"No. But she can't come anyway because of her work."

"How do you ski?"

Larry said, "Passably."

Perri was a good skier, although she had learned skiing late, at twenty-five. She had simply followed her instructor's movements, ignoring the confusing things he said. Having taken dance class for years, she had caught on to combinations rapidly. She had a natural ease of movement and no fear. So she became very good very fast. It would be fun to ski with Larry and show him her style.

"I ski okay too," Perri said, although he hadn't asked.

"The runs are really long," Larry said, "and you go up in a cable car."

Claudine, who had entered the room, asked, "What is a cabble car?"

Perri went back to the corner office. Fenley, uncharacteristically, was standing by the window looking at the river.

"Did you miss the river?" Perri asked.

"I missed some things about being here, yes," Fenley said.

Perri had an awful hunch he was going to say he'd missed her, so she quickly pulled the phone to her and lifted the receiver. The only way she could get them both out of this situation with dignity was to discourage him before he made a pass at her. An explicit advance, flatly rejected, would only make things worse in the corner office they shared. But Fenley just said, "You know, you did pretty well on the Hanson Hall shoot."

That night, Perri lay musing in her bathtub, in fragrant, oily waters. The worst thing about an office crush was also the best thing: if it didn't work out, you still had to—or got to

—see the person every day. Got to hope, got to agonize. The agony was essential. But she remembered Sara once saying, "For you and for Proust maybe—not for me."

Perri nudged the tap with her foot and added more hot water to her bath. A hot tub in the moonlight in Park City, Utah. After a day on the mountain, she and Larry are pleasantly fatigued and muscle-sore. They take off their towels and lower themselves into the wonderfully hot, frothy water. At first they just sit gratefully. Then they bob. They rub their backs against the water jets to massage different sets of vertebrae. They still haven't kissed, so when their limbs bump underwater, neither knows if it is intentional. Their movements are tentative; their sensations intense. The uncertainty about whether or not they are touching by accident persists for some time, and then, driven mad by her slender body and plump little breasts, Larry pulls her to him and—

"Help, help! Daddy! Stop it! Stop!"

Through a vent in the bathroom floor, Perri heard Roland yelling. She leaped up from her bath. She heard Sara screaming in the background. Perri threw on her robe and ran downstairs to their door, knocking and ringing their bell. They didn't come fast enough: she let herself in with her key.

Gordon said, furiously, "Oh, great, just what we need, my good friend and ally upstairs."

But Roland ran to her. Rory clung to Sara. It was eleven-thirty at night. The children were in pajamas, Sara was in a robe, and Gordon was dressed in a suit.

"I heard Roland screaming," said Perri. "What's going on?"

"What's going on," Gordon said, "is I come home to tell my wife what happened with the audit and I find her in bed with the help!"

"That just isn't true!" Sara yelled. "Don't tell the children that! I was just in Carlo's room to talk about tomorrow's schedule."

"Dressed in your robe!"

"Is it against the law to walk about in my own house in my own robe?"

"Don't play the innocent with me, Sara. Not now."

"Come on, kids," Perri said. "We'll let the grown-ups quarrel by themselves." She led the boys to their room.

Roland said, "He threw a chair at her. That's why I yelled."

"And then I yelled because he yelled," Rory said.

Perri said, "Grown-ups fight sometimes. I'm sure he didn't throw the chair *at* her. I'm sure he just threw the chair."

Roland said, "I bet they never make up. I bet they get a divorce."

"Don't be ridiculous," said Perri. "They're just having a fight."

"Yeah," Roland said. "And Daddy's just going on another 'business trip.' "

"Maybe," Perri said. "Maybe not. Maybe everything will be better than you think."

"How?"

"Life's full of surprises."

"Oh, sure." Roland turned away from her when she kissed him good night. But little Rory hugged her, with both hands hard around her neck.

As Perri returned to the living room, she could hear Sara say, heatedly, "I'm telling you, nothing was happening! We were just talking. Jesus!"

Perri had to admire her sister's aplomb. Sara really seemed indignant.

Gordon said, "I came back to see if you want to make up . . ."

Sara didn't say anything.

Gordon said, "If you want to make up, then Carlo has to go."

"Now?"

"Yes, now. When do you think—next summer?"

Perri came into the room. Gordon said, "As long as you're here, Perri dear, you can be the one to do the honors. Go downstairs and tell Carlo to start packing. He has to leave. Now."

Perri said, "Gordon, it's almost midnight . . . Sara?"

Sara said to Perri, "Go downstairs. Do what he says."

Perri said, "You're sure?"

Sara nodded.

Perri reluctantly went down the basement stairs. Sara ran after her. "Take him to Lucy's," she whispered.

Perri nodded. Lucy had left that morning for a conference: the apartment would be empty for a week.

Gordon called down the stairs, "What's going on there?"

"Nothing," Sara said, hurrying back upstairs. "You were going to tell me. What happened at the audit?"

Perri heard something about only owing six thousand dollars. Then she reached Carlo's room. The door was open, and his suitcase was on the bed. He said, "You don't have to tell me. I heard. I must leave."

Perri asked, "Where will you go?"

"I don't know. I'll find somewhere."

"You can stay upstairs at Lucy's place for a few days. She's away in Chicago this week."

"Yes? Would that be possible?"

Perri nodded.

"Thank you, then," Carlo said.

Perri said, awkwardly, "I'm sure Sara wants to talk to you."

"But her husband is back."

It was a simple statement of fact: he didn't even sound bitter. In fact, Perri thought, Carlo sounded relieved.

_19_

WHEN PERRI LOOKED IN ON HER sister the next morning, Sara was sitting in the armchair nursing Zoe. "Sara, what's been happening? What did Gordon walk in on last night?"

"Nothing. Absolutely nothing. I was in Carlo's room, but we were just talking."

"God—you were lucky."

"Yeah, real lucky," Sara said bitterly.

"Well, you _were_."

"Perri—Carlo _can't_ anymore. In bed."

"But I thought you two had such fabulous sex."

"We _did_. It was wonderful. Then last week he was talking about the beautiful babies we'd have and I had to tell him . . ." Her voice trailed off.

"You told him you'd tied your tubes."

Sara nodded. "And he said, in such a sad voice, 'But I wanted children with you.' " She was silent for a while. Then she said, "You know, I brought this on myself. It was my choice. Cutting my options forever."

"But you didn't want any more children."

"Not with Gordon. I didn't imagine a Carlo . . ."

Perri said, "And he hasn't made love with you since?"

"He tries. But he can't. He's just not turned on anymore. What he loved was me as Mama—making dinner, talking to the children. He desired me because I was fruitful. Fecund."

"He says that about 'fecund'?"

"His body does." Sara's face was stony.

Perri said, after a pause, "At least you've got Gordon back, it seems. If you want him—the beast."

Sara said, "You know, he was terribly anxious about that audit. He's become human again. We owe far less than he thought."

"You always apologize for him! No matter what he does."

"Well, he hasn't done anything so terrible, has he?"

"What about with Zoe?"

"Has he hurt her? Has he talked about not wanting her in front of the boys? Has he hit me? Has he been unfaithful and thrown it in my face? He's not the very worst of men."

Perri looked away, disgusted. Now that Carlo was impossible for her, Sara was talking herself into staying with Gordon. Or could it be that she loved him?

Sara said, "Roland really wants us to get back together."

"You can't decide things just because of him—"

"—and Rory—"

"You *can't.*"

"I'll tell you what I can't," Sara said. "I can't break up a long marriage with a good man because I'm in love with some student au pair who's stopped wanting me."

"I'm sure he still wants you—" Perri began.

Sara said, "He wants a woman who can give him a family. And he has every right to one." She brought Zoe to her shoulder for burping.

Perri stood up. "I'm just curious," she said. "Did you and Gordon make love last night?"

Sara looked away and nodded.

"More than once?"

Sara nodded again.

"You're blushing—how quaint!"

"I guess I feel guilty."

"Did you feel guilty last night?"

"A little."

"It probably made it more exciting," Perri said.

Sara said, "I've always liked Gordon in bed."

" 'She said evasively.' "

Sara said, "You know, Perri, marriage isn't some steady settled thing. It's not a lake, all shining and smooth. It's more like a mountain stream, with shallows and rapids and waterfalls and pools. It keeps changing."

Perri rolled her eyes upward. "You'll never leave him," she said.

When Perri came into the office, Fenley was busy on the phone, arranging the porno-mag shoot. They were going to do a segment, after all, on the class-action suit against "Different Strokes." They would film a writer reading from her work in front of the publisher's offices. They would try for an interview with an editor. They would interview both the Grievance Committee chairman and the former Union president about the suit against the magazine. It was one way to contrast the two Union factions: with a current issue they viewed differently—for some of the ousted elitists objected to a major Union presence in a porno dispute. She and Fenley had decided that while they wouldn't emphasize the Union schism, they wouldn't ignore it either.

Down the hall, Larry and Claudine were at work trying to liven up a slow part of the film. Nancy was out tracking down archival footage of the early days of the Screenwriters Guild. Perri enjoyed thinking that five people were gainfully employed because ten months ago she had had an idea. She hung up her coat, turned on her computer, and sat down. Today, she was working on narration for the history section of the film.

She had lost the narration fight with Fenley the week before. "We're not making cinema verité," he had said. "Narration is the quickest, most efficient way to impart basic information. And like it or not, this is an informational documentary. Not an art film."

"Narration is so heavyhanded."

"Not if it's done right. You can have a shot writing it. Unless you'd rather work on the Endowment application . . ."

"No! No! No!"

So now she was mired in narration. She wrote four or five lines. Then Fenley came and stood in back of her. She didn't think she would ever get used to writing so publicly, to tapping words from brain to screen to be read by any passerby.

Fenley said, "Shorter sentences. This isn't *The New Yorker*."

Perri said, "This is just the draft. I'm thinking aloud."

"Think snappier," he said and left the room.

She muttered, "Snap, crackle, pop" and cut the sentences in half. She deleted several words. She reread. It was better, punchier. She saved the text she had written. Where was Fenley? Maybe he had gone to some meeting. Perri pulled the telephone toward her and called Park City, Utah. She had just reserved a ticket for the festival and was inquiring about housing when Fenley walked into the room. She said, "I'll call back" and hung up. No one from the office must know in advance of her trip to Park City. At worst, she could ski and see a lot of good films. She needed new ski pants.

157

Fenley came up in back of her and read the new text. He said only, "What footage would we use this narration against?"

Perri hadn't given that part any thought. "I don't know . . . something visually arresting."

Fenley said, "Naked women."

She pretended not to hear. "Maybe a montage of writers' faces. Thoughtful ones, craggy ones . . ."

"Naked women," Fenley repeated, "if you want to make this stuff exciting."

"How can you talk that way? In this day and age? Aren't you embarrassed to be such a sexist?"

"What's a sexist?" he shot back. "Someone who likes a lot of sex? Why should I be embarrassed about that?"

Against her will, Perri spluttered. She said, "That's a very juvenile joke."

"But you laughed," Fenley said. "I got you there."

"You got me there," she agreed.

"I'll get you someday," she thought he said then.

She asked, in disbelief, "What?"

"I've got your number," he said, and that, if true, was just as bad. She guessed that Fenley reveled in sex and that he suspected she did, too. Fenley certainly spoke of it a lot. So what? She could never, never—although sometimes people who didn't attract you were dynamite in bed. This did not mean she had to find out. Fenley said, "Do you want to have dinner tonight?"

"I'm busy," she said.

"Tomorrow?"

"It's not a good idea," she said, "to get involved with people at work."

"Then you're fired."

"I can hardly be fired," Perri replied coolly, "when I'm scarcely getting paid."

"Jesus! Don't I have any power over you? None at all?"

There was a moment, there, when she felt sorry for him—

and that was his power. She could make him happy and she wouldn't—because she didn't like the way he looked. He had the power of those whom we wrong: he made her feel guilty. She said, "Of course you have power over me. I want to earn your respect. I want to do a good job. I want to learn from you. I want you to consider me a thorough professional."

"And that's all."

"That's plenty."

"You're a pretty shrewd cookie."

She said jokingly, "Chauvinist—don't call me 'cookie.' "

"Does that make me some kind of *crumb*, for using a common expression? It's no fair."

"You know what they say—'that's the way the cookie crumbles.' "

"God," Fenley said, "you're as bad as I am."

"Worse," she assured him, standing up. "Much worse." She went down the hall to the editing room, aware, and ashamed, that at times she *did* flirt with Fenley, even though he didn't attract her.

She entered the editing room and saw that her beloved was wearing a jade stud earring that matched his green shirt. Larry hadn't shaved; he had a four-day stubble, the kind that is deliberate. Macho bum meet disco earring. Perri admired the effect. "Hi, Larry," she said shyly. "I have to look at the history section for the narration, take a couple of notes . . ."

"Sure. I'll just be a couple—five minutes more, then I'll wind back the reel and you can view it."

He turned to look at her. She saw that his eyes were the exact shade of brown as the roll of magnetic soundtrack by his elbow.

Larry said, "Do you need to get stoned for this?"

"Very funny." She found herself warmed by Larry's teasing, as she was when he said anything remotely personal to her. "No hurry. I don't mind watching you work."

He was removing a couple of frames from a shot. He

marked the film with a grease pencil, then put it into the splicer and brought down the cutting blade. He handed the trim to Claudine. Perri watched him view and mark and cut. A piece of doggerel was forming in her mind and she tried to work out the last of it so she could rip it off her mental notepad and throw it away. Here she was again, writing Valentines she could never send, elated and alive! She finished the quatrain:

> *His eyes were the color of mag track*
> *His shirt was the green of Kilgarry*
> *She sat in the gloom of the editing room*
> *And tried to write poems to Larry.*

When the phone rang, Perri jumped, but Larry didn't notice. Since Claudine had left for lunch, Perri picked up the phone. It was her friend Ann, calling to revise their evening plans. They would meet at the reading, not at the restaurant. Ann asked, "How's your great crush?"

Perri said, "A little worse than usual today." *He's wearing a new earring.*

"Is he around now?" Ann asked.

"Uh-huh." *I want to creep up on him from behind and put one hand on his mouth and the other on his heart.*

"I hope you're being cool."

I only devour him visually and analyze his every word. Perri said, "Arctic, of course."

"Somehow," Ann said, "I doubt that."

Perri said daringly, looking at the back of Larry's head, "You think he knows?"

Ann said, "Absolutely. You're a terrible actress. You probably blush and stammer a lot when he's around."

Perri held the phone away from her ear and called, "Larry? Do I blush and stammer a lot?"

"Hadn't noticed," Larry said.

"See?" Perri said to Ann.

"I can't believe you," Ann said. "You've gone mad."

"That's nothing." Perri whispered into the phone, "I'll tell you tonight what else I'm going to do."

_20_

TEN DAYS LATER, PERRI WAS
aloft, flying to Salt Lake City, toking up in a tiny steel lavatory.
She preferred being stoned at takeoff, but there was no one
to drive her to the airport and she wanted to get there straight,
in case of hassles. And there was too much security in the
airport to smoke there. So once again she was puffing away in
a bathroom. Airplane bathrooms always had a "No Smoking"
sign—and a prominent ashtray. The acknowledgment that
some would disobey the sign—an ashtray so the bad ones
wouldn't start a fire in the trash receptacle—always encouraged
Perri to disobey the sign too, even though to do so, she had
to disconnect the smoke detector (which was a federal offense,
the flight attendant had announced). Perri figured that under
the circumstances a joint was no worse than a cigarette. She

wondered if constipated nicotine addicts needed a cigarette while moving their bowels. That was the trouble with getting stoned in bathrooms. Your cravings led you shitward. Perri was grateful for the vigorous ventilation system and the equally aggressive air freshener, which mimicked lavender. She combed her hair, and decided she needed more color. She put on blusher and lipstick. The bathroom smelled fine when she left, and the walk back to her seat had that special glow, that aura of significance she loved so dearly. . . .

Perri edged past four male knees to her seat by the window. She sat down and closed her eyes. It was the moment she had been awaiting. Ahead lay hours of enforced passivity. A drink, a meal, a movie. Maybe she'd talk to her neighbor, maybe she'd finish her book. The luxury of filling time instead of chasing it. Getting away was always so hard, and what kept her going through all the arrangements for the trip was the thought of this moment at peace on the plane, with all the details and dilemmas resolved and stoned hours ahead with no work at all. Her only task was her own amusement. Intriguing hypnagogic images danced on her eyelids: blue cartoon characters she had never seen before. They took her with them, and she dozed, missing the drink part of the plan.

A crowded party in an elegant townhouse. Italian furniture, Persian rugs, French porcelain. Attractive waiters glide through the room bearing trays of hot tidbits. We see a Picasso on the wall.

Narrator (Tom Fenley), voice-over: This is a very special publishing party, to celebrate the latest Duke Stevens thriller. Not many authors get parties thrown for them at Asa Pons's New York townhouse. But then not many authors sell as many books as Duke Stevens.

The camera isolates Duke Stevens, a hearty man with a muttonchop mustache. He is laughing drunkenly, surrounded by people. Perri approaches.

Perri: Do you have a moment?

Duke Stevens: Sure.

Perri: Congratulations on your latest.

Duke Stevens: Thank you.

Perri: I hear you got two million dollars.

Duke Stevens: Less agent's fees. And taxes.

Perri: Do you know what the average author gets per book?

Duke Stevens (mocking): Less than I do?

Perri: You could do a lot for other writers, you know.

Duke Stevens: Really? How?

Perri: You could join the National Writers Union. They need celebrity writers like you.

Duke Stevens: How about you? Do you need a celebrity, uh, date?

Perri: Have you had any dealings with Asa Pons?

Duke Stevens (piously): A fine human being.

One of Asa Pons's male assistants walks toward the camera.

Male assistant (to Duke Stevens): Are these filmmakers friends of yours?

Duke Stevens: I'm hoping one of them will be.

Male assistant: Well, they all have to go. Ma'am, tell your crew to pack up and leave. You have no right to be here.

Asa Pons comes upon the scene and spots Perri.

Asa Pons: You again! When are you going to learn that no means no? I simply won't waste my saliva on the so-called National so-called Writers so-called Union. End stop. Finito. Enough.

[From *Against Goliath: The National Writers Union.* Produced by Tom Fenley and Perri Jennings. A Fenley Films Production.]

In Salt Lake City, Perri rented a car and drove north for an hour to Park City, a ski town in the mountains. Perri arrived too late for the last movie of the evening, so she picked up her key and went right to her room. Festival visitors were being housed in various places around town, and she was in a spacious condo right at the ski center. In her room, up three broad steps, a hot tub was steaming. She didn't know where Larry was staying and hadn't been able to find out. But she would see him the next evening, at his screening, if she didn't lose her nerve.

For it suddenly seemed crazy, what she had done. Larry had avoided her for months in New York—so she had followed him to Utah in the hope of getting him at last. Anyway, she would spend the next day skiing. Build up her confidence on the mountain, then try the more slippery slopes of romance. Block that metaphor! She thought: and I'm not even stoned. She went into her handbag and soon changed that. Then she sat in the hot tub while the water bubbled around her. If nothing else, she told herself, you're a woman of action. You want this man, and you came here to get him—or to know you never will. She reached for the festival program and flipped through the pages. A woman she knew, a director in her forties, was here with her first feature, *Family and Friends*. Elyse Melman was more Ann's friend than hers, but Perri had called her in New York and established a festival rationale.

Perri spent the next day on perfect snow, in perfect weather. It didn't take her long to remember skiing from the year before. She sang aloud as she glided and swooped. She went through a slalom course, leaning back on her heels to make grand slalom turns. Then she did a run for speed: went down a whole trail without stopping.

At lunchtime, she had a charbroiled hamburger at mid-station, at a table in the sun. The temperature was forty-five degrees. She applied more sunscreen. One of her friends had skin cancer from too many hours in the sun. How sad to have to trade beauty for health! Perri loved the look of a caramel tan, on herself and on other women, and men. She wondered if Larry got dark in the sun. It was her first thought about Larry for hours. Sports were great the way they forced you to live in the here-and-now: this turn, this ski, this knee. Perri tightened her boots and clipped on her skis and set off again. There were so many ways to get up and down this particular mountain. What a good hill. When she got to the bottom, she decided to take a cable car to the summit. She was the only one around, so she had the car to herself. It was a car for four, with padded benches and a bubble top and a fifty-mile view. Now, this would be nice with Larry. Cable-car necking. Cool hands, hot mouths, crude talk. "Did you always want to fuck me?" "From the very first minute I saw you."

Perri reached into her jacket pocket for her lipstick and came across an old matchbox instead. She opened the little box absently and saw with surprise half a joint. She didn't know when it was from, and it probably wouldn't even give her a buzz. Perri made it a policy not to ski stoned, as marijuana made her colder and compromised her confidence and coordination. Now, though, she found herself taking the joint out of the box and bringing it to her lips. I mean, it's right here, she thought, surely God wants you to have it, letting you find it like this in an empty cable car! She lit the ancient joint, sucked the smoke deep into her lungs. After all, you're skiing fine, and it's a lovely warm day . . . Meanwhile, she was getting high right away, which made her inhale all the more eagerly, especially when she suddenly remembered which grass this might be, the stuff Tony had dubbed "two-toke Hawaiian." Uh-oh! If it was *that* grass, she was already many tokes over the line . . .

She stared down into the wide valley below her, all white and black and evergreen. The land seemed to pulse up at her as she sat in her bubble and glided over it. To her left, now, she saw a very steep, slick-looking trail. She certainly wasn't going to choose that run. To her right was something kinder. She took out the ski map and frowned at it. Was the easier run "Mathilda's Matinee"? The cable car arrived at the station and bumped to a stop. Perri got out of the car and took her skis off the outside rack. Then the car, untenanted, moved on. Perri clomped out of the dingy cable-car station. Outside, on the flat part of a slope, dozens of skiers were adjusting their boots and getting into their bindings. Perri did the same. She put on her hat. It was definitely colder than at lunchtime, and some of the runs were already in shadow. Perri was decidedly chilly. She followed the sign for "Mathilda's Matinee."

The run began with a narrow trail through the evergreens. It wasn't steep, but she had to keep turning. Perri felt okay except for the fatigue. She paused to catch her breath. Still, she had broken the taboo against stoned skiing, hadn't she? And wasn't it lovely here in the woods? She skied around a curve, and suddenly she didn't see the trail anymore, it seemed to drop away. She skied to the edge and looked down. Way below her was the mid-station lodge, sugar-cube size. Between her and it was a seeming precipice. It seemed "Mathilde's Matinee" was not the easier slope, after all, but the steep one she had seen from the cable car. It looked even more treacherous up close.

Perri stood there, looking down. Other skiers dithered near her, gathering courage for the plunge. Most people skied the slope lurching and jerking; many fell. But sometimes a skier would zip down with style and seeming nonchalance. Perri was agog. Skiing was a humbling sport. There were bound to be dozens of better skiers than her on any mountain; she could tell at a glance who they were. And these really good ones came in all sizes and ages and styles. Some wore fluorescent body suits. Some wore shabby parkas and jeans. This year, some very macho men were skiing in funny hats with animal ears or horns. Perri didn't see how those hats could be aerodynamic.

She had now been waiting on the edge of the steep hill for fifteen minutes and she was shivering and also rather frightened. She didn't see how she was ever going to ski that slope in front of her. She told herself she had skied on slopes that hard before, but she didn't really believe it. Not today, she hadn't, and not stoned. What a terrible idea *that* had been. On this beautiful day on this beautiful snow, Perri was exhausted and anxious and cold. Five more skiers, she told herself, then I'm going to try the hill whatever happens. It took a full five minutes for three skiers (two lurchers and an expert) to go past her. The fourth skier, a woman in aqua overalls, looked very good as she skied toward Perri. When she got to the rim where Perri was waiting, she didn't even pause, just went fluidly down, oh, it was pretty to see, edging without effort, and then—bam! She was down and over, over and over, and even as she was rolling, Perri was thinking, *If such a good skier wipes out—what about me?*

The woman stopped rolling and lay on her back in the snow, one ski tip caught in the ground. She shouted, "Help!"

Perri looked around. She was all by herself on the ledge.

The woman cried again, "Help!"

Then Perri was over the rim and skiing down to help the woman in the aqua pants. Perri miscalculated her last turn and had to sidestep down the final few feet to get to the woman, who was moaning, "The ski, the ski. Take off my ski." Perri awkwardly maneuvered herself closer. Then she tried to release the boot from the ski. She had never used a binding quite like it.

The woman begged, "Please, take it off. Off."

Perri said, "How? What do I press?"

"The little white circle." The woman began moaning again.

But the little white circle was designed to be pressed from above, not from the side, and with the extreme pitch of the slope and her skis in the way, Perri couldn't get a good angle on it. She quickly bent down and began taking off her own skis. The woman yelled, "No—*my* ski! Take off my ski."

"In a second. There." Her own skis were off, and Perri got close to the woman's ski. "Now I can get to it." And she pressed, and pressed again, and there was a click and the binding released. Perri lifted the boot out of the binding and laid the woman's leg gently on the ground.

"Thank you. Oh. That was terrible."

"Where do you hurt?"

"In my knee. I must have twisted something. Damn! Such a stupid fall"

"No, it's a very hard hill."

"I've skied it before. It's not so bad." She began to struggle to her feet.

Perri helped her up. The woman stood there shakily. Perri looked up at the hill they had come down. It was the steepest third. The incline below her was manageable. Perri said, "What do you think? Are you able to ski?"

"I think so." But when she tried to get the injured leg into the binding, she winced. "No, I can't, I have to sit down."

A young boy, maybe thirteen, was staring at them from the rim, and Perri yelled, "Help!" With a great deal of flailing and upper-body motion, he skied down to the women. Perri said, "Could you get the ski patrol over here? We have an injury."

"Sure," he said, "right away." And he left with his mission, making time.

"It won't be long now," said the woman. "You don't have to stay with me."

"Don't be ridiculous."

"Well, thank you. I'm taking up all your time."

"Not at all. If you hadn't fallen, I'd probably still be on that rim, gathering courage."

"It's not such a hard hill," said the woman. "We're over the worst part. Did you ski it okay?"

Perri said, "I don't remember. I wanted to get to you fast." She was really shivering now, and still rather high, and starting to feel guilty. Would she have helped the woman more quickly if she had been straight? Taken that painful ski off any sooner?

When the ski patrol arrived with radios and a toboggan, the woman thanked Perri again and again, and Perri didn't feel so bad about her habit or herself after all.

Two hours later, Perri arrived at the Egypt Theater for the

Robeson screening, dressed inconspicuously in black pants and a black silk blouse. She didn't want Larry to see her before she saw him and where he was sitting and whether or not he was here with a woman, so Perri had slicked down her hair under a turban and worn a pair of heart-shaped lavender-tinted sunglasses. It was such a good disguise she had scarcely recognized herself in the ladies room mirror.

Larry wasn't in the theater yet as far as she could see. The place was two-thirds full: not bad for a documentary program. The other film was a portrait of Judy Collins. The lights dimmed halfway, and the audience became quiet. Then a woman from the festival committee introduced Lawrence Mercator to the audience.

Larry walked out from the wings, his earring gleaming. He said, "This film is dedicated to Paul Robeson—to his memory, to his art, and to his politics. Thanks for being here tonight. I'll be here to answer questions at the end of the program." He left the stage by the stairs, walked back several rows, and sat down near—Perri craned her neck. Larry sat down between two men, one of whom seemed to be his friend. No, both of them. Great! Fantastic! She removed the heart-shaped glasses. She watched the film. (Larry ducked out after the first few minutes and ducked back in before the second film.)

As the lights came on after the program, Perri put on her sunglasses again. Most of the audience stayed to listen to Larry and the other filmmaker take questions from the floor. The questions all concerned funding and distribution: practicalities rather than aesthetics. Larry seemed at ease and happy on the podium, and he responded generously to the questions. The other filmmaker was a curly-haired woman named Tina Tremont who strode around on skinny legs as she gave her answers.

The couple in front of Perri stood up and left, and she sank a little lower in her seat to avoid Larry's attention in the semidark auditorium. "One more question," the moderator announced. Perri put on her new ski jacket, and waited in the shadows by the door. She wasn't sure what she was going to do, but she felt unable to approach Larry yet.

Ten minutes later, Larry and his friends came out of the theater, one last questioner trailing along with them. Perri followed the group up the block, past her rented car, and along the next block. They reached the Mermaid restaurant. Then they must have said good-bye to the questioner, for, dismissed, he waved awkwardly and came back down the street in Perri's direction. Perri loitered in the street for a couple of minutes, then peered into the cafe window. The Mermaid had a little bar up front and a dozen tables toward the rear.

When Perri walked into the restaurant, she saw that Larry and his friends were sitting three tables in. Larry had his back to her. One of his friends, a blond man of about thirty, was facing her, looking at her. She took off her ski jacket and hung it on a hook. She opened the top two buttons of her blouse. She glanced back at the table again. The blond man was still looking at her. She gave him a small, shy smile and turned away on her barstool. This was going to be a cinch. She couldn't believe her good luck. She ordered a glass of wine, revolved half a turn on her barstool, then got up and went to the back to make a phone call to no one. She averted her face from the group at Larry's table, but she knew she was being looked at—and hard.

When she climbed back onto her barstool, a glass of wine was waiting. "Compliments of that gentleman over there," said the bartender.

Perri looked toward Larry's table. Her blond admirer held up his glass and smiled at her. She held up her glass and smiled back. He said, and mimed in case she didn't hear, "Come here."

She shook her head.

"Come on."

Perri got off her barstool and crossed the room. The blond man took the coats off the empty chair at his table, and Perri sat down and turned away from him. She said to the man at her right, "Hello, Larry."

Larry gave a spasm of surprise. "*Perri?* What are you . . . ?"

"You *said* it was a good festival . . ." she teased.

"That's *it?*"

"Well, there's a little more," Perri said, feigning reluctance. "A friend of mine made a movie that's being shown here, *Family and Friends*. I'm helping with publicity."

"But you never told me," said Larry. He finished his drink and signaled for another.

Perri said, "It was all very last minute."

The blond friend, miffed, asked, "How do you two know each other?"

"We're working together," Perri said.

The third man said to Larry, "You mean this is the broad you were griping about?" He winked at Perri, who didn't know how many cons the wink covered.

Had Larry really been complaining about her? More than likely. She certainly complained enough about him . . . But tonight they were away from all that, and she was a little drunk, and for once she felt she had the right line. She said, lightly, laughing, "Larry will do *any*thing to hide his secret passion for me."

Larry put down his drink and said, with a very small smile, "I guess I even hide it from myself."

"As best you can," Perri said huskily, dramatically. "But you can't hold back passion forever. It just doesn't work." Ostentatiously, she placed her hand on Larry's leg and gave a squeeze.

"Oooh, ooh," said the blond man, shaking his head in envy. The third man gave a whistle.

Larry looked down at her hand on his leg. Then he put his

172

hand on top of hers and pressed down. He said, "Whatever you say, boss."

They sat like that until dinner came. Perri was silent. She felt her heart bruising her chest. The waiter laid down their plates, and then she had to fake eating. She had to fake heavy flirting for the "dragon lady" show she was putting on for Larry's friends. Later, with Larry's hand on her leg, she had to fake watching a movie. And after the movie was over, she had to fake nonchalance when Larry asked if her place had a hot tub.

21

THEY DIDN'T MAKE IT TO THE hot tub or even to the bed. As soon as she closed the door of the condo behind them, he reached for her, she grabbed him. Their mouths met hungrily, pushing, mashing. They fell onto the pale blue wall-to-wall carpeting. They pressed against each other, tumbling and rolling. Shameless beasts, unable to wait another few seconds, Perri told herself. But then she thought guiltily, It's *Larry*—why must you fantasize *now*? Or *is* it a fantasy, when I tell myself what's sort of going on?

Meanwhile, Larry was below her, stretched out on the carpet, and she brought both his hands above his head and held them there against the rug. She leaned over his face so her breasts, beneath her blouse, brushed against his face. He sighed and moved his mouth back and forth against the silk.

Then they turned over and did it in reverse: he held her hands as if they were bound. His free hand went beneath her jacket to undo her blouse. Then he was browsing beneath, learning her feel and response here and there. They were kissing all the while, and she was finding out what he was like and showing him what she could do. Discovery and exhibition: making love with someone new. The special thrill of sex with someone new you know well: how sex extends the other knowledge, reveals the person from another angle . . .

She would never have guessed that Larry would be more aroused by rubbing and tickling her under the arms than by petting her breasts—nor would she have imagined her own intense excitement when he pressed his thumbs into her armpits. Almost for spite, to get even, Perri began mouthing his ear, the one with the earring, and now he began breathing fast. When she put in her tongue, he made a whimpering sound and tried to pull away. She held his head tightly against her mouth and sucked on his earlobe. She could feel the gold stud in her mouth, against her tongue, and she heard herself sigh. Larry brought his body hard against hers and began rubbing himself rhythmically against her very middle. It was getting sweeter and sweeter, like high school but better, no battle, just this warm ache, this yearning arc, this . . .

Perri opened her eyes and tried to multiply thirteen by thirteen. But it was too late, her body was surging and soaring, she tried to stay relatively still. Perhaps he wouldn't know. He gave her a few seconds. Then he said, in the cranky voice she knew so well, "Didja have a good time?" And she almost came again.

"Well?" he demanded.

Perri felt one final quang between her legs. She said, cautiously, "Fair."

"Good," he said, "'cause I'm just getting started."

They still hadn't removed any of their clothes, although Perri's jacket and blouse were open. She got up and walked across the room. She took off her jacket. Then she sat down on the edge of the bed and pulled off her boots. Larry joined her, boots off, shirt open, belt unbuckled. His pants were unsnapped and unzipped. She began opening the top to her own pants. He said, "Never mind" and pushed her down on the bed. He kneeled over her and thrust his hips forward. He said, "Take it out."

She wanted to tease him for a while, to assess and caress him with her hands. But without even pulling his pants all the way down, he rudely stuffed himself into her mouth. She did his bidding. Soon he moaned on the brink, and she pulled her lips away. He jammed himself once or twice into her neck, against her chin, and spurted onto her hair and her blouse.

She let him lie against her for a while. But when she felt her shoulder getting numb under his weight, she eased out from under him. He had fallen into a doze, although she herself was very much awake. She watched him sleeping. She had never seen his face in repose before, and she saw a new gentleness there. Asleep, he looked something like a child. She pulled a blanket over him and turned off the overhead light.

She crossed the room and sat in the kitchen area. It was one-thirty-five. She should be sleepy, after a day on the slopes and an evening of tension and fulfillment. But Perri was restless. She thought, You haven't smoked dope in over twelve hours—no wonder you can't get to sleep. She glanced at Larry, asleep across the room although they hadn't even fucked yet. It didn't look like it was going to happen for a while.

When she went to bed with someone for the first time, Perri liked to be drunk and not stoned—hot and crude and not at all mental. But since intercourse didn't seem imminent, she made herself a mid-size joint of her ordinary, workaday grass. Workaday/playanight grass, Perri thought. An herbal nightcap for my nerves. Otherwise, I might be up for hours.

She opened the sliding glass door and stepped out onto a small balcony. She lit her joint and leaned on the rail. A fingernail moon shone lemon over the mountains. Long gray clouds lay furry near the mountain peaks. She began to feel calmer. After all, the gamble had paid off. She had him in her bed. She was spending the night with Larry Mercator—although getting stoned while he slept had not been part of her plans. She tossed the roach over the railing. Perri Ganja-seed.

She went inside and took off her clothes. How would she explain her blouse to the dry cleaners? Would she need to? Was there a different solvent for milk, say, than for sperm? Was it worth the embarrassment to save a favorite blouse? She took off her underpants with regret, for Larry hadn't even seen them. They were a new pair, pink, with tiny satin ribbons, but they were too slimy to put on again. Sex was so messy. Had she been God, she would have divined—designed— *devised* something more aesthetic. And maybe more ecstatic. Like a ten-minute orgasm. How would that have changed world history? At all?

Perri rolled back the hot-tub cover. Chlorine-scented steam billowed into the room. She stepped into the very hot water and sat down on the underwater seat. She didn't turn on the water jets or bubbler, out of deference to Larry. She looked across the room at him and thought: my sleeping lover. Or aren't we lovers till we fuck? Why is intercourse always considered the supreme act between a man and a woman? Because it is best? Because it is trickiest? Because it has, potentially, the most consequential results: new life, perhaps, new death?

She closed her eyes and extended her limbs in the water. She was half afloat, half asleep, when the bath became fizzy like soda—the bubbler was on, and Larry stepped into the hot tub.

"Aiieee," he said, lowering himself into the water. He sat down opposite her and stretched out his legs. His toe nudged her breast. He said, "How are ya?"

"I'm pretty good."

"You're pretty stoned," he said. "Your eyes are all red."

"You found me out."

He asked, "Got any more?"

"Of course. I'll get it." She stepped out of the tub, tucked a towel around her torso, and went to roll a joint.

He said, "I don't usually use grass."

She said, "I do."

"How often?" he asked.

"Couple times a day." This was true if you defined "couple" liberally.

He said, "I've smelled it on your breath."

She said, "I use mints most of the time."

"I know that too." He turned off the bubbler, then turned on the jets. She returned to the hot tub with a lit joint, which she passed to Larry. He inhaled and passed it to her.

To be companionable, she joined him. Soon, he said, "I can feel it already. How can you *work* high like this?"

She said, "A) Since I smoke quite a lot I don't feel it that much, and B), I don't often use it for work—only for certain things. Not for being persuasive on the phone. But for creativity, for answers to an impasse, for ideas . . . You have to admit, it's good for ideas."

"I admit nothing," he said, putting the dead joint into the ashtray. "But it's sometimes a good pleasure drug." Then he came toward her. They rubbed against each other in the water. Their arms and legs and mouths were busy. And again there was this competitive edge, this "I'll show you" aspect to their play. She murmured, while rhythmically mouthing his neck, "Take this and this and this."

He said, "Take this," and tried to get inside her.

She pushed him off and said, "Wait."

"Wait? After you hijacked me into your hot tub?"

"You didn't put up much resistance. Anyway, I didn't say 'no,' I said, 'Wait.' Go put on a condom."

He said, "I don't have any."

She said, "I do." Once again Perri left the hot tub, hoping

he would follow her. Hot tubs were good for foreplay, she thought, but she didn't like to fuck in the water. Oddly, she felt drier then, less sexy. And she was already very dry from the grass. But Larry remained in the water, so after she brought him the package, she felt she had little choice but to join him in the bath again.

"You travel with condoms," he observed.

"On occasion."

"Pretty sure you'd get me?"

"Well." She thought of Sven in Stockholm and said mildly, "It just makes sense to have them around."

"If you sleep around."

"Well, I don't—not anymore. But what's the big deal? Women buy sixty percent of all rubbers sold."

"You sound like a condom ad."

"Well, it's common knowledge. Condom knowledge." She giggled. He didn't.

He said, "You're so superior."

She said, "I'll take that as a compliment."

"You would." He was very erect as he put on the rubber. She could hardly refuse him then, although somehow she wasn't aroused. He had trouble getting into her: the water had washed off her lubrication. And her mind was all aprickle, not the way she liked to be (mindless, burning) during sex. He pulled her down upon his lap again. She moved her leg up—and suddenly he was all the way in. She'd been more aroused when he'd touched her arm in the editing room. But thinking of her yearning then, of her emotional abjection, Perri began to get interested. Slowly she moved up and down. He might ask her again if she'd had a good time. She shimmied her hips against him. He pulled her buttocks hard. "Ohhhhh," he groaned.

After a bit, he slipped out of her.

She teased, "Didja have a good time?"

He said, "What about you?"

"Sure. But I can never come in water."

"We're getting all waterlogged anyway." He stood up, a dripping pillar.

She said, "You're so skinny."

"You, too. Except for these." He dried her with a towel. "This is nicely rounded, too," he said, his hand on her behind.

When they were both dry, they lay back on the bed. His index finger moved slowly on her in a single stroke, from the tip of her nose down her lips across her chin and neck then between her breasts across her belly, down, inexorably down. His hand stayed there and established a rhythm.

So he was a gentleman, he wouldn't leave her all alone aroused . . . though considering an earlier round, *perfect* etiquette, perhaps, decreed cunnilingus. Imagining his mouth, she came abruptly on his palm. He pressed back against her. Then he patted her thigh and sat up. He swung his legs over the side of the bed and went to the bathroom.

Perri put on her nightgown and pulled down the bedspread. She got into bed. Waiting for Larry to join her, she fell into a doze, but when she felt him getting into bed, she awoke. She lay still to see what he would do. He lay down on his side of the bed, facing away from her, without touching her at all. He fell asleep almost at once. Perri, piqued, was awake for another half hour. With even the most casual encounter, she liked to lie entwined through the night. But these days there were very few casual encounters.

At least she knew Larry well. She moved over to him, snuggled against his back, put her arm around his shoulder. He shook her off him and moved to the very edge of the bed. He liked to sleep alone, untouched, inviolate. She was disappointed but not surprised.

They fucked again in the morning, and that time, by imagining three men watching, Perri came okay with Larry hard in her. After his own silent orgasm, which followed hers by a minute or two, Larry got out of bed and began putting on his clothes.

Perri said, "It's only seven-thirty."

"The ski lift starts at nine. And I've got to get back to my place and get on my ski clothes and have breakfast and rent skis . . ."

"Well, if you don't want to miss any skiing . . ."

"I don't," Larry said. "The ticket's too expensive."

"Want to meet over there?" Perri asked.

"This morning I'm going to take a lesson."

"And lunch?" Was this being pushy? But she felt so sad at his leaving—even though it hadn't been, *especially* because it hadn't been, a night of the most perfect bliss. And now he didn't want to have lunch with her. Perri turned away from him and lifted up her chin. It did no good to feel sad about these things, none at all. But how else could she feel when the seconds ticked away and Larry said nothing?

Then Larry said, "We could meet at that mid-station bar-becue place around one."

"Yeah? Great. Okay!" She grinned at him from the bed. He came over and they hugged good-bye. And she hugged that hug to her after Larry left, striding out into the morning.

Perri stayed in bed and put her head under the sheet to inhale deeply. She thought of what she and Larry had done together in the last eight hours: the flavor and dynamic of each sexual act. The first thing had been really great—when they were just rolling on the floor in all their clothes and she simply couldn't stop herself. Surely, surely that had been best, Larry in her arms at last—and against her very center. Think-ing of it, she was getting hot again. Sex was like dope: when you had it good you wanted more and more—if, that is, you were really obsessive. Perri lingered on in bed another hour.

22

"I'M CURIOUS," PERRI SAID. "Why did you walk out of *Robeson* last night?" Perri and Larry were having hamburgers at the ski slope.

Larry said, "After the mix, when I can no longer change things, it's just torture to see a film I've cut. I see all the mistakes. All the awkward things I should have fixed."

"No one else sees those things," Perri said.

"Perhaps not."

"The audience liked the film fine. So did I." This was an exaggeration, for she had found the film predictably doctrinaire. "You did a good job."

Larry said, "I had a great subject. I still remember hearing him sing in a church when I was only three years old."

"Already a radical?"

" 'Red diaper' baby," said Larry. "Every year, my mom and dad would wheel my carriage in the May Day parade. They stopped in 'fifty-six, when they left the Party entirely."

"Understandably enough."

"Not to me."

"Well, after Khruschev's Stalin revelations . . ."

"Stalin made some mistakes," Larry said. "It doesn't invalidate scientific materialism."

" 'Made some mistakes'?" Perri was incredulous. "Stalin caused millions to starve and executed millions more!"

"Let's get going," Larry said. He picked up the bill and scowled at it. "You owe me six-seventy."

Perri counted out the money. Larry paid with a credit card, which meant he could deduct her meal too. She reached for his nose with a napkin. He pulled back at her touch. "You have a little ketchup there," she explained. He wiped it off with his own napkin.

Outside, Perri soon saw that Larry was a lousy skier. He was heaving around on his turns, moving his hips and shoulders too much. When they paused by the side of the trail, Perri said, "Try facing right down the hill and keeping your upper body very still."

"I took my lesson this morning," Larry said coldly. "We don't all have the time and the money to ski for weeks each year."

"Huh? I don't ski for weeks each year, if that's what you mean."

"You just act so superior."

"Hey, I just thought you might want a pointer. I didn't think you'd blow up."

"I'm not blowing up," he said between his teeth.

He fell twice. The second time, he dropped his poles. She picked them up and skied down to him. As she handed him the poles, Larry said, "You must really be enjoying this."

"It sure is great snow."

"My falling," he said.

She pretended not to understand him and said laughingly, "Don't talk about falling in love—I'll think it's a *snow* job."

As she skied on ahead, she heard him shouting out to her, "No, no, I meant . . ."

Humorless wimp! Perri thought. Then she was shocked. How could she think that about Larry, whom she'd been adoring for months?

Perri arrived early for the *Family and Friends* screening and helped Elyse and her husband hand out press releases. She asked Elyse, "Is it hard for you to see one of your films once it's finished?"

"Not at all. I love to see it with an audience. Every time, it seems different." Perri sat next to the Melmans for the screening.

Afterward, Elyse said, "It was wonderful watching you. Laughing and crying."

"I couldn't help it," Perri said. "I was so moved. It was so passionate. And tender."

"I wish you could review it."

"Well, reviewing your plans for the party," Perri said, "I was wondering about the music."

"Music?" said Elyse. "I haven't even thought about the music."

"You have to have music," Perri said, "or it will seem dead."

"Know any Utah bands who'll play free tonight?"

"I have a couple of tapes for my Walkman. I can buy a couple more. All we need is a system."

Elyse looked at her.

Perri said, "I'll find something. Don't worry. Go get some dinner."

Two hours later, John Cougar Mellancamp was blaring from a borrowed deck and speakers, and Perri had just finished writing with magic marker on a hundred helium balloons. Some said "Family," some said "Friends," and a few said "and." People started arriving. Perri went outside to smoke a joint—her first of the day, she noted with surprise. It was another crystalline night. The moon was even smaller now, a single yellow eyelash. She went back inside. There was quite a crowd by the drinks table. Elyse, looking flushed and happy with a dozen people around her, was telling a young man with a ponytail her original inspiration for the film. "As it happens," she said, "we had to cut out that image in the final version. It just didn't work. But it started everything."

"It was the grain of sand that started the pearl," he said admiringly.

Perri asked Elyse, softly, "What do you think? Should we start people dancing?" Elyse nodded.

Perri left to put on a Huey Lewis tape. She returned to Elyse's group and said, "Let's begin." Since she needed a partner, she took the ponytailed man by the hand. Elyse danced with her husband, and a third couple joined them.

One couple dancing is two people putting on a show. Two couples dancing aren't that different. But once there are three or more couples dancing—depending on the size of the room—some critical mass is reached, and it all changes, dancing becomes the focus of the evening, the activity that offers itself irresistibly to graceful and clumsy, to gazelle and camel alike. When Larry walked in half an hour later, he walked into a dance party, and Perri had discovered that her parter, an actor from Los Angeles, was really fun to dance with. She spotted Larry watching her and danced the better for it.

When the song ended, she went to Larry's side. "Hello, Larry."

He said, "Your eyes are red."

"I'll put in some eyedrops."

"Smoking dope again?"

"My first joint of the day." Larry hadn't seen *Family and*

Friends because he had already bought a ticket for the new caper movie starring Michael Michaels, which was playing at the same time. Perri didn't see the point in seeing a big studio movie at a festival, but she asked, "How was *Cahoots*?"

"Terrific sound effects," Larry said.

Of all things to notice! Perri grinned and said, "Want to meet Elyse Melman?"

"Sure."

Perri introduced the two. Larry said to Elyse, "What's your next project?"

"I'm not really sure. Lots of maybes. Meantime, I'll go on teaching."

Perri knew that Elyse had been teaching film in the same place so long she had tenure.

Larry said, "Where do you teach?"

Elyse named a community college in New York and wrinkled her nose slightly.

Larry said, "I know what you mean. I taught there once and I don't even put it on my resumé."

Elyse's face froze and she turned away. Perri said to Larry angrily, "Maybe you should. Your resumé's not all that fabulous."

Larry said, "Yeah, maybe it would help me get better jobs than the low-budget documentaries I always seem to get stuck with."

"Low-budget, high-minded," Perri said. "I'm proud of our film."

"You would be," he said.

Perri said to Elyse, "As you can imagine, he's utter bliss to work with."

"I can see that," Elyse said.

A red-haired woman in a black dress kissed Elyse and began congratulating her.

Perri and Larry walked away. Perri said, "How could you insult her like that?"

"I didn't mean to. Why did you sabotage me? Saying I was hard to work with?"

"I was just smoothing over a touchy situation." They stared at each other, unsmiling.

The young man with the ponytail signaled a dance invitation to Perri. She mimed "later." Larry asked, "Who are you signaling to?"

"No one important. Want to dance? Want a drink?"

"I want to get out of here."

"Oh."

"Coming? Little hot tub et cetera?"

It was the most intimate thing he had said to her all day. It reminded her that they were lovers and that she had been crazy for him.

She said, "Let me say good-bye to Elyse."

They went to his place this time, and the hot tub was on the terrace. They had sex and slept apart, had sex and slept apart. In the morning, they sat across the table from each other and ate Cheerios and milk. Perri was leaving Park City that afternoon; Larry was staying another two days. He suddenly said, "Howzit going to be in New York? You and me?"

Perri stared at him in surprise. To her it was perfectly obvious. "Well, Larry. Surely, um, surely . . ."

"What? Surely *what*?"

"You must know this was only for Utah."

"Whatever you say, boss." He sounded bitter.

"Come on, Larry. We're not right together. We make each other angry. We don't laugh enough."

He didn't say anything.

After a pause, Perri said, "In fact, I'd like to pretend it never happened. I don't want anyone at work to know. Especially Fenley."

"Okay. And I don't want Maude to find out."

"She won't."

Larry said, "I hope you and I will get on better now. In the editing room."

"I'm sure we will. God, I was obsessed."

"And now?" He reached for her face across the table and ran both hands up along her jawbone, pressing her cheeks with his thumbs, stroking her neck with his fingers. "How is it now, pretty Perri? Now that you've satisfied your little yen?"

"It wasn't so little—that's what I'm trying to tell you."

"It was pretty damn small if two days together was enough."

"Stop it, Larry." He didn't say anything then, and Perri stumbled on. "I feel awful about all of this. Chasing you here. Hunting you down. And now saying stop. But, Larry, I'm not right for your real life. Just think about who I am! A decadent dope-addict dilettante sex-fiend."

He didn't smile with her then or make a joke or tell her she was more than all of that. He said, true to form, "Put it that way, you're right." After a pause, he mumbled, "Maybe that's why the fucking was so good."

"Maybe," she said to be kind.

In the taxi going home to Morton Street, Perri thought about Sara and wondered how she was doing. She was probably all cozy again with her brute of a husband. Perri herself preferred Carlo and hoped he had found a place to live. She had been surprised, when she left, to learn he was still staying at Lucy's, although Lucy had been back from her trip for a week. Perri had told Lucy that Carlo could use her place while she was in Utah—"As long as he's gone when I'm back." Perri didn't like houseguests. For one thing, she didn't want anybody to see how much dope she smoked.

"Right here," she told the cab driver. "By the lamppost." It was after midnight. She counted out some bills.

Upstairs in her apartment, everything was just as she had left it. There was no sign of Carlo. The place smelled musty, so Perri opened a couple of windows. She got into her nightgown. Now she would smoke her midnight joint and think about Larry. No! Not Larry, not anymore. She felt empty in the middle. Her obsession had been cotton candy spun around a hollow paper cone. How stupid, how idiotic she'd been. Depression rolled in on her like a giant gray wave. Pathetic fool, she told herself as she made a joint. This will probably make you feel even worse. Then she got into bed with the joint, an ashtray, and a book of matches from Nell's. She lit up and inhaled. She turned off her bedroom lamp and watched the tip of the joint glow orange in the dark.

PART III

∽᠍᠍᠍᠍᠍᠍᠍᠍᠍᠍᠍᠍᠍᠍ LUCY ᠍᠍᠍᠍᠍᠍᠍᠍᠍᠍᠍᠍᠍᠍

| January 1987 | January 1988 | June 1988 |
| * | * | * |

SARA * · * · · · · · · · · · · ·
conceiving Zoe · · · · · · · · · · · · · · · · · loving Carlo

PERRI * · * · · · · · ·
meeting Fenley · · · · · · · · · · · · returning from Utah

LUCY * · *
Paul dies · · · · · · · · · · · · · · · · · reconciliation

23

Afterward, Paul would say "Lucy" and sink into sleep.

This time, it wasn't very different. Perhaps he called me louder, held me harder: we'd been apart for weeks over summer vacation and this was a reunion. We fell asleep. I loved those light naps with him, his body patterning my dreams. We were still somewhat conjoined when I awoke an hour later. His eyes, near mine, were open, and his body, in my arms, was cool.

"Paul?" I said, and then I screamed because I knew. I pulled away and got out of bed to turn on the light, although it was sunny and bright in my cheerful bedroom, and absolutely evident that he was dead.

I was sobbing and shuddering as I called Perri, who I knew

was working at home. I said, "Perri, come up here alone right away."

I went back to Paul, who, in death, looked only a little dismayed. I closed his eyelids and smoothed down his hair. The doorbell rang.

I opened the door to my sister. "What *is* it?" she asked, and I led the way to the bedroom. She looked at Paul and said, "Oh." She rushed to his side and felt for a heartbeat. "He's cold. When did it happen?"

"I was sleeping—maybe an hour—I don't know. Perri— what should we do?"

"Get dressed," said Perri. "Then we'll have to dress him and get him to the living room. There'll be police, perhaps an autopsy. You should wash him."

"Wash him?"

"His penis."

I went back to Paul. I put my head to his chest one last time. Then I got a washcloth from the bathroom and did what Perri had asked. I thought: I had him dead inside me. I ran to the bathroom, kneeled at the toilet, and vomited a purple acrid mush of crackers, wine, and cheese. When I stood up, my hands were shaking and my throat was sore. I put the washcloth in the hamper. I got dressed.

In the bedroom, Perri had got Paul into his shirt and underpants. I helped her with his pants and socks and shoes. It wasn't so different from dressing a very large doll. Perri and I hauled him to the living room and lowered him into the armchair. "You were having a meeting," said Perri. "Aren't you both in that torture group?"

"Antitorture. Yes." We had first met at the Amnesty reading, although he taught at Columbia, too, in the Chemistry Department.

"You were having a meeting, and I was here with you," Perri said. "Where's the coffee?"

I brought out three coffee mugs and a thermal carafe of coffee I'd made before. I poured Paul's cup only halfway.

"Get out your clipboard," Perri said, "and jot down some notes."

I found my clipboard and hastily wrote: Campaign to free Jonas Dykstra: letters, event, concert? reading?

"Brush your hair, put on lipstick," said Perri.

"I never wear lipstick," I said, "you know that."

But Perri was dialing the police. When she finished talking, she put down the receiver and turned to me. "Lucy, they're going to ask how come we didn't see it happen. Where were we?"

"We were talking to someone long distance who wanted to speak to both of us, so you took the phone in the kitchen and I took it in the bedroom and—"

"No—that's the kind of thing they can trace. How about, we thought we heard someone in my apartment, and went down to check—"

"Without Paul? It doesn't make sense."

"Then where were we?" she asked again.

"We were in the kitchen making coffee," I said slowly. "And when we got back to the living room we thought that he'd fallen asleep . . ."

"So we thought we'd let him sleep," Perri said. "And we went down to my place. I showed you these new pants I'd bought . . ."

The doorbell rang. I pressed the bell for the downstairs door. Two police officers came up the stairs: a man and a woman. The woman was black, my age, with a soft voice and direct eyes. The man was also thirtyish: short, thin, Hispanic. He prowled through the apartment while his partner, Officer Dorothy Chaney, asked us questions and wrote in her notebook.

Fifteen minutes later, an ambulance and two medics arrived.

They put Paul on a stretcher and covered him with a sheet. "Who's coming?" asked Officer Chaney. "One of you has to come with us to the hospital."

"I'll do it," I said.

Perri said, "Are you going to be okay?"

I nodded. As the cops left the room, I tried to catch what the man was saying to the woman, but my Spanish wasn't good enough, and Perri was jabbering about going to see Sara and the baby at the hospital, a different hospital. I locked up the apartment. Ahead of me, under a blanket, my lover Paul was being carried down a narrow flight of stairs.

In the ambulance, I sat beside the shape on the stretcher as we sped up Eighth Avenue. The siren was screaming, as if it really mattered now when we would reach the hospital. Maybe the ambulance crew was paid by the job, and if they hurried back to their station they could pick up an extra fare.

Inside the hospital, they took Paul away, but I had to wait for the next of kin to arrive. I had to wait for my lover's family: his wife, an executive in the perfume business, and his grown daughter, a masseuse. A whole life I couldn't fathom. He wouldn't talk about them. I was, he used to say, his vacation from home. "Not that they're not wonderful," he would add.

Did he talk about me to anyone at all? I used to worry that if his car crashed in the summer, I wouldn't learn about it till the academic year. How embarrassing to have a homely mistress!

Perhaps I exaggerate the importance of appearance. But I do not exaggerate my lack of physical appeal. I have a lumpy face, sallow skin, thin brown hair often awry. When people praise my shapely hands, it's out of desperation.

Paul's wife was a pale-skinned brunette in her elegant forties. We met in the windowless waiting room: she held out her hand and said, "How terrible for you." She meant that he died in my apartment.

"Terrible," I said. *He died in my arms.* What would she do if I should say that? Her poise infuriated me. I thought, *You lived with him for twenty-five years. Why aren't you crying?*

But she wasn't cold, just controlled. As soon as her daughter arrived, Paul's wife ran to her and began sobbing, and I had to leave so I wouldn't start too.

At eight o'clock the next night, I was surprised by a ring at my door.

"It's Officer Chaney," a woman's voice called up. "Professor Jennings? Could I talk to you a moment? About Paul Granides?"

"Of course," I said. "Come in." But I felt adrenaline rush through me. I had lied to her and her partner, and I knew my face was either white or red. I closed the door behind us and hurriedly went into the kitchen. I called out, "Would you like some coffee?"

"Thank you," she said. "I'd appreciate that."

I measured the beans into the grinder and turned on the motor. When I turned it off, my face felt okay, and Officer Chaney was sitting on the cane stool observing me in the kitchen.

"Smells great," said Chaney.

I put in the water. I turned on the coffee-maker. I poured half-and-half into a creamer. I put cups and spoons on a tray. All the time, I was wondering if I should call a lawyer. But I'd done nothing wrong and I liked Officer Chaney. I emptied a package of shortbread cookies onto a plate and began arranging them. The small orange light on the coffee-maker came on.

"Let's take this to the living room," I said. I carried the tray; she took the coffee.

We sat sipping on the couch. "Delicious," she said. It was the blend Paul preferred. *Had* preferred. "Professor

Jennings—may I call you Lucy?—there are some inconsistencies in our reports, and I was hoping you could straighten things out for us."

"I'll do my best," I said. "Did you get the autopsy report?"

"Yes, he died from a brain clot."

I nodded. "It must have happened very fast." I remembered the story. "While we were in the kitchen."

"Making coffee."

"Exactly."

"The coffee's one of the problems," Dorothy Chaney said.

"Excuse me?"

"When Officer Perez and I came in, we saw the coffee cups from your meeting. Two empty ones. And a third, near him, half full. Now, if you were making coffee when he died, why would his be half full? And why would it still be warm to the touch?"

"I guess my sister made herself another cup and set it down somewhere . . ."

"*After* you discovered he was dead? After you called us? This sister business doesn't make much sense. What was she doing up here? Why did you both go to her place?"

"She was helping us brainstorm," I said. "Paul and I were planning a benefit." I told her about the kind of work we do at the organization. "Anyway, when we noticed he was sleeping, we went downstairs . . ."

"Yes, that's what you told me before. To look at some pants. Come on." Officer Chaney looked weary. "Why don't you just tell me what happened?"

I stared at her. What was the reason she had to know?

"The autopsy revealed the presence of sperm. Was Professor Granides having an affair . . . with your sister?"

"No! Not with my sister!"

"With you?"

How dare she act surprised! This was my apartment! I stared "yes" at her but didn't say a thing.

Officer Chaney put down her cup. "This doesn't have to go any further than here. He died of natural causes. You're not under suspicion. But there are these inconsistencies, Lucy. He had been dead longer than you said. So I'm going to tell you what I think happened. And then I'm going to say good night and that will be the end of it."

Officer Chaney took a cookie from the plate and studied it. "My guess is that Professor Granides wasn't here for a meeting, and your sister wasn't here at the time of his death. You and he were romantically involved. You had sex. You fell asleep. When you woke up, you found he was dead. You called up your sister to help you."

I said at last, "His family doesn't have to know about this guess of yours, does it?"

"Certainly not."

"That was my worry." I looked her in the eye. "It's a pretty good guess."

"Thank you," she said, standing up. "This must be hard for you."

I said, "He was a wonderful man. You can't know . . ."

"I believe it," she said. "Get some rest."

So much for my efforts at deceit! I closed the door behind Officer Chaney. I lay on the new couch and closed my eyes. I thought about how Paul and I had met.

At every lecture or symposium I attend, I make a point of asking a question. This forces me to focus, and if I ask a good question early, it helps shape the question-and-answer period. I was called on first after the benefit reading for Amnesty International.

I stood up and said, "Tonight we've heard some beautiful works by writers who've been imprisoned and tortured by right-wing regimes. Are no good poems and stories being written in the prisons of Cuba and the Soviet Union?"

"Uhhh?" The moderator turned to the five readers on the

stage in back of him. They were all well-known New York writers, pleased to do good for an impeccable cause (the abolition of torture), flattered that their names were considered big enough and their voices expressive enough to read the words of heroes and martyrs. None of them had chosen the program; none of them was ready to defend it. I remained standing.

Finally, a young woman in a brown dress walked onto the stage. "I'm on the Programming Committee. We selected the materials," she said. "We decided that this year our focus would be writers from Africa and South America."

"No stirring writing from the Communist prisons in Mozambique?"

"I'm not aware of any," the woman said, "but I'll make a note and check."

"Are there any other questions?" the moderator asked smoothly.

Three hands went up; I had broken the ice. Sure enough, the next person responded to what I had said. "I think what the last questioner meant was that we seem to regard right-wing torture as somehow more terrible, more objectionable than torture by left-wing regimes."

"What is the question?" the moderator asked.

"It was a clarification," said the speaker, who sat down before I could see him.

"Yes, in the back?"

Half an hour later, the meeting broke up. It was a mild night in May. I didn't need my jacket; I kept it on my arm as I walked out of the theater. Someone stepped from the doorway and asked me, "Are you the woman who asked the first question?"

I turned to look at him. He was in his forties, unkempt, intellectual looking. I asked, "Are you the man who came to my defense?"

He nodded.

"Thank you," I said. I began walking.

He fell into step beside me. "Going downtown?"

"Down to the Village."

"By subway?"

"Actually, I thought I'd walk awhile."

He said, "I love walking at night in Manhattan."

"Me too." Darkness masks the dirt, and there are lights against the sky.

"The sidewalks are emptier then," he said, "you can stride."

We walked all the way to Seventeen Morton Street together.

The next time, we walked across the Brooklyn Bridge at night. Later, I learned Paul was married. Later, I discovered I didn't mind too terribly. Later, we began our joyful rituals.

Five years: once or twice a week.

Afterward, Paul would say "Lucy" and sink into sleep.

24

I MISSED MY FIRST DAY OF classes because of Paul's death, so I had a lot of catching up to do on the following Tuesday. I only teach on Tuesdays: I lecture to a hundred sophomores and meet with my graduate seminar of twelve. The rest of the week I devote to research and writing. It's not a hard life. I have been, academically, very lucky. A university is the best place for women like me: well-intentioned, brainy, plain.

The first day I walk in for my undergraduate lecture, I know initially I disappoint. The students all want to fall in love. They want the professor's charisma to buzz them, make them hum and glow. Then their burning interest in the teacher may even extend to the subject. No chance of that, one glance tells them, with me. I put my pile of books on the lectern and begin. My sophomores take notes until the end of the hour. Sometimes they nod with interest or blink with surprise. They raise their hands to object. It's a lively time: no one ever falls asleep. But after the hour, they don't swarm around me.

My graduate students are different. Some of them even chose this department because of me. All feel privileged to be here. I shine for them. They don't notice my looks or object to my homeliness: I am Lucy Jennings, of the "Jennings corollary." Jennings of the Stanford monographs. Some are surprised that I am still so young, but none seem dismayed that I'm not a pretty woman: my mind is the reason they're there.

One of my new graduate students was much older than the others, a familiar-looking man of forty-five with fading brown hair and a gray mustache. After class, he came up and said, "I was just sitting in for today."

"Oh? Deciding on the course?"

He shook his head.

I looked at him, puzzled. "Are you in the department?"

"No," he said, "I just wanted to meet you. I'm George Kutcher. I was a good friend of Paul's."

I found myself staring at him like a simpleton.

He said, "I was hoping we could have some coffee or maybe a drink."

"A drink," I said.

We went to the Ivory Tower, a popular, monastic-looking bar nearby. At that time of day, it was nearly empty. We sat in a booth and gave our orders.

"I'm in the Chemistry Department," he said. "Paul hired me ten years ago."

"He's mentioned you," I said. What was it Paul had said about his friend George? Something faintly unsavory but funny? But what? "Photosynthesis in primitive fauna? Is that you?"

"That's me," he said, flattered.

Oh yes! Paul had told me that George, a bachelor, often got

to know women of his age and education through the personals. He would meet them first at a coffee shop so they could look each other over before proceeding further. "But what if it turns out he knows the woman?" I had asked. "How embarrassing for both of them."

"That's exactly what happened once. It was a woman he went to college with, a woman he detested who also hated him. When he saw her alone at a table, *New York Review* in hand, he realized what had happened and slunk away."

"How mean."

"His rationale was that it was better to be stood up by a stranger than revealed in all your neediness to an old college classmate you despised."

Now George said, "I'm going to miss Paul enormously."

The waitress laid down our drinks, and I lifted my glass. "To his memory," I said. Orange juice and vodka slid down my throat. I swallowed once, twice, again. I put down my glass and asked, "How long have you known about me?"

He said, "I guess since the beginning. After that reading? When you began walking downtown and ended up going eighty blocks?"

"He told you all that?"

"Well, Lucy, you were the joy of his life."

"Please," I said. *"Please."*

"No, no, I didn't mean to . . ."

"It's not that," I said. I looked away. When I could, I said, "I killed him. He died in my bed."

"That's ridiculous—he would have died anyway. You didn't kill him, you kept him going."

I mumbled something to the tabletop.

"What's that?"

I said, "He kept me going, too." Then I concentrated on the ice in my drink. I moved the glass so the cubes hit the sides.

"Are you sorry he told me?" asked George.

"No—your knowing makes it more real. Our whole time as a couple we were illicit, alone. No one was there to see us together. I'm happy he told you. One of my great fears was . . ."

"What?"

"It seems so silly now. So ironic."

"Go on."

"I worried he'd get hurt or something and I wouldn't know. No one would tell me."

"Actually," George said, "he thought about it, too."

I looked up. "Really?"

"Sure. Being so much older. He told me if anything ever happened I was to tell you. And give you this." He handed me a manila envelope.

I wanted to tear the thing open, but I put it on the table and folded my hands demurely on top of it.

"Paul always said you had beautiful hands."

I opened the envelope. Inside was a book, a first edition of e.e. cummings's *Collected Poems*. The date was 1938. I turned a few pages. On the space at the top of the table of contents, Paul had penciled, lightly, the words "The Lucy Poems." There were several small circles around page numbers beside the poem titles.

George said, "I have to go now. Committee meeting. Walking back?"

I shook my head. "I'll stay here a little longer."

George stood up and put some money on the table. "It was good to meet you, Lucy. I'd like to help, if there's any way I can . . ."

There seemed to be a hint of flirtation in his voice. Was it my unattainability in this first month of my mistress-widowhood? Or simple curiosity: What had Paul seen in me? Just how had I given him joy? Men like George rarely even spoke to me at parties.

"Thanks," I said. "I'm okay."

He left. Perhaps that night he was meeting SWF, slender, pretty, 36, seeks prof SWM 35–45 for granola and la Grenouille, fandangos and frolic, photos please. At the door, George turned and waved. Then I got another drink and turned to one of the poems Paul had marked with his small penciled circle—the first of what he'd called "The Lucy Poems."

I read the damned thing. It was unbearable. Had I really meant all that to him? I moved my glass so the ice hit the sides again. I reminded myself about the world. While I'd been in the Ivory Tower with George, out there on this planet a hundred men and women had been murdered, some at war and some at home. Others were being raped and tortured even now as I finished my drink. They were being held under faucets so that they couldn't breathe. They were shrieking under electric cattle prods. They were having their nails pulled out, and fainting, and being revived for some more. I made myself read the poem again. This time it wasn't so bad.

25

It was one of those balmy seventy-five-degree Indian summer days in October that come along every year in New York—yet always arrive as a happy surprise. Even I, a mistress-widow of six weeks, felt an unreasoned pleasure in the day. I got off the subway one stop early and strolled down Seventh Avenue South in the sun. After several blocks, I turned into Traber's.

I'm a great bargain hunter, like my father was. Sara only likes shopping for yarn and for food, and Perri only likes shopping for clothes, but I enjoy buying anything, especially if it's on sale. I am, of course, a sucker for Traber's.

Traber's is a large discount outlet store in the Village owned and run by Arabs. It carries different goods from one day to the next. At various times, you can find boxes of luxury cosmetics at one-fifth their original price, eight-piece screwdriver sets for a dollar, furry ape-slippers with toes, hand-embroidered tablecloths, clear plastic boxes, and red and green candles, scarcely cracked, very cheap. It's best to go in when you don't need anything in particular but can meander around with your basket, accumulating a variety of unexpected, underpriced items. I thought I might find a toy for Zoe there—or my own favorite bath soap at one-quarter the supermarket price.

Today, the store was almost empty and the bargains were good: a tiger-striped terry-cloth robe for six ninety-eight, tortoise-shell hair ornaments for a quarter, a set of wood-carving tools for a dollar. I put these things and some others into the plastic shopping basket on my arm. I couldn't quite picture myself in the tiger-patterned robe, but it would be something nice for a gift or a guest: "One size fits all." The wood-carving tools were for Roland and Rory.

The two Arabic men at the front of the store were talking to each other excitedly. They sounded angry, but I thought that they probably weren't. Vehemence seems as integral to the Arabic language as coquettishness is to the French. Two Syrian girls lived with me at Yale for a year, and they always sounded acrimonious but were really only vivacious. One rainy Sunday, they taught the rest of us in the suite the basic Arabic curses and showed us how to do the gutterals. It became a brief craze among us to curse in Arabic.

Because of that, I knew what the cashier at Traber's was saying when I approached the front of the store. He gestured at me and said, impatiently, "Over here, *khara*."

I asked, "Excuse me? What did you say?"

He said, "Bring your things over here, *khara*."

He had called me "piece of shit." I said furiously, "*Khara* yourself. How dare you talk to me that way? What have I done to you?"

He shrugged and smiled at his friend. I said, "Keep your

junk!" and shook the shopping basket so the contents flew out at him.

I was trembling as I left the store. Had he called me *khara* because of my looks or from general ill will? I had been inoffensively filling my basket. I had been absorbed, almost happy. Now on the street the sun seemed too bright and once more I knew that Paul was dead. I remembered our afternoons together, the sun through the skylight, the well-being I might never know again.

Of course, it might have been different with Paul if we had been married. Fights about the garbage and the bills. Old tensions building over the years. "Points" and "score," as with Sara and Gordon, whose lifetime "I-was-right" competition had intensified of late. If Sara and Gordon's marriage was the model, it was little wonder that Perri and I had avoided matrimony. Not that we were avoiding it exactly, but given my physiognomy and Perri's taste in men, marriage seemed unlikely for us both. I turned down Morton Street and went up the stoop of Seventeen.

In the small outer foyer, impulsively, I rang Perri's bell. Perri buzzed me in. She had just come home from work—she hadn't even taken off her watch and shoes. I watched her change out of her dress and into some pants. I couldn't help noticing that Perri's once-pert little butt seemed a bit flatter and lower—and wasn't that a trace of cellulite on the back of her thighs?

Perri proceeded to talk, at some length, about her current crush, an obnoxious-sounding film editor named Larry. His only virtue seemed to be his general lack of interest in my very desirable sister. I told Perri about *Love and Limerence*. She talked about *moments* with Larry when she was flooded with joy. She said, "Then he's cranky and rude for a week."

I said what Mother used to tell Sara and Perri in turn— "Why don't you go out with some nice, cheerful man?"

We made faces at each other. Then I headed upstairs to my

apartment. I opened the door, hung up my coat, sat down at my desk with the mail. I found a letter from the American Psychological Association concerning the paper I would be presenting at the annual convention.

Last spring, by happy coincidence, Paul and I had each been asked to present a paper for the four-day meeting. (His: "Chemical Imbalances in Mild Depressives." Mine: "Emotional Effects of Extreme Precocity.") We had planned to book adjoining rooms and relax between presentations and sorties. He had invented some research reason to stay on in Chicago, and we were going to have a week, in all, together. Seven days, six nights, *six consecutive nights*.

I put the letter on my bulletin board. The convention wasn't for another two months, but I was already dreading the ordeal. I would have canceled the trip if I hadn't been on the program. I knew it would hurt being there without Paul. I shoved the rest of the mail to one side and stood up.

It was five-thirty. If I hurried, I could just make the six o'clock yoga class. I'd discovered yoga just the year before, had found that the chanting and the poses calmed me, seemed to cleanse me, gave me that serene and oceanic feeling others, apparently, get from religion. I opened the closet and took down my yoga bag. It held a pair of loose white pants and a loose gray T-shirt. One of the things I like about yoga is that for much of it, people keep their eyes closed. Another thing I like is the sleeping.

The instructors vary from one day to the next, but they all follow the same routine. The third quarter of each session is devoted to deep relaxation, and as I lie down on my towel, tightening and loosening each part of my body in the darkened room, I always ease into a glorious sleep. You're not supposed to nod out during deep relaxation: you're supposed to be conscious of the peace so you can derive benefits from it. But few stay awake: there are snores from all parts of the room. I'm

210

amused that I routinely walk a dozen blocks and pay five dollars just so I can sleep in public.

Today, there were fewer people than usual in the room: perhaps fifteen, so there was no need for crowding. The instructor was lighting incense by the shrine, and I sat on my towel and looked around the room. The two rows of towels were lined up down the middle of the room, and I was facing a woman of sixty in a lavender leotard. Across the aisle and to my right was a black woman who looked vaguely familiar.

The instructor sat down at one end of the room and said, gently, as they always did, "Good evening. This is Hatha Yoga One. Would you all please close your eyes?"

We chanted. We worshiped the sun. We expanded our chests in the fish pose and massaged our thyroids in the shoulder stand. Then it was time for deep relaxation. I tried very hard to stay awake, but failed, happily, as usual. When the instructor croaked the wake-up chant, I awoke fully refreshed. I opened my eyes and, as instructed, assumed an easy cross-legged position for the breathing exercises.

It wasn't until the nerve-cleansing breath that I recognized the black woman to my right as Dorothy Chaney—Officer Chaney of the New York City Police Department. She was wearing a forest-green sweatsuit. She looked smaller and softer out of uniform.

After class, I smiled at her as we walked into the dressing room, although I doubted that Dorothy would remember me. But Dorothy said, "Hello. It's Lucy Jennings, isn't it?"

"Good memory," I said. I smiled again. "Unless you're following me or something."

She laughed. "I'm off duty." She took off her sweatshirt. She was not wearing a brassiere. "Very off duty." She pulled down her sweatpants.

I became very absorbed in putting on my socks. It occurred to me that this was probably the first time I had ever seen naked black breasts. Dorothy dressed in blue jeans and a plaid flannel shirt.

We left the dressing room and the yoga center together and walked to Seventh Avenue. "What did you think of the instructor?" Dorothy asked.

"Very mellow," I said, "but she can't hold a tune."

"I know—when she sang to bring us out of deep relaxation, it was like a broken alarm clock!"

"Did you sleep?" I asked.

"Of course," said Dorothy. "Always do."

"Me, too."

We reached Greenwich Avenue. Dorothy said, "I'm just going to go to that Syrian place up the block and get some of their babaganoush. Would you like to join me? I suppose you're busy . . ."

"No, no, I'm free," I said. "That sounds nice."

26

THERE WAS A NOTE FROM
George Kutcher in my department mailbox two weeks later.
He wanted to know if I could meet him later for a drink. I
saw no reason to refuse and no reason to accept.

I gave one of my better lectures, and many students asked
me questions afterward. I had to lead a trail of them, like a
parade, into my office. Last on line was George.

"Did you get my note?" he asked.

"Yes, thanks . . ." I said absently, vaguely.

"Yes, thanks or no thanks?" he asked.

"Well, yes, thanks, I guess, since you're here."

We walked to the Ivory Tower. "Our place," said George.

I didn't reply. I couldn't see why he was trying so hard.
Then it occurred to me that in a way he was like the male

prisoner my father had told me about. He knew all about me
long before meeting me; he knew something of my life and
ways in advance. He first knew the inner me, and so to George
Kutcher, my frowsiness mattered little. Advance knowledge
worked in reverse in his case. From hearing stories about him
for years, I felt I knew the inner him, and so his physical
appeal left me unmoved.

In the booth, I was tracing wet circles on the dark wood
and feeling it was wrong to be there when George asked why
I was nervous.

"I'm not nervous," I said. "I have no reason to be nervous."

"You don't seem to be having a very good time."

I said, "It's just . . . I don't know you that well."

"Would you like to know me better?" he asked. "I could
cook us one of my fabulous Mexican dinners tonight . . ."

After a while, I said, "I guess not."

"Mexican food too hot for you?"

"Sort of."

He said, "I guess you're still in mourning."

I nodded again. The truth was, I didn't really trust George
and didn't really like him. This was unfortunate, I knew. For
most women, he was certainly a catch. Indeed, on Manhattan
island, men like George were all too rare: SWM prof., attractive, likes women. If only he could make me laugh, or make
me cry, or even intrigue me a little. But as we went through
our chitchat, I heard nothing to hold me. I said at last, "I
really should go now."

He spread his fingers, signaling *Be my guest.*

I went to the ladies room. A little later, on my way out, I
looked back at George. I was pleased to see him in animated
conversation with another woman.

Dorothy Chaney finished her wine, wiped her mouth, and
put her napkin on the table. She gave a sigh of contentment.
"Fabulous."

"It is good," I agreed. We were in an Italian restaurant. Our plates were empty; our stomachs were full. Dinner out together after Wednesday yoga had become our pattern: it was the third time we had gone out together. I was very pleased with our friendship. I didn't have many friends—I had colleagues and relatives—so to know a new woman was an event. I also liked Dorothy's race, and profession. I had always wanted to have a black friend, and this one led a daring life and did a perfect shoulder stand.

"So what's happening, Lucy?" she asked. "You ready to date someone new?" Last time, I had told her about Paul.

"Apparently not," I said. Then I told her about George Kutcher's pursuit. "I wish I liked George a little—men don't exactly batter down my door to get at me."

"And women?"

I laughed. "I don't know any gay women." She gave me a funny look, so I quickly added, "Except you, I guess."

"Whatever makes you think that?" she said, grinning. "Do you mind?"

"No. Uh-uh." But though not surprised, I was rather dismayed. I wasn't sure how many differences our good-natured rapport could bridge.

"I have lots of straight friends. Straight lovers, too. Oh, yeah." She grinned.

I said, "Straight women lovers . . . ?"

She said, "Come on, Lucy, surely you know that every woman is a little 'bi.' Who first cuddled and kissed and caressed us? Our mothers! It's no mystery some of us prefer women. The mystery is that any woman would prefer a man."

"You can't mean all this!"

"I do too! It's the most natural thing in the world. We were first held in female arms, nourished through sucking a breast. We crave female flesh all our lives. Except most women are too uptight to admit it. And most women are too chicken to try. Maybe they're worried they'll like it too much."

I said, "That's ridiculous. For many it's a perfectly normal, instinctive aversion. They aren't attracted to women."

"Nonsense," Dorothy said. "They just won't let themselves try it. And then they miss the thrill of a lifetime."

"But not for them! Straight women don't insist that everybody's hetero. Why do gays insist that everybody's really gay?"

" 'Bi,' at least," Dorothy said. "Because it's true. And look at it this way. No man can understand a woman's body like another woman. Isn't that obvious?"

I thought of Paul's hands and shook my head.

"I don't mean me, of course," she said, "but sometime, when you're ready, you should think about meeting a woman. There are so many more of us out there . . ."

"And yourself?"

Dorothy said, "I'm looking for somebody permanent. I want to have a child. But I want to have a partner first."

"Tell me about her," I said. "The partner you want to have."

"She's gentle," Dorothy said. "Kind. Very sensual. Maybe an artist. She stays home and cooks me dinner."

"Is she white?"

"Sometimes, yes, a pale blonde. But sometimes I imagine an Asian. That doesn't matter so much. The gentleness does. The directness and honesty. That's what I like about you."

I said nothing but I was pleased.

"Why don't you come dancing tonight?"

"In a women's bar?"

"Well, yes."

"It's just not my scene, Dorothy. I'd be ill at ease. I'd embarrass you."

Dorothy said, "You would not."

"I can't tonight," I said and patted her hand.

She pulled hers away and said jokingly, "Don't get fresh."

After dinner, she went off to the gay bar to meet her friends and I went back to Seventeen Morton Street. Halfway down

216

the block, I saw Sara's au pair Carlo coming toward me. I nodded hello, unsure if he remembered me, but he said, "Hello, Lucia" and smiled. A sunny and attractive young Italian. I wondered how Gordon liked having him around in a situation ripe for romance—or for farce. But Sara had told me that Carlo was Gordon's idea in the first place. "Of course, we didn't know what he looked like," she'd said with a smile.

As I climbed upstairs, I could hear Sara's boys racing through her apartment. Stamp stamp stamp giggle giggle, "Don't!" "Yes!" "Time out!" Marijuana smoke seeped out from under the door of Perri's apartment. What worried me about Perri was that she found so many pretexts for smoking. She smoked dope for inspiration, pain relief, and sleep; for meals out and showers in, for TV shows and rainy afternoons.

I opened the door to my empty apartment. Perhaps I should have gone dancing with Dorothy, after all. I also wanted a child and seemed unlikely to get one. It was one important thing we had in common. I wanted our friendship to continue; it had a certain crackle to it. But I didn't think I could be life-companions with Dorothy or any other woman—or even experiment in bed for a night. I've never fantasized about a woman, although perhaps a skilled lesbian could help me over this initial lack of sexual interest in my gender. But it goes against the grain to push for pleasure without passion.

Besides, in the gay world as in the straight, my general homeliness would surely hinder me. Or is that necessarily true? At times, I've seen—at a distance or in the rain—a person I've taken for a rather cute man. Up close, it turns out to be a rather plain woman. Would gay women think I was cute? Or sexy? Watch out for Lucy—she's *hot*. I couldn't help but smile at the thought.

Better to smile than to cry. Better not to brood one more time on how appearance affects a woman's existence—and not always in expected ways. I thought of Lily and how being very pretty had probably spoiled her life. She had left a high-school boyfriend and a small town in Texas because everybody said she was beautiful enough to be an actress and had a real sweet voice as well. Now, at forty-five, Lily was a waitress at the Peacock. She was still single, still taking lessons, still waiting for the right man, the big break. If her nose had been a little bigger or her eyes a little smaller, she would have stayed in her town, married her Bill, and been happy raising children.

Or was that utter nonsense? Just because I'd love to raise children doesn't mean everybody else would. Maybe in Texas Lily would have hit the bottle, hit her kids. You never can tell.

And it does no good to lament that life is unfair, all people should be equally attractive. Nothing will change the natural aristocracy of the good-looking . . . nothing except time. Aging is apparently most traumatic to beautiful women: the wrinkles and sagging sadder for Perri than for me. But as I walked about in my empty apartment, I thought, What about our lives now? What about being Perri wearing white jeans and her leather jacket?

I went into the study and turned on the computer. While it was whirring through its initial preparations, I took out the most recent issue of the Amnesty International newsletter and thumbed through the pages.

The computer was ready for me. I opened file PRSNRS. Some of the letter could remain the same, whether I was writing politely to the Prime Minister of Turkey protesting the thirty-six-year prison sentence given Recep Marasli for publishing books about the Kurdish culture or whether I was writing respectfully to the Minister of Justice in Santiago about Rodrigo Rojas, doused with flammable liquid and set on fire by the Chilean police.

It was very important, said Amnesty International, that our letters of protest be courteous.

218

27

"LUCY, THIS IS VERY GOOD OF you," said Sara.

"Hurry back," I said. "I've got a ton of things to do." I was leaving for Chicago the next day.

She placed the red portacot beneath the window in my study. Zoe, visible through the mesh sides, was on all fours. Slowly she lifted her fuzzy dark head. Sara said, "I've just fed her and changed her. Give her this and she'll soon go to sleep." Sara held out a pacifier and said, "The magic plug."

"An old one of Rory's?" I asked. Rory and Roland had both used pacifiers, too, when Sara wanted them to sleep. Perri thinks Sara's the perfect mother, but I think she's too controlling.

"I did buy her one or two new things," Sara said.

"Where's Carlo, anyway?"

"At class. He has a seminar now."

"How's he working out?"

"He doesn't work out as far as I know," Sara said, smiling.

"Come on, Sara—do the boys like him?"

"Sure. He plays with them and takes them on nature walks and teaches them secret codes."

"And he's okay with Zoe? And Gordon?"

"He's learning, with Zoe. He and Gordon, however . . ." Sara shook her head. "There seems to be a natural antipathy." She looked at her watch. "Y'okay now, Lucy?"

"Just fine."

She said, "See you later. And, really, thanks a lot." She was on her way to a postnatal exercise class. "I got into shape so much faster with Roland and Rory—and it didn't even matter then."

I looked up, curious. "Why does it matter now?"

She said, vaguely, "Now? Oh. Well . . ." She was stalling. "I'm closer to forty now."

"Sara, you're years away."

"Two."

"What does it matter, anyway?"

"You'll see," she said.

She did look heavier lately. Although still not chubby, Sara was no longer girlishly slim, as she had been until Zoe. I had never been as thin as Sara; now our shapes were similar. Her clothes were tight, mine bagged. I had apparently got thinner since Paul died, but since I didn't have a scale, I wasn't really sure.

Sara peered at me and asked, almost accusingly, "Have *you* lost some weight?"

"Perhaps."

"You look good." Then she looked at her watch and said, "Gotta go." Raincoat swirling around shiny blue tights, Sara turned and walked out.

From my desk, I watched Zoe inside her red portacot. The infant pushed against the mattress with her feet, raising her bottom high, keeping her head on the mattress. Now one foot pushed through the mesh against the wall, and I watched, mesmerized, as the baby wedged herself higher and higher—and over she went! She lay, on her back, as surprised and helpless as an upside-down turtle. For a few seconds, she was too startled to cry. Then she closed her eyes and opened her mouth and began.

I rushed across the room and picked her up. Good-bye to the letters I was sorting, good-bye to the bills. I held Zoe high on my shoulder and rubbed her little back. "There, there, there, there. You were the strong girl, you turned right over, you got surprised. Didn't you, little one?"

Zoe's sobs subsided. Now I held a warm and quiet baby. I bowed my head to smell hers and found myself kissing her forehead. She straightened her legs against my arm as if about to launch herself over my shoulder and into the room. I held her tight and brought her to the couch. We sat there happily nestled. Then I held her away from me, so I could look into her face. Her eyes were lighter than at birth: they would be blue, like Sara's. Her mouth turned down, like Gordon's, and her nose was a blob, a miniature version of mine and my father's—the grandpa she would never meet.

As with many three-month-old babies, Zoe looked preternaturally alert. If she followed the usual pattern, as her brothers did, with each passing month she would get plumper and dumber looking, until at about a year she would begin to talk in words to match her baby face: "mama," "cookie," "bye-bye." At fifteen weeks, however, tiny Zoe looked like she could give a lecture on paradox; in her eyes lay the wisdom of the ages.

Such entertaining creatures babies are! With babies, as with lovers, what they give is partly what they are, partly what you read into them, and partly what you are with them. So I love babies because of one: their essence; two: their mystery; and three: the me I become when I'm with them—kindly, caring, crooning.

Zoe gave me her steady, wise gaze and tried to stand up in my lap. I told myself: Enjoy every moment, you might not get a baby of your own.

Actually, since Paul's death, I had devised a baby-plan, but I wasn't sure if I'd be brave enough to go through with it. I knew it was unlikely I'd marry, but I didn't see why that should bar me from motherhood. If by the age of thirty-four, I wasn't living with a man, I intended to visit a sperm bank. My sabbatical year would begin when I turned thirty-five.

Remembering my plan, I stopped feeling sorry for myself: Zoe was not a substitute child but a rehearsal opportunity. Sara always claims she rehearsed motherhood with *me*—but surely she exaggerates. She cannot have been fully maternal at ages six and seven—although she was already bossy and controlling. What irritates me is the way she idealizes our childhood. We did not always play together like angels. And Mom and Dad were not great parents. Mom was not deeply interested in us, and Dad was almost always tired and withdrawn. Their marriage, while companionable, seemed dry and passionless: boring.

I left Zoe on the living room rug for a moment and went back to the study for her portacot and my legal pad, which had my list. We're all of us list-makers, Sara, Perri, and I, although Perri's lists are absurdly detailed. Number two on my day-before-departure list read "go to bank." Number three was "wash clothes." Perri would have written:

bank
    deposit check
    go over balances
    get cash

clothes
   sort
   wash
   dry
   fold
   put away

Then she'd have the pleasure of making many check marks. As for Sara, I have seen her add chores she's already done to a list—just so she can run a pencil line through them, savoring each completed task. Or is she establishing evidence, for Gordon, that she works hard keeping house and raising the children? Apparently, he wanted her to go out and work instead of having Zoe, although he makes what seems to me quite a lot of money.

In the study, I consulted my legal pad. Number four on my pre-Chicago list was "polish shoes and handbag." I felt this would be easy with Zoe on hand.

Bringing her cot back to the living room, I placed Zoe inside it. I put on a Bach concerto, then spread newspaper on the floor near the baby and got out the polish and rags and brushes. She stared at my every action. What fun to be watched and admired as you go about your chores! I'd much rather do housework with a baby or a child as company than do it alone. Sometimes Roland and Rory come up on weekends when I'm cleaning up. They each have a dresser drawer that I fill with things they may like: novelties I used to get at Traber's, magazine clippings, unusual candies.

Last month Rory said, "Mom doesn't want us to eat candy between meals." Roland said, "Shut up, geek. Aunt Lucy, don't listen to Rory." I said, "I don't give you much—and you don't have to tell her." Rory stared at me, unaccustomed to this concept. Roland looked delighted.

I had finished polishing the shoes but not my bag when the phone rang. It was Dorothy. She wanted me to know about

"V," this great women's bar in Chicago, in case I'd feel freer to "explore my sensuality" in a strange city. I had to laugh at her persistence.

On my way back to the rags and the polish, I glanced out the window and saw Sara running up the outside steps. "Mommy's coming," I said to Zoe. I worked on my handbag, which hadn't been cleaned or polished in the two years I'd had it. A trip forces you to do at once all the things you've meant to do for months. I rubbed the polish into the leather, then wiped away the residue. I buffed the bag with a brush. I held it up for Zoe to see.

But the baby was asleep (without having needed the pacifier, I noted with a certain pride). And Sara still hadn't come up, which was very inconsiderate of her—I had to get to the bank before three. Granted, Sara didn't know it—but she did know how busy I was. She always had been careless of my time. I decided to leave Zoe sleeping in her portacot while I went down to the basement to put my laundry in the washer—why risk waking her moving her? I transferred my dirty clothes from the hamper to a laundry bag. Then I left my apartment.

There are two ways to get to the basement from my place. You can go outside and down the stoop, which puts you on the street, from which you go down another half-flight of stairs to the basement entrance. Or you can go in through Sara's apartment and down the inside stairs to the basement. It was raining, so I went in through Sara's. I unlocked her door and called, "Sara? Sara, it's only me." But she didn't answer. I went down to the basement, still calling "Sara" so I wouldn't frighten her, and opened the door to the hot tub. But she wasn't there, either. I decided to do all the clothes in cold water, rather than do them in two smaller loads of hot and cold, as I prefer when I have time. I stuffed the clothes into the machine and added detergent. Then I went back upstairs, puzzled by Sara's absence.

Fifteen minutes later, she came up to my place, dressed in

jeans. Seeing Zoe quiet in the cot, she said, "I told you she'd sleep."

"We had a great time together. Busy as I am, I was sorry when she nodded off. With*out* the rubber plug."

"She's a good baby. I always had to hold Rory for hours."

"Sara," I said, "where were you just now? I saw you come up the front steps half an hour ago."

"I needed a shower," said Sara. And indeed her hair was wet. But I thought it was odd that I hadn't heard the shower when I'd gone through her apartment with my laundry, and odd that she hadn't answered when I'd called.

I said, pointedly, "I just hope I don't miss the bank." It was two forty-five. "I have a deposit."

She said, "Do it by machine."

"It's my paycheck," I said. "I like to hand it to a teller."

"Well, run along, if you're paranoid about your money." She took up the portacot in one hand and turned away.

"Sara? Is anything wrong?"

"Wrong? No."

"You seem so down. So dejected. Not like you usually are after exercise class."

"I'm fine," she said. But her face seemed drained. "Thanks for sitting. And have a good time in Chicago, in case I don't see you."

"I'll try," I said, "but I don't expect much."

"Sometimes that's the best attitude," she called up the stairs. "Then you can be happily surprised."

Yes, Pollyanna, I thought. Sticking the envelope with my salary check into my newly polished handbag, I grabbed my raincoat and ran. I made the bank by three minutes. I gave the teller my paycheck, tucked the validated deposit slip into the zippered compartment of my wallet, put a bunch of twenties in the billfold, and left the bank. On my way back I stopped to buy a small tube of toothpaste. Sometimes when I'm doing one of these dull little chores to maintain myself, I find myself picturing somebody very famous doing the same thing (even though the very famous mostly have others to do their small tasks). Henry Kissinger picking up his dry cleaning. Jacqueline Kennedy buying Vaseline. Madonna choosing oat bran cereal. In all the stores, such a brush with celebrity would be the highlight of the day, perhaps the year, to be savoured again and again, to be analyzed. "Did you see the stain on Kissinger's pants?" "I wonder why Jackie needs Vaseline." "Do you think Madonna has high cholesterol?"

If such speculation by strangers is the fruit of fame—no thanks. I prefer name recognition by a small group of peers —which I've been fortunate enough to achieve. I'm known, when I am known, for the products of my mind; I'm esteemed for what I value most about myself.

I reminded myself about this as I found myself walking behind a very pretty, somewhat punky girl of twenty. Great bones, blond hair, skinny body, perky breasts. She wore tight black clothes. Men turned to stare after her, jaws slackening. Even women turned to look.

I bobbed in her wake.

28

Now, if a woman like that had been in the gay bar, flirting at me from across the room with her hair and eyes, coming over and asking me to dance —I might well have had a passionate initiation in Chicago, despite my inhibitions and aversions (touch those? kiss *that*?). But V's did not offer me anything like that. I sat at a table with my beer amid very young girls who looked rough. Most had what I consider the "international dyke look": short hair, no makeup, earrings. The women at V's seemed drabber than straight women—less attractive. That was odd, I mused, since gay men tend to look better than straight ones, especially past the age of thirty.

It was the fourth day of the convention. I had given my paper the morning before and had thoroughly enjoyed the session. I felt as if each audience question, even the hostile ones, had been designed to best elicit the additional information I had gathered. Afterward, I had lunch with some of the other specialists in my field. In the afternoon, I'd gone to seminars, lectures, discussions. But I had eaten dinner alone, and breakfast alone this morning. Lunch today had been a sandwich during a lecture. I was alone again at dinner.

I missed Paul acutely: we should have had this time together. We could have showered together. He might have rubbed soap on my shoulders, his worn face streaming love. I came out of the shower and dried myself off. I wondered once again if another man would ever love me. Certainly not tonight in Chicago. Even if I were pretty enough to pick up someone in a bar, a strange man might get violent, weird. Women were more trustworthy, kinder as a gender.

And so, remembering Dorothy Chaney's suggestion, I found myself in a room full of lesbians. I wouldn't want to go to bed with any of these women, and surely none of them wanted to go to bed with me. What I wanted, I could never have again: Paul tightening his grip on me, then relaxing, saying "Lucy."

The music hurt my ears. Near me, two broad-hipped young women wearing blue jeans were dancing suggestively, looking into one another's eyes. I couldn't tell anything about their relationship: whether they had just met, whether they were longtime lovers (they looked so alike!), or whether they were just friends, cruising together. Dorothy had warned me about this situation. She said sometimes she was blunt, asking, "Are you two together?" Sometimes she did it with her eyes. Sometimes she went home with a stranger. Sometimes it was great.

I ordered another beer. Although erotically disappointing, V's was a comfortable place. I liked sitting in the room with local women: local men would have jangled me. What I didn't like was sitting all alone, passively awaiting contact with another, knowing it depended on how I looked, how I dressed. Actually, I'm quite a good dresser, I think—but does any woman think she dresses terribly? Does any person honestly believe he has bad taste?

Just as I challenge myself to ask one question after every lecture, now I challenged myself to speak, however briefly, to three women here before leaving. And then I would go, because I was getting more and more depressed.

"Excuse me," I said to the woman on my right, "where's the bathroom?"

"In back," she said.

"Thanks. Do me a favor. Don't let the waitress take away my beer."

"Okay."

That wasn't much of an exchange, but it counted as one toward my three.

The graffiti in the bathroom were not as diverting as I had expected. I had hoped to find rather more literary and romantic odes to Sapphic love, but these, in both picture and text, were every bit as crude as one might expect in any barroom bathroom. On the way back, I stood by the far side of the dance floor. I watched long enough to know the woman watching on my left was also alone. I said to her, "Do you have the time?"

She looked at her wrist. "Ten-thirty." She glanced at my wrist and said, "Doesn't your watch work?"

I couldn't tell if this was accusation or pursuit. I said, "I was just checking. I can't believe it's only ten-thirty."

She said, "It gets better later, after midnight."

"I'll never last."

"I know what you mean. I have to be at work at eight."

"What do you do?"

"I'm a nurse."

"I'm a psychologist," I said.

She nodded once, then looked away. Had she thought I was pulling rank? Or had she thought I was trying to pick her up? Never mind. It counted as two. One more and I could go.

The music got louder still, but I didn't mind, it was a song I loved. And I suddenly wanted to dance. As a teenager, I'd often danced with my sisters, so dancing with a woman wasn't novel. Now I walked back toward my table, looking for somebody lonely. I chose a solitary chubby redhead and said, "Hey, want to dance?"

"Sure," she said, to my surprise, and she followed me onto the dance floor.

We danced for dancing, not for courting. It was fun, working up a sweat to the beat. When a slow song came on, we sat down and talked. Her name was Peggy and she worked in a department store. She was waiting for her girl friend, who was meeting her here later on. I was relieved to hear this. We danced one more dance. Then I left.

A gay bar was one way to meet women in a strange city, I decided, especially when it wasn't tennis weather. But I wanted to go back to New York. I didn't see the point of staying in Chicago for the weekend, as I had planned before Paul's death. When I got back to the hotel, I called to change my flight.

So when my taxi turned down Morton Street the next night, no one expected me home, and from out in the street I could tell: somebody was, or had been, in my apartment. When I'm away, I always leave the kitchen light on, not the living room light, which has a lampshade tricky to remove when you want to change the bulb. I climbed the stairs and listened through the door before opening it. Vivaldi seeped through the cracks. I unlocked the door, put down my bags, and walked toward the living room. Flutes and violins courted and fused. The music was very loud.

Because he was so low, stretched out full-length upon the yellow leather couch, first I saw his feet, which rested on the armrest. I moved into the room and saw the rest of him. A young man, blond, familiar-looking—of course, it was Sara's au pair. His eyes were closed, but he was not asleep. From time to time, he raised one finger to "conduct" the music.

"Hello," I said.

He opened his eyes, saw me, jumped to his feet, ran his hand through his hair, and reached back to turn down the volume. "Sorry, Lucia," he said, pronouncing my name Lu*chi*a, with his lovely Italian accent. "You escared me. I didn't hear you enter."

"You scared me, too. I didn't expect any visitors." What was going on? What was this guy doing here?

"Sara said I might stay until Sunday. You didn't know?"

I shook my head.

He went on. "We expected you back Sunday night."

"What happened to your own place in the basement?"

He said, stiffly, "I am not working for the Lenoxes any longer. I am no longer living there."

"Did you and Gordon have some sort of fight?"

"You can ask Sara about it," he said after a pause. "She said you wouldn't mind if I stayed here while you were away."

Pure Sara, I thought—always free with other people's time and things. "Gordon's back?" I asked then.

"Papa came home," he said briefly.

I said, "Ricardo, I don't know what—"

"Carlo," he said. "My name is Carlo. I'm a student, you know, and I don't have much money for hotels. I'm hoping to find a place at semester break. On Monday, I'm going to see a room in Brooklyn, but until then perhaps . . . Sara said . . ."

"Sure. Stay till Monday." As long as *Sara* said so, I thought but didn't say.

I brought my suitcase into the bedroom. My bed was unmade, and there were several books near it on the floor, including one I had written. Some socks were scattered about on the floor. I called to him, "The couch pulls out in the study."

Carlo came into the bedroom. "Thank you so much," he said. "I am very gratified that you will let me stay in your so beautiful apartment."

I said, with a small smile, "Be my guest."

"An idiom?" he said eagerly. "But now you mean it literally?"

"Yes," I said, surprised at his grasp.

He said, "You could say it was a sort of . . . *literalidiomo*."

He pronounced it with Italian gusto. I tried out his portmanteau word, trying to roll the syllables as he had done. "A literalidiomo."

"No, Lucia," he said. "Like this." And he said it again, even more expressively, following the curve of the word with the bunched and graceful fingers of one hand. Then he asked, "Tea? Would you like some mint tea? I will put on the kettle, and then change the sheets . . ."

"Thanks," I said, "that would be great." I sat down heavily in the corner chair.

"You must be very fatigued," Carlo said.

I nodded.

"Take a hot bath. Here. I'll run it for you."

He went into the bathroom, and soon I heard the water hit the tub and smelled my favorite bath oil. The kettle whistled, and Carlo headed for the kitchen to make tea.

A couple of minutes later, he placed the cup of steeping tea on the table beside me. "It's the balance that's so good. Hot water inside your body, hot water outside. Drink hot, sit hot, stay hot."

I reached for the string of the teabag. He brushed my hand away. "Let it stay two minutes more," he said. "You should perhaps check on your bath."

He was right, the water was getting too high. I saw that I was almost out of bath oil: Carlo had apparently used it himself a few times. His razor rested on the sink. The towels were damp and mussed on the racks. Would it be like this to live with a man?

He called from the kitchen, "Shall I bring to you lemon and honey for the tea?"

"Yes, please," I called. Maybe also like that: somebody thinking of me.

When I came out of the bath, my bed was freshly made and the books and socks were off the floor. He had brought in a small Boston fern and put it on the night table by my bed. He was certainly trying to be nice. Well, he *was* nice, I decided. I wondered what had happened downstairs, between him and Gordon.

In the middle of the night, I opened my eyes in terror. There was a person in my bedroom. Then I recognized the intruder as Carlo, tiptoeing past my bed to the only bathroom in the apartment.

When he came out, I said, "Hi."

"Hello."

"Are you sleeping okay?"

He came over to the edge of my bed, sat down, and said, "No."

"Is the bed in the study all right?"

"It's not the bed."

"What's wrong?" I asked softly.

He shook his head. "Lucia, I don't want to bore you. A woman of your intelligence and perception."

"What's all this . . . ?"

"I read your *Prodigies*. I so much admire your mind! And my problems are personal, petty, and boring."

We were both sitting on my bed, in the dark. I was wearing a blue cotton nightgown and he was wearing underwear. "I'm not easily bored," I said.

"It's the little hours of the morning and you are perhaps tired."

"Actually, I'm feeling very wide-awake. You can talk to me, tell me what's the matter."

"It's only everything!"

"Like what?"

"First, I lost my job . . ."

"You'll find another—it won't be so hard."

"And I need someplace cheap to live."

"That's harder—unless you want to be an au pair again."
He shook his head. "It takes too much time!"

"Still," I said. "You're a student. You're flexible. You'll
find something."

"And the INS is on my trail. On my tail?"

"Either. Both. What about?"

"My student visa's running out. I thought I could get it
renewed, but I can't. I just can't do anything right," he said
feelingly.

"Do you have a decent lawyer?"

"I don't have money for a lawyer. I just feel so powerless.
So im . . . im . . . ?"

"Impotent?" I suggested as he groped for a word.

I felt him staring at me. Then he said, sharply, "I was going
to say, 'imbecilic.' "

"You're not imbecilic, Carlo. You're just a foreigner caught
in the system. I know an immigration lawyer. Maybe she can
help."

"Really, Lucia? Could we call her in the morning?" He
leaned toward me eagerly. He seemed about as young as Roland.

I smiled. "Yes, Carlo."

"You are very good to me," he said. "Thank you." And he
leaned over a little further, I guess to kiss me on the cheek,
but something happened in the dark, and a corner of his mouth
met mine. And within seconds, it became not a thank-you kiss
at all, but an enormous *please*.

I put my arms around him, my hands sliding under his T-
shirt. Then I was lost in the smoothness of his back, the
roughness of his face, the persistence of his mouth.

_29_

Sara let herself in with her key two days later. On seeing me, she said, surprised, "Lucy! When did *you* get in?"

"I came back early."

"Oh. I see. Well. Fine."

I could see her looking around for traces of Carlo. She said, "I was just making sure that everything was okay up here before you came back. We've been in Connecticut all weekend."

Gordon's parents lived in Greenwich. "Everything's fine," I said, smiling, for everything was very fine indeed.

Sara said, "Is, um, Carlo still here?"

"Not at the moment." He had just gone out to shop for our dinner.

"But he hasn't left yet?"

I shook my head. "You might have asked me if he could stay here."

"I thought he'd be gone by the time you got back."

"That's not the point, Sara."

"I didn't know how to get in touch."

"There are phone lines from here to Chicago."

She didn't say anything.

"Anyway, it's okay," I said. "What happened downstairs? Why was he fired?"

"He didn't tell you?"

I shook my head. "Some kind of fight between him and Gordon?"

Sara nodded.

"But what about?"

"Oh, just a silly thing. Nothing important. But Gordon got furious and said that Carlo had to leave. He had nowhere to stay, it was midnight, and your place was empty . . ."

"How convenient."

She asked, "Is he all packed to go?"

I said, "He can stay for a while. It's all right with me."

"Honestly?"

"Sure. He's no trouble at all."

She looked worried. "I just hope Gordon doesn't find out."

"What? That Carlo's here?"

She nodded.

"Well, Sara, of course he'll find out. They'll run into each other in the hall. Or Gordon will see him come up the front steps."

"You're right. He's going to be furious. At both of us."

"Well, let him *try* to get angry with me. It's not his apartment. And I'm not his wife." I paused. "Or his doormat."

"You think I'm a doormat with Gordon?"

"Sometimes."

"Well, think again. I stood up to him about having Zoe."

236

"Why didn't you stand up to him about keeping Carlo?"

Sara looked away and said, "It was complicated."

"What happened down there? What started it off?"

Sara said, "I can't tell you now. I'd better get back before Gordon misses me."

"God forbid."

"Well. He's been much more attentive since his return."

"Is that good or bad?"

"Good, I guess," Sara said. "And he's sweet with the baby." For a few seconds, she lingered by the door, as if she had something else to tell me. Then she said, "Welcome-home dinner tomorrow? Maybe Perri can come."

"Sure, Sara."

She left. She didn't know I'd been welcomed home already.

When Carlo came back, we kissed as if we'd been apart for weeks. Then we began making dinner together. He cut up the chicken, I crushed the garlic. It's hard to describe happiness. The glow sounds boring; sadness, madness glitter more compellingly. I diced an onion, crisscrossing it first, then slicing vertically to make small squares of white translucence. Carlo put the iron pan on the stove, his every gesture graceful. I poured us some wine. Chicken skin hissed as it touched the hot pan. I said, "Sara was here. She wondered if you'd left."

"What did you tell her?"

"I said you could stay for a while, that you were no trouble at all."

"Ah, Lucia." He put his hand on my neck.

"But, Carlo. She wouldn't tell me either. Why were you fired?"

For a few moments he said nothing. Then he said, "With Gordon and me, it was, how you say, 'hate at first sight'? He was just looking for some reason to get rid of me. And he thought he found one."

"You won't say any more?"

"I can't. It would be a betrayment."

"Betrayal," I said. "All right."

He opened the spice cabinet and said, "Tarragon, tarragon."

"Bottom shelf."

We spent the next day together, too. It was Monday. Carlo did not leave to look at the room in Brooklyn, and he didn't have any classes. We lounged about luxuriously. I read his thesis outline. We went for a walk in the steely-cold rain. We dried off. We cooked. Dinner at Sara's was canceled: Perri was busy and Sara had a cold. Carlo and I went to bed early. There was just enough reflected light in my room so I could see his face and body above me, or below me, or relaxed by my side.

On Tuesday I had to go teach and he had to see his thesis adviser. Coming home, I saw Perri in the hall, opening her mailbox and balancing some packages. I asked, "What did you buy?"

"Some ski things."

"That's right, you're going off to Utah to chase that guy you see every day at work."

"But it will be different out there," she said. "I just know it." I opened the front door with my key, and we both climbed the stairs. At her landing, she said, "I hear Carlo's still staying with you. He can stay in my place when I'm gone."

"Thanks, Perri."

She said, "Come in for some tea?"

"I can't." I was longing to get home to Carlo, and I didn't feel like another long talk about Larry, Perri's unworthy limerence object.

"Don't you want to see my new ski outfit? And have a chat?"

"Passionately," I replied. "But not today."

"Oh, all right. I'll call Ann."

"How is Ann?"

Her friend Ann was in bed with a bad back.

Perri said, "She's found a way to write her novel with the

keyboard on her knees. I told her she should stop writing during this attack, that maybe it was stressful. But she said it was more stressful *not* to write . . ."

"I understand the feeling. Toward the end of a project, you just want to finish."

"She wants to finish so she can start her next book."

"Say hello," I said. I like Ann, but I don't like her novels —not enough plot for my taste. I climbed the stairs to my apartment.

Carlo was in the bath. I bent down and kissed him.

"Come in?" he asked.

I shook my head. "Come out?"

He pulled out the plug and stood up, water running down his body.

I held out a terry-cloth bath sheet and wrapped it around him. He followed me into the bedroom and sat down on the bed. I began rubbing his hair with a small towel.

He closed his eyes and said, "Ahhhh."

"You like this?"

"I love it," he said.

"Then I'll do it some more."

That soft blond hair. Those golden, muscled shoulders. I toweled his hair lovingly. After a time, he sighed and pulled me down with him.

"You really do like having your hair dried," I said half an hour later.

"Oh yes. The head's my erogenious zone."

I said, "Erogenous, darling," the "darling" just slipping out. I gave him an anxious glance, but he looked happy and at peace, not scared by my endearment.

We went to the movies that night. I paid for our tickets, and he bought the popcorn. He brought my hand to his knee and held it there. I leaned against his shoulder. I was thirty-two years old, and it was the first time I'd been on a date at the movies. I closed my eyes to bask in the experience. Perhaps then I missed a crucial visual clue, for the movie seemed very confusing to me—and yet beautiful. The theater was beautiful, too. And the audience: as we walked out, I looked at them and felt awash with happiness.

"Are you hungry?" he asked me on the street. "Want an ice-cream cone?"

"Perhaps some of yours."

He bought a coffee cone and I had a bite, putting my mouth where his had been.

And so the week passed. Perri went to Utah. Sara took care of Rory, who had caught her cold. Roland came up and told me about it; I rummaged through Rory's drawer for something new to keep him busy. I found a small hand-puzzle, the kind you tilt back and forth to make things float around. This one was a "cocktail": you had to get the straw, the soda bubbles, the lemon wedge, and the cherry into the glass. "Here," I told Roland. "This will keep him busy for a while."

Carlo asked after Roland had left, "You keep toys for them here?" I nodded. He said, "Such a good aunt!"

"They're wonderful nephews."

"They are. But I bet you like all kids."

"Most of them, yes."

"You see?" He was delighted.

"See what?"

"I know you so well, my Lucia."

I said, "I haven't held anything back"—although that wasn't true, strictly speaking. "Almost anything," I amended myself.

"We all have certain secrets," Carlo said. "A person always has some things he keeps to himself."

"Shouldn't lovers tell each other everything?" I teased.

"Lovers last of all," Carlo said. "Last of all? Least of all?"

The day after Perri came back for Utah, I knocked on her door on my way home from yoga. She told me all about Utah.

Park City *had* made a difference with Larry—she had got him into her bed. But his great allure had been his indifference to her—once she had him, she found him a bore. "Standard-issue Marxist," she said. "So predictable."

"You're pretty predictable too," I remarked. "A man responds and you get bored. A man spurns you and you get aroused."

"Not *any* man, Lucy," she remarked after a while.

"All right. Any tolerable-looking, tolerably smart man between twenty-five and fifty."

She said, "Maybe you're right. I wonder if I would like Fenley if he turned me down."

"Is he still giving you a hard time?"

"Yeah—makes dirty jokes and treats me like shit. But I know he really likes me."

"No chance for him, then," I said.

Perri said, "Do you think I could change?"

"Possibly. Do you really want to?"

"I don't know," she said. "How's life with Carlo?"

"It's okay. Well, more than okay."

Perri looked up sharply. "More than okay?"

"Actually, blissful."

"Lucy, don't tell me . . ."

I nodded. "Uh-huh. I still can't believe it."

"Jesus," said Perri.

"What's wrong?"

"You really don't know?"

"Know what?"

"Why he had to leave Sara's?"

"Well—he won't tell me. And *she* won't. What happened?"

"Lucy, can't you guess?"

"What? He and Sara?"

Perri nodded. "She was crazy for him."

"And Gordon found out?"

"He came home unexpectedly and found her in the basement. Although Sara insists that they were just talking—that time."

"Then Gordon kicked him out?"

Perri nodded. "I brought Carlo up here."

Something hurt in my chest. I said, slowly, "So I'm some kind of substitute Sara, is that it?"

Perri said, "I doubt that. They were having problems even before Gordon found out . . ."

"What kind of problems?"

"Ask Sara."

"Sara! She's the last one I'd ask! She never even hinted they were having an affair."

Perri said, "And I swore I wouldn't tell."

"Why?"

"I guess because you're the youngest. She doesn't want to shock you—disillusion you about marriage or something." Perri suddenly looked anxious. "Promise me you won't tell her you know. Or him."

I stared at her. "I can't do that, Perri." For a few moments, the room was silent. Then I burst out, "But what should I do now? Confront him? Confront *her*?"

She said, "Why do anything at all?"

"To find out the truth."

"Whose truth? Sara's? Carlo's? And how will it help you right now?"

"Well, once I know . . ." I paused. "I mean, once I know more, I'll know what to do. Whether I should keep Carlo here. Whether I should make him leave."

Perri said, "Lucy, don't be a fool. You said it was blissful with him. Be smart and play dumb. Let it be."

"You honestly think I could do that?"

"Why not give it a try? I took your advice about Larry . . ."

"What advice?" I asked numbly. Sara and Carlo. Carlo and me. I didn't want to hear another word about Perri's stupid crush. But Perri prattled on.

242

"You said the only way to end an infatuation was by extinction, absence, or consummation. So I decided on the last. And now my sickness is over."

"Your infatuation."

"Yeah." She paused. "But why don't I feel healthy again? Why do I feel so depressed? As if something had died. Maybe love—in a way. Maybe I'll never love like that again."

"Maybe you dignify the word 'love,'" I suggested. "Maybe next time you'll really like the guy, too."

"Maybe there won't be a next time."

It was too silly a statement to answer. I just looked at her. She was wearing a pink silk kimono trimmed with blue peacocks. Her eyes were very blue. Her face was blank and beautiful. She said, "Do you really like him, Lucy?"

I nodded.

Perri said, "Then do as I say. Pretend you don't know."

30

I WALKED SLOWLY UPSTAIRS TO my apartment. Carlo was home: I could hear Bach's A-Minor Concerto. Carlo and Sara, Carlo and me: one sister after another. Would he try for Perri next?

There was a note from Sara under my door. "Come down to welcome-home dinner tonight, for you (belatedly) and Perri, just back from Utah—and Larry!" That exclamation mark told me Sara thought Perri had triumphed in Utah, just because at last she had lured her editor to bed. But to me the episode was very sad. If you get what you want and then you don't want it, how can you trust in what you want again?

I stared at the note. Dinner at Sara's: knowing about her and Carlo, knowing *she* didn't know about me—and Perri watching the sister show! This was not my idea of enjoyment. I folded up the note and put it in my pocket. I'd tell Sara I was busy.

But would it be better staying home with Carlo? Telling him I knew—or pretending ignorance?

Now I understood why he had been so sad that first night: he had lost his lover as well as his job and his place to live. Yet he'd sat on my bed and talked to me and leaned over to kiss my cheek. And his lips had met mine and begged please.

I walked into the kitchen. I smelled tomato sauce. Carlo came toward me with a wooden spoon in his hand. He kissed me and exclaimed, "Lucia! I have made the most wonderful marinara!"

I nodded, unable to speak.

He went on. "I needed to get things: I took ten dollars from the sugar bowl. You don't mind, do you? . . . Surely, not. Say something, Lucia! Maybe I should not have used your money, but I did not think you'd mind."

"No, that's fine," I mumbled. I didn't see how I could go on like this with him, pretending I didn't know. "Look," I said, abruptly. "I have to eat downstairs tonight. At Sara's."

"Am I invited?"

"No, Carlo." Did he think we were—officially—a couple?

"I am glad."

I gave him a questioning look.

He said, "It's awkward with Gordon."

I nodded. He turned off the gas. "The sauce will be even better tomorrow. As for tonight . . . do you have any sardines?"

I nodded.

"You don't mind if I open a can for my dinner?"

"Carlo, don't be ridiculous."

"You seem very cast down, Lucia."

"Downcast," I said, automatically. I looked at him. Tell

him, I challenged myself. Another voice said "Don't!" I sat down. "Something sad," I said at last. "I lost a student. He was stabbed in Riverside Park."

He took me in his arms. "How terrible," he said. I nodded against his shoulder.

But my student had been dead for three months—stabbed after a sexual encounter—and I was using his death for my own convenience. "A young man of twenty," I said against Carlo's green sweater. "Gay. Very promising."

"Gays have it so hard. And now AIDS."

I pulled back to look at Carlo's face. I asked, "Have you been with any man?"

"Not since I was fifteen, with a schoolmate."

"And women? In New York?"

Carlo inserted the key into the sardine can. "Two. It didn't work out with either of them."

"Why not?"

He concentrated on rolling the tin evenly on the key. He said, carefully, "One was a student in my program. A fanatic about bees. A little too crazy for me."

"And the other?"

"She was older. And married, with children. I want my *own* family," he said fiercely. He opened the refrigerator and took out a lemon. "My own kids."

"You'll be a good daddy," I said. "Sara said you were great with the boys."

No comment from Carlo on this. I went into the bedroom and saw he had unpacked his suitcases completely. A tweed jacket hung in my closet alongside a familiar-looking, tiger-striped terry-cloth robe. Carlo followed me into the bedroom. "I hung up a few things," he said, "and put some clothes in this drawer here. It's okay?"

"Yes, Carlo, it's fine." I pulled out the tiger-striped robe. "Where did you get this?"

"You know that cheap store, Traber's? We must go there sometime."

Downstairs at Sara's, Rory opened the door. I inhaled deeply. The air was fragrant with eggplant and meat. "Moussaka," Rory said.

I smiled. "When you were really little, Rory, you used to say 'moussaka' every time you saw a motorcycle. You'd scream, 'Moussaka, moussaka!' "

"Why?" he asked, puzzled.

"That's how you pronounced 'motorcycle,' dummy," Roland called from his room.

"It's really unnerving," Sara said, coming toward me in an apron and giving me a hello kiss. "They're tucked away in their rooms and you forget about them—then they join in the conversation without missing a beat and reveal they've been listening all along."

"I've been reading my book!" Roland hollered.

In the dining room, Perri was playing with Zoe, bringing the baby's moist fists together to clap them. "Patticake, patticake, baker's man . . ." Rory looked forlorn, so I hauled him onto my lap.

Sara brought the salad in and set it on the table, beside two small casseroles. "Roland," she called up the stairs. "Dinner's ready." Rory hopped off my lap and went to his place at the table.

"Where's Gordon?" I asked. "Working late?"

Sara nodded. "Roland! I'm serving!" She turned to me and asked casually, "Is Carlo still living upstairs?"

Perri looked up at this, to see what I'd say. And I suddenly knew what I would do. I said, "Yes—and it's working out great."

"Oh, really?" Sara asked.

Rory said, "Which one is for us?"

Sara began serving him from the casserole without the eggplant.

I said to Sara, "I think I'm in love."

"He's a sweetheart," Sara said, unperturbed. She dipped into the adult casserole, the one with the eggplant. "Perri, your plate."

I said, *sotto voce*, "And the sex just gets better and better."

Her serving spoon stopped in midair. "You and Carlo *are sleeping together?*"

"Uh-huh. This eggplant looks great."

"Lucy, he's using you," Sara said.

"Sara!" said Perri indignantly.

Sara said to Perri, "Lucy needs to know. So she doesn't get involved."

"Needs to know what?" I asked.

"Just be careful—Carlo only needs a place to live."

"Oh, really? How do *you* know?"

She said, "I have my reasons."

"What?" I was furious. "Because you had him first? This makes you the great expert? You think he still loves you or something?"

She looked at me, startled.

"Well, think again, Sara. That was then. This is now. Besides, you never even told me!"

Roland came into the room belatedly and sat down at the table.

Sara was saying, "You should have guessed why Gordon threw him out!"

Perri said, "Sara, the kids!"

I said, "Yeah, Sara, the kids."

"Don't just smile like some demented Cheshire cat!" She was furious. She stood up and said, "Is Carlo upstairs now? I'm going to go ask him some questions."

Perri said, "What good will that do? Come on, Sara, calm down."

But Sara began walking toward the door. I jumped up and held her arm. "Don't do it, Sara," I said. "Leave him out of it."

"Let me go!" she replied, trying to pull away.

I tightened my grip and said, "Don't get him involved."

"Well, he's *already* involved. Up to his neck—or should I say up to his prick?"

"Sara!" Perri said. "Don't be so coarse!"

"You're a fine one to say that—Miss Lay of New York! Lucy, let me *go*."

She pulled free and made for the door to get Carlo. I grabbed her from behind. The more she struggled, the more tightly I gripped her. I lifted her clear off the ground and headed back with her to the table. I had no idea I was strong enough for that. She tried unsuccessfully to kick me. I said, "Come on, Sara, control yourself."

"Let me go! Let me go!" She began yelling, "Carlo! Carlo!" I clapped one hand over her mouth and kept walking her back to the table. "Mmmmf! Mmmmmrrff!" She couldn't say anything more.

"Oh, really? 'Mmmmf, mmmmrrff'? Very intelligent." I found myself laughing at her. My older sister, helpless in my arms, mad with jealously because of me! "Back to the table with you. Until you calm down." I took another few steps. "Now, be a good girl," I said as she struggled silently, "and we'll all have a nice meal." Roland and Rory stared at us, stupefied.

"Lucy, let her go!" Perri said, standing up. But she still had Zoe in her arms and couldn't get between us.

"Not while she's still in this rage," I replied. Sara's body bucked against me, but I contained her easily. "Behave yourself!" I told Sara. It was fun to play mommy, fun to be in control.

She twisted her mouth away and began yelling.

I got my hand over her mouth again and shut her up forcibly.

She shook her head wildly to get free, but I only tightened my grip. Then she thrashed forward and back, opened her mouth—and sank her teeth around my thumb.

"*Animal!*" I shrieked. "Ow! Ow! Let go!"

Perri screamed, "Sara! Lucy! Stop it!" Zoe began howling, and Perri passed her to Roland. "Get to your room with the others."

The children fled. Blood flowed from my hand. "You fiend! Let go!" I yelled. Sara's teeth clamped deeper, gnawing. In pain, I lost my hold on her, and she opened her mouth and pulled away. She spat out my blood. I held my hand up to look at the damage.

"Oh my God," said Perri.

"She wouldn't let me go," Sara panted. "I had to make her let me go!"

Blood poured down my arm. There were two deep gashes around the base of my thumb, and I could see to the bone. "You almost bit it *off!*" I yelled at Sara.

"No, no!" she howled, and ran to her room. I heard her throw herself down on her bed.

I sank into a chair. Perri came toward me with a wad of gauze bandage. Blood dripped onto one of Sara's rugs. Perri began rolling gauze around my thumb. The white got red at once. "God," she said, "God!" She finished rolling the bandage and ran to the phone. I heard her call Carlo and ask him to get me a taxi. I heard Sara sobbing in her room. The walls were swaying and seething and the room was getting dim. My bandage was already soaked through. The air swirled around me, graying to black, and I slipped from my chair to the floor.

When I could see again, Perri and Carlo were squatting around me. Carlo said, "Lucia, can you stand up?"

With their help, I got to my feet, and they guided me into a waiting taxi. I think I blacked out again during the ride, but I was fully conscious walking into the emergency-room entrance, half held up by Carlo and Perri. I held up my dripping bandage to the admitting nurse. Another nurse guided me into a little operating room, and sat me down on the table. Carlo sat on a chair beside me. Perri went outside to present my insurance card. A nurse approached me with a needle. "You're not pregnant, are you?" she asked cheerily.

I was silent for a moment. Then I told her, "I might be. It's too soon to tell."

The nurse said, "Planning to abort?"

I shook my head.

"Then I'd better give you something else." She left the room.

Carlo stared at me. "You mean . . . *us?*"

"It's possible, yes." I hadn't used anything with Carlo—not the first time, nor any time after. This was what I hadn't told him. No doubt my affair with Carlo would be brief—it might even end with this revelation. But maybe we'd already made a baby. Better his genes than some stranger's. "Are you very angry?" I asked.

He shook his head. "Angry? No. I am *flattered*. My baby? You want him? Or her?"

"Yes, Carlo. Yes."

"And we could get married?"

I stared at him, speechless.

"Not if you don't want," he said, hurriedly. "But for the baby's sake . . ."

A very young doctor walked into the room, flanked by two nurses.

They made the injection right into the wound, and I was blown upon a wall of pain. Then numbness oozed into my hand, and the doctor began sewing. The thread was black. The stitches were ugly. There was a lot of blood. I made myself watch.

31

"WOULD YOU LIKE ME TO SLEEP somewhere else?"

"Like where?"

"I could go back to the study."

"What for?"

"So you can sleep more peacefully. So I don't bump on your thumb."

"No, Carlo. I want you here with me."

He turned out the light and climbed into bed. "Are you comfortable like this?" He lay very still on the far side of the bed.

"No, I need this." I brought his hand to my cheek. "I need nursing and mothering."

"I will do what I can," he said gravely, "but I may not know how. You must always to tell me."

I smiled. "I will always to tell you." We lay close, snuggled spoonwise, and soon, despite my throbbing thumb and arm, I dozed off.

Sara's letter came under the door the next day. I sat down with it on the yellow leather couch, which already looked soiled. With difficulty, because of the enormous bandage on my thumb, I opened the envelope. I read:

Dear Lucy,

I'm too deeply ashamed to see you or call you right now. I don't expect you will ever forgive me, whatever I say, but I need to write to you so you will understand—perhaps so I will. To say "I am sorry" after my animal act seems an insult to both of us. I am mortified, anguished, in pain. I grieve as for lost innocence.

To have done that. To you. In front of the children. What if I'd bitten it off?

You should know that I tried my best to do so. I was wild with fury, insane with the need to escape your strong arms lifting me so easily. I couldn't even squawk: you wholly dominated me, humiliating me before my family. As I struggled to get free, as I used all my might and got nowhere, what began as a jealous pique became another state of being. I am tempted to say another self came out, but that excuses me too easily. That self is part of me. That self said I will do anything to get free, anything at all. That self came out when you held me and I couldn't get away. For a moment in time, a self I didn't know was me would have killed.

If that self is there in all of us, maybe it emerges

253

during physical combat and constraint. Lucy, do you know that before last night I have never been physically assaulted? Whatever you say about Gordon, he has never slapped me, never pressed his physical advantage.

It occurs to me that—perhaps like many middle-class women—I've never known violence firsthand. Can you imagine Daddy beating us with his belt? I've never even witnessed a live fistfight! Certain things have been incomprehensible to me. I could understand lust but not bloodlust.

What I will never understand is how for so many men blood and lust go together. I know in your Amnesty work you come across case after case of men torturing women before raping them. How can men be aroused by tears and blood and mucous? Can you imagine making a man scream and bleed and faint and getting hot, not sick, by doing it—then fucking him, hurting him, more? Surely women do not act that way.

But women as men can revert to a primitive, savage state. For me, the goad was physical. Your strength. Your hand on my mouth. I was helpless, trapped, and I had to get out. I felt I would die if I didn't escape. I bit into your thumb as hard as I could.

How can I look my kids in the eye? And you, Lucy—with your bandage, hand throbbing—how can you ever forgive me?

I was all wrong about Carlo—irrationally jealous and mean. You should know it was over with us a week before he moved up to your place. I wish you luck with him, if that's what you want—but he may have to leave soon, his visa's running out.

Any time you want to talk, my door is open.

In deep remorse and love,
Sara

I got off the couch and walked to the study. I sat at my desk and found some notepaper. I stuck the ballpoint between my first two knuckles and wrote, laboriously. Oddly enough, holding the pen this way didn't change my handwriting much.

Dear Sara,
*   I appreciate your letter, but you'll understand if I can't see you for a while.*
*   Lucy*

Her teeth had severed a tendon in my thumb, and the doctors said it might never be strong enough to hold something tightly again. Say, to grip a tennis racket hard for an overhead. The joy just after you've hit the ball cleanly and well. The joy of feeling wholly healthy. I was in a lot of pain.

But Carlo looked after me, cooked all my meals, and Perri came up once a day. By the end of the week I could sit at my computer and work. The following week, I went back to school. Carlo came with me. He carried my books, picked up my mail, walked me to the lecture hall, took a seat, listened attentively, scribbled in his notebook.

"Let me see your notes on my lecture," I said later in my office. He handed me his notebook. His handwriting was elegant; his spelling made me smile. But he was a good student: he had taken down the main points. I asked, "What do all these asterisks mean?"

"They are things I don't understand. Terms you'll explain to me maybe?"

"Of course I will. Are you really interested?"

"But certainly."

"It's somewhat removed from your studies."

"I'm not a horse with blinkers," Carlo said. "I like to graze in many fields."

On the way home, we stopped at a drugstore. And that night, we learned I was pregnant.

Carlo said, "This is wonderful news! Is it not?"

"It is for me."

"And you have considered my marriage proposal?"

"Not seriously."

His eyes shone golden in reproach.

I said, "I just can't box you in like this. You're young, you have your whole life ahead of you, we barely know each other . . ."

"I know you very well," he said. "I have been happy here. I have been hoping for this baby. I'm a thirty-year-old man. Not so very young. I am ready for marriage."

"And you want to stay in New York," I said flatly.

"Yes, it's true. If we marry, you know, I could stay."

"That thought has crossed my mind," I remarked. If we were still speaking, Sara would tell me Carlo just wanted his green card.

Carlo put his arms around me and said, "But that isn't the reason, you know."

I said, "That and this apartment."

"And the baby!" said Carlo. "And you. It's a bundle deal."

"A *package* deal," I said.

"Yes, a package deal." He said into my hair, "And what about you? Do you like what the package brings you?"

I was silent.

He said, "You're thinking of what Sara will say?" I nodded. "Forget about her," Carlo said. "Think about you."

I thought about me: plain Lucy, dumpy Lucy married to this glowing, blond Italian. Everyone would wonder at our pairing; everyone would speculate. That very afternoon, the department secretary, seeing Carlo's hand on mine, had shot me a curious look. Everyone would think he was using me. In fact, I would be using him. Using him for sex and company. Using him as daddy to my child.

But perhaps we all use people anyway, even lovers with the "purest" desires. Take opposites who attract. He "uses" her warmth and vivacity; she "uses" his coolness and calm. Completing each other, they are mutually "useful"—and no one condemns them or clucks in dismay.

Carlo asked, "Will you let what people might say stop you from marrying me?"

It seemed a feeble argument indeed—yet I remained silent. Something else bothered me. Carlo hadn't mentioned love.

The doorbell rang. It was Perri, with a bag of my favorite coffee blend from Balducci's. "Anybody want some?" she asked.

"I'd love a cup," I said.

"Not for me," said Carlo. "I must do some reading." He closed the study door behind him.

Perri busied herself measuring water and coffee and told me that Sara was very depressed.

"As well she might be," I said, cutting Perri off. I didn't want to hear another word about Sara. She had her beauty, she had her hands, *let* her wallow in remorse. She even had Gordon. I asked Perri, "How's it been at work?"

"You mean, with Larry?"

I nodded.

"It's funny," she mused. "In the mornings, I still get this quang when I see Larry's jacket on the hook. 'He's here,' I think and my pulse starts to pound—and then I remember Utah. About his cranky carping. About feeling bored with a humorless Marxist. Then he becomes just another colleague."

"Like Fenley?" I asked.

"Well, Fenley's another story. I think he's, um, *dating* Claudine. I'm glad for both of them, I guess."

I remarked, "You don't *look* all that glad."

"Well, naturally he has a certain, shall we say, *allure* now that he's seeing someone else. And I really admire him professionally. He's teaching me a lot."

"She said lamely."

"No, it's true. He insisted we film a segment dealing with

some writers' claims against a porno magazine. I really opposed
him, thought it was exploitive, cheap. But it's an exciting part
of the film—not just because of the sexual aspect, but because
it's a point of polarization. Fenley's smart, he instinctively saw
that."

"And you want to learn from him," I said, smiling. "That's
all."

"Well, Lucy, I realize it's stupid of me to want more. This
is a man who's constantly putting me down. And I don't like
his looks. I never did, I never will."

"Methinks the lady doth protest too much. You're probably
beaming at him."

She didn't confirm or deny this. "I guess it's just my competitive nature," she said. "And a certain pity. I just know
Claudine's using him."

I observed, "One way or another, we all use each other in
love."

"How did Mommy use Daddy?" asked Perri.

"As provider. And companion."

"As companion? Then we all use people all the time."

"It's true."

Perri said, "Then there's something wrong with your defi-
nition. Ah, the coffee's ready."

"Just half a cup for me."

"Worried about getting to sleep?"

I shook my head. I put my hand on my belly.

"Indigestion?" asked Perri.

I said to her, "Can you keep a secret?"

She nodded.

I said, "It isn't indigestion. Guess again."

32

I WAS OFTEN TIRED, THOSE early pregnant weeks, so Carlo did most of the housework. I hadn't decided whether or not we should marry; he let the subject drop. He was certainly sweet, charming to live with and observe. Yet it was not a grand passion. We made love very nicely but never more than once a day nor in peculiar places. We liked to talk, but we also liked to be quiet together, listening to music or reading. We never fought. It was cozy, I admit. Yet was this enough for a marriage?

Two weeks went by. My original stitches were removed. Surgery was done to reconnect a tendon, and I had new stitches now: a whiskery line of them. The operation had been a success, the doctors told me, but I was still in great pain, especially by the end of the day. I took as few pills as I could. They made me feel unreal: floaty, disconnected, irresponsible.

One day, I met Sara by the mailboxes. "Hello, Lucy," she said.

I nodded at her, but I couldn't speak.

"Okay, if that's how you want it," she said, turning away, her head stiff. She unlocked the front door and hurried into the inner hall. The front door swung gently closed behind her. When it met the doorframe, it hesitated for a moment, then caught the lock with a small, gobbling sound. Only then, when she couldn't hear, did I say "hi" to my sister.

Oddly enough, I saw something of Gordon in the next couple of weeks. One night he came up and showed me how to modify a computer program I was using for my work, and three days later he returned to give me some other ideas. Another night, he and Rory came to borrow some needle-nose pliers and had juice and cookies with me in the kitchen. Carlo stayed in the study on these occasions, but there were signs of him everywhere. In the kitchen, the odd plants he had foraged were drying out in brown-gray bundles tied with string.

Gordon didn't ask me about Carlo and I didn't ask him about Sara. But when he left with the pliers, he said, "Sara misses you, Lucy. You should talk to her."

I shook my head. "I can't yet. I'm sorry."

I was out when the letter from Immigration arrived. When I opened the door, Carlo held the letter out to me before I'd even taken off my coat. I scanned the few lines. If Carlo didn't leave in two weeks, the Agency would initiate deportation proceedings. "So, Lucia," he said. "Now you have to decide."

I sat down.

Carlo joined me on the couch. He said, "I want to be here when you have your baby."

I said, "Here in New York."

He said, "Here with my family. Here with the woman I love."

Tears filled my eyes.

He held me to him. "Lucia, of course I love you." He stroked my hair gently, from the top of my head to my nape. I drew back to see him. I wanted so much to believe him. I looked into his beautiful eyes.

"What do you see, Lucia?"

I shook my head; I saw too much. I saw the speculation our marriage would inspire: insulting to him and to me. I saw my life changing form, my privacy invaded, my time not my own. I saw my solitude gone.

"Tell me, Lucia." Carlo's eyes were tender and his mouth was kind. And I saw a dear man who would be my companion, a man I certainly could love, a man who loved me, or pretended to, at least.

A week later, we went down to City Hall and got married. I insisted on secrecy: only Immigration was to know. There were so many things to get used to: Carlo in my house, a baby in my body, I wasn't ready to be a wife and talk about it yet. "You are a strange one," said Carlo, but he humored me. "We will have a big wedding party in Florence," he said in the taxi coming home. "And then everybody will know."

"When will that be?"

"In May, perhaps. When you finish teaching."

"That's a nice plan."

"And you can meet my family."

"They'll be rather surprised."

"Why, Lucia? I have always liked intelligent women."

Could it be that he just hadn't *noticed* my looks? "Look, Carlo!" I pointed to a weedy, brown abandoned lot.

He took out the pocket notebook he carried even on his wedding day and noted the location of the lot. "In three months," he said, "it will be green and growing. And in six months, we will come back and pick some of those plants for our salad."

"In six months I'll scarcely be walking, let alone climbing fences and harvesting dubious greens."

In response, he slid his hand into my coat and stroked my belly through my dress. I closed my eyes. Perhaps he closed his.

The taxicab came to a stop. "We're at Seventeen," the driver said.

Three nights later, I was dreaming of Italy. The sun was hot and and all the women wore black. Carlo and I were walking down a country road. Huge blossoms crowded the hedges. "They must be watered every day," Carlo said, "or they dry out and die." We walked on; now the flowers on the bushes were withered. "You see, Lucia," Carlo said. The leaves were brown, and clouds of dust filled the air. Dust on my arms, dust in my throat—I sat up in bed with a start. I prodded Carlo awake. "Do you smell anything?"

He sat up, too, and inhaled. "Smoke?"

The smoke seemed to be coming from below us—Perri's bedroom. I jumped out of bed, threw on my robe, and ran to the kitchen. The smoke alarm began to ring as I took Perri's key from the hook. I ran downstairs and pounded on her front door. Then I opened the lock with my key. I rushed in through thick smoke, yelling, "Perri, Perri!" and coughing. I couldn't see much in her room. I turned on the light, but the electricity was dead. Her mattress was smoldering, but she didn't seem to be in it.

There was a crash at the window, and I saw Carlo outside on the patio, breaking her glass door with a poker. Again and again he smashed at the glass to make a big hole. Then he stepped into the room, keeping low, ducking. Little flames rose up as the air rushed in. Carlo had a flashlight—the one

I keep in an electric socket in my bedroom—and he swept it back and forth across the floor. There through the smoke I saw Perri. She was lying naked between the bed and the window, face down, utterly still. A lick of flame jumped from the sheet to her hair. I screamed, and Carlo began smacking Perri's head with his bare hands.

"Here," I said, taking off my robe. He snatched it from me and mashed it down on Perri's head. When he pulled the robe away, Perri's hair was charred and her cheek was meat-red. I put my head to her chest. I couldn't tell if she was breathing or not.

Carlo said, "Out. We have to leave now." He put Perri around his shoulders. The smoke was worst by the bedroom door, so Carlo left through the patio, cutting his arm on the broken glass. He didn't seem to notice. Carefully, he climbed down the fire escape to Sara's bedroom, Perri's limbs dangling around him. I followed them down. Cold air reached up under my nightgown as I went down the metal stairs.

We knocked at Sara's window. "Open up, open up!"

Gordon jumped up and ran to the window. Opening it, he demanded, "Is this some kind of joke?" Then he saw Perri. He helped Carlo into the room with her and got her off Carlo's shoulders.

I said, "Perri's bedroom is on fire."

Sara called 911 from the bed.

Carlo and Gordon carried Perri outside. Sara ran to get Zoe, and I went to wake up the boys.

Then we were all in the street. Carlo kneeled over Perri, who was lying on the sidewalk, wrapped in a blanket. He was breathing forcefully into her mouth. His arm was bleeding all over the blanket as he tried to bring life to Perri's body. Gordon held Roland and Rory by the hand. Sara hugged Zoe tightly in the wind.

The fire truck and the ambulance arrived at the same time. Billows of smoke were rising from the back of the building.

The firemen jumped from the truck and began dragging their hoses. The captain asked me, "Is everyone out of the building?"

I nodded. But we both saw Gordon running back into the building.

"Hey—you can't go back in there!" the captain yelled, but Gordon was already inside. The fire wasn't near the parlor floor, but the captain was furious. "Guy's gotta rescue his *things*."

The paramedics got Perri onto a stretcher and into an ambulance. One of them started resuscitation.

"I'll go with her," Sara said.

"*I'll* go with her," I said.

"There's only room for one of you," the driver said.

"I'll go," Sara said. "I'm the oldest—and I'm dressed."

It was true. Sara wore a coat and shoes, but I was standing barefoot in my nightgown. She thrust Zoe into Carlo's arms and pushed me aside to sit by Perri in the ambulance.

Rory said, "I'm cold." It was twenty-five degrees.

Gordon came out of the house, carrying some of Sara's rugs and hangings. He threw them down on the sidewalk and reached for Zoe. He said to Carlo, "Get your arm treated."

Carlo said, absently, "Yes, my arm."

Roland wrapped Rory in one of Sara's rugs. Then he put a larger rug around his own shoulders.

"Come on, Carlo," I said. "We're going to the hospital, too." We ran toward Seventh Avenue to get a cab. Roland ran after us to give me a hand-woven rug.

33

PERRI SURVIVED. THE PARAMED-
ics got her breathing before the ambulance reached the hospital. When Carlo and I got to the hospital, she was being
treated for her burns, which were severe, but localized. Only
her face and neck had been burned, and some of her scalp.

She regained consciousness at five in the morning, after
Carlo had gone home. I was in the intensive-care unit with
her; Sara was getting some coffee.

Perri moaned and said, very clearly, "Where the fuck am
I?"

I said, "Saint Vincent's. In intensive care."

She brought her hand to the bandages on her face. "I hurt
so much." Her voice was weak and raspy. "What happened?"

"There was a fire in your bedroom."

"Is everyone okay?"

"We're all fine."

"And the house?"

"I'm not sure . . . Perri, were you smoking in bed?"

She didn't say yes or say no. I heard her raspy breathing.

I said, "You're lucky you're alive. Oh, Perri!" Then I couldn't help myself, I was crying.

"Lucy, what's wrong?"

"You weren't breathing. You had us so worried. Are you trying to kill yourself or something?"

"No, Lucy, of course not."

"Because if you are, leave the rest of us out of it."

"Don't scold me now, Lucy. Please."

"I thought you were dead. I thought we'd lost you."

"Well, see, you were wrong, here I am. Hello, Sara."

"Perri!" Sara said, returning. "Darling, thank God!"

"Bye, Perri," I said. "I'll be back." Then I went home.

From the front, Seventeen Morton Street looked unchanged. But the back was badly damaged. Perri's room was charred and sodden, there were holes in the ceiling, and black debris was everywhere. The floor in my bedroom and study would have to be rebuilt: through the gaps in the boards I could see the gray ruin of Perri's bedroom. My back rooms smelled foul, but the living room was okay.

Carlo was asleep on the living room rug, rolled up in a red blanket. I got us pillows and another two blankets, for it was very cold. Then I lay next to him. He put his arm around me. We slept on the floor until noon. When I awoke, I saw Carlo near me, watching me.

"Good morning," he said.

"Good morning. Brrrr."

"The electricity's still off." He began rubbing my shoulders. "Getting warmer?"

"Perhaps a little."

He drew me to him. His mouth was mellow on mine—

warmth to the back of my head. Another kiss, another. Our faces were twisting together. Then we made love on the living room floor.

To be honest, a bed is much better, at least for the one underneath.

I went to the hospital the next day. Perri was alone in a semiprivate room. Her bed had been cranked high so she could sit up. An intravenous drip was attached to her left arm. Bandages covered most of her face and neck. Her streaky hair was damp. I walked to the bed and kissed her as gently as I could, but she said, weakly, "Lucy, don't joggle me."

I sat down in a chair by the bed. "How are you?"

"I'm in terrible pain. At least until my next shot. Which I should have gotten already. Eighteen minutes ago, to be precise. I keep telling them I want a higher dose, but no one will listen to me."

"You'll leave here a Percodan addict."

Perri said, "I don't have an addictive personality." From the side of her cheek I could see, I recognized her mocking smile.

I said, "I brought you some tapes and your Walkman."

"Great . . . You saved my life." She was quiet a moment, then said, "You did, you know. Save my life."

"It was Carlo who carried you out."

"It was you who woke up," Perri said. "It was almost too late."

Sara came in, holding peonies. She drew back when she saw me. She said, "Maybe I should wait outside till Lucy's gone."

"Of course not," I said.

Perri said slowly from beneath her bandages, "I wish you two would stop your feud."

"That's up to Lucy," Sara said. She put the peonies in a vase and filled it with water from the bathroom.

A nurse with a needle came into the room.

"Thank God," said Perri, holding out her right arm to the nurse.

"How bad's your pain?" I asked. "With ten being most?"

Perri said, promptly, "Ten." Then the nurse gave Perri her shot. She said, slowly, "That's better. When do I get the next one?"

"Not until eight."

"I'll need one sooner," said Perri.

"You'll have to speak to a doctor about that."

After the nurse left, Perri remarked, "Five hundred dollars a day and the room service sucks."

Sara said, "What do they say? About your face?"

Perri said, "They'll need to do skin grafts. Then they'll see how the scars heal. I can have further surgery later. Even then, I'll have scars for the rest of my life. But maybe with makeup, I won't look too freaky."

Sara said, "You've still got your beautiful body and your beautiful hair."

"Most of my hair," Perri amended. "A big chunk burned off."

I said, "You're lucky you're alive! You should talk about how you're going to *live*, not how you're going to look."

Perri said, "You mean I should stop smoking pot."

"Of course you should stop smoking pot. Go to Narcotics Anonymous."

"Lucy, pot's *okay* for me. If I hadn't been drinking at that awful party, I would have been perfectly fine with the joint."

"Talk about denial." I looked away, exasperated. "Anyway, if you'd been drinking so much, why did you bother with the joint?"

"Different kind of head. Relief that I was home. Celebration. Habit."

"Well, break the habit. See a therapist or something. And stop thinking about how you'll look."

Sara said, indignantly, "Stop moralizing, Lucy. She has

every right to worry about her appearance. When you've lived thirty-five years as a beautiful female, you get used to it. You do. You get used to the attention. The *friendliness* of men on the streets and in stores, the way women look at you, with this flattering interest and speculation. You get used to all that and to being nice in return and to getting special treatment just because of the way you were born."

"I wouldn't know," I said.

"Perhaps not," said Sara. "But when you're looking good, even riding a bus can be fun. For me, the worst thing about being pregnant was the way I stopped getting the attention I'd grown used to as a pretty woman. I felt I'd disappeared behind my belly. When I stepped onto a bus, I didn't get admiring looks—I only got a seat."

"I guess I inhabit another planet or something." Then I felt an inner excitement. My jaw hummed as I added, deliberately, "For me, the worst thing about being pregnant is the fatigue."

The color drained from Sara's face.

The nurse put her head into the room to say, "Visiting hours are over." Then she went on down the hall.

Sara said to me, "You and Carlo . . . ?"

I nodded.

Sara said, "Are you going to get married?"

I said, "You might as well know—both of you. We got married last Monday."

Perri gave a little shriek. "You did? You sneak! Congratulations!"

"So Carlo gets to stay in New York," said Sara. "Lucky Carlo."

"You've got it wrong," I said. "Lucky Lucy."

The nurse came back to tell me and Sara, "You'll have to leave now."

We put on our coats and said good-bye to Perri.

"Going home?" asked Sara in the lobby. I nodded. She said, "Share a taxi?"

"I thought I'd walk."

"Good idea," Sara said. We left the hospital, and she fell into step beside me. She asked, "How's your thumb?"

"Okay. Hurts in the cold."

"What about tennis?"

"They're not sure yet."

We crossed West Eleventh Street. Sara suddenly, angrily, said, "Are you going to accept my apologies now? Or are you going to hold a grudge for the next fifty years?"

I said, equally angrily, "Leave me alone, I don't know."

Sara said, "After all, you got his baby."

I stopped walking to face her. "You wanted *that*?"

Sara nodded. There were tears in her eyes, perhaps from the wind.

I said, "Oh, Sara" and held out my arms. Our wool coats pressed together. People leaving the Elephant and Castle restaurant stared as she sobbed on my shoulder. My shoulder bag was squashed between us, and my eyes were wet, too, though why I couldn't tell.

When Sara said, her voice quavering, "Congratulations, Lucy," my tears, my heart overflowed.

EPILOGUE

June 10, 1988

Dear Lucy,

I hope this letter finds you on some sunny balcony, with flowers all about and a cup of cappuccino in your hands. A honeymoon in Italy! How are Carlo's relatives? I used to try to imagine his childhood, his mother and father. Do write and tell me all about them. Let me know how you are feeling—and, please, no more two-sentence postcards!

Even as I write, the workmen are hammering overhead. You chose an excellent time to be away—while your floor is being rebuilt. I know how much you hate noise. That's something you and I share: Perri doesn't seem to mind as much.

Of course, most of the time she's at work, writing one last grant application while the others get ready for "The Mix," whatever that is. (I always tune out when she tries to explain.) Half of her face is very scarred—but the other half is as lovely as ever. How strange: in profile, different ways, she must inspire radically different emotions. She'll have more surgery in September. The doctors say she won't be badly disfigured, but she doesn't seem to believe them. In any event, she's being very courageous.

Meanwhile, I must let you know that late last night I heard her and some guy going upstairs—and Perri was giggling, "Fenley, stop it!" Can this be the same man about whom she used to complain?

Gordon and I are getting on rather well these days. I'll always be touched that he ran in and brought out my rugs the night of the fire. We've taken up roller skating at an indoor rink. He's much better at it than I am, which is a happier dynamic for us than the other way round. (How he sulks when I beat him at Ping-Pong!) Last night, I learned to skate backward, and today my thighs feel black and blue.

Gordon got his finances in order and discovered that he's having a good year after all. So in August, we're renting a house in Montauk. Gordon plans to catch fish and play golf, and I plan to sit with Zoe on the beach, underneath the red and yellow umbrella, watching the boys as they frolic.

Roland made up a riddle. "Why is a typewriter like a present? Because they both have a ribbon." Rory is trying very hard to make up a joke of his own, but hasn't quite mastered the form: "Why is a bicycle like a car? Because they both have wheels." Zoe is getting quite plump and is of course engrossing to observe as she discovers one thing or another. When my children

*are all in one room (and I can see that none is im-
mediately endangered, for a halo of possible mishap
surrounds almost every activity)—when I see their
faces around the dining room table (we prop Zoe up
in the high chair now), I sometimes gaze at them until
happiness tingles my forearms.*

*You and Carlo have all this ahead. He will be, I
predict, a wonderful father. He is very eager for a
family of his own. In fact, he stopped desiring me when
he learned that I couldn't have any more children. Ours
was just a brief affair: but for me how brightly it
burned! I can't regret it; I can only regret how it led
me to behave toward you.*

*I have finished the rug I was working on when you
left. It is mainly beige and gold, with the head of a fox
in the middle. Gordon claims it's the best thing I've
done, and he's hung it up in our bedroom. The eyes of
the fox are golden and kind.*

Be happy and well.

> *Love,*
> *Sara*

> *June 15*

Dear Lucy,

*Got your stingy postcard yesterday—you don't de-
serve a letter! Never mind, I have some time, we made
the deadline on the distribution grant application and
I can breathe again.*

*Last week—just to please you—I went to a meeting
of Narcotics Anonymous. I set off feeling like Arlo Guth-
rie, arrested for littering, on a bench with murderers.
I mean, I just smoke some grass and I was sure the
others would all be ex-mainliners. It wasn't that way
—there were all kinds of people, with all kinds of
problems—all kinds of users, all kinds of drugs. But I*

was bummed out by the hearty cheer, the revival-meeting spirit.

It's true that I caused the fire by smoking pot in bed. But it's also true that I'd drunk three glasses of wine at a party. And I hadn't checked the smoke alarm battery in months. I don't think marijuana is my real problem. Romantic obsessiveness is—and dreaming when I should be doing. I do need some help (beyond your and Sara's advice), so I've made an appointment with a cognitive therapist who's helped my friend Ann. He works very short term: in and out in three months! Wham-bam—sounds good to me.

The bandages came off my face two weeks ago: my skin is very shiny and a bright salmon-pink. They say it's healing well, but I can look in the mirror and see for myself. Then I look away from the mirror and do my work. Or eat a peach. Or turn up the music and dance. And then nothing's changed, I'm still me. So I'm getting used to my life as another woman, not lovely—scarred.

The film is essentially finished; there's just some follow-up mopping up to do. Larry pals around with Nancy now and lends her books like Tristes Tropiques, *poor girl—though her whole face comes alive when he indoctrinates her. Claudine is working somewhere else. Fenley's got a new project, a "Front Line" for PBS, and he's busy planning that.*

Well. I guess you deserve to know more, having suffered through the Larry episode with me. When I went back to work, I found I was still glamorous to Fenley, even with my bandages—and later, even without them. His sexual jokes and jibes continued.

The day before our grant application was due I'd been typing at the terminal for hours. It was seven o'clock; everyone else had gone home. The letters danced green on the screen. And then I felt these hands on my back, caressing and kneading. "You must be very stiff," he said. Those hands felt so great I just nodded and let him go on. After a while, I closed my eyes and leaned forward so my forehead rested on the desk. His thumbs worked my shoulder blades; his fingers kneaded my ribs, then my sides, then—then was the time I should have stopped him, if I was going to. Because of course soon his fingertips worked their way forward. And it was just too good to stop. My hunch about him was right. So, Lucy—I did it at the office after all! And elsewhere, too. The man is a maestro. You know I've never liked his looks, but I talked him into a new haircut and out of his nylon turtlenecks, and, really, he's almost attractive! We're keeping it a secret from the others at work, and this sense of the forbidden makes everything even hotter for me. Maybe this therapist will help me straighten out my sex life— but somehow I doubt it!

You seem on the right path anyway, Lucy. You write how lucky you are, but you made your own luck, too. Enjoy it all—and for God's sake take an hour off from bliss to write to me!

Love,
Perri

June 22, 1988

Dear Sara and Perri,

You both reproach me for my postcards—but, remember, this is my honeymoon—not a time when brides engage in lengthy correspondence! I probably risk another round of recrimination by writing this, a single letter to you both . . .

I write from a sunny balcony—Sara, you were right—and the flowers are purple and red. Pots of oreg-

ano perfume the air. I sit at a wrought-iron table. I look at ancient stone houses and the river Arno. We are in Florence, with Carlo's mother Franca. She's not exactly a middle-aged matron wearing black. She's a slim and pretty redhead, loud and vivacious, used to admiration from all sides. (You don't have to be a model to be a professional beauty.) Now married for the third time and the mother of two very little girls, she inspires mixed emotions in Carlo. You can tell that he's deeply attached to her . . . but wary. It's clear that he doesn't like Giorgio, Franca's husband, who is rather younger than she and heir to an olive-oil fortune. Before that there was a movie actor. And before that there was Luigi, Carlo's father, whom I've only met once. He never remarried; we met in a restaurant. They look so alike! Imagine Carlo—fifty, balding, in a three-piece suit. Luigi works in government. When Franca married the actor, Carlo wanted to live with his father, but Luigi refused and Carlo has never forgiven him: "He abandoned me in my minute of need." I tell him, "You ended up happy enough with your mom." He says he'll be glad to get back to New York and his thesis. As for me, I don't relish the idea of returning in July. Carlo's never spent a summer in New York, but he insists that we'll have fun. Frankly, I'd rather have fun in France, but funds are getting low . . .

I'm in that serene and happy part of pregnancy the books all extoll: late in the middle trimester (every new endeavor brings its attendant jargon). I'm feeling hearty and robust—but Carlo and Franca fuss about, feeding and tending me as if I were an ailing rose.

The baby moves energetically now . . . the bubble, the bud, the fish . . . Bring me no metaphors! That baby feels just like an animal inside an abdomen would feel. Its kicks are like the kicks of something small and vigorous within: the belly, the baby insists on what is.

I kiss you both, and Roland and Rory and Zoe, and even Gordon, yes—all of you at Seventeen Morton Street.

Much love,
Lucy